GONE: A PSYCHOLOGICAL THRILLER

WHEN BAD THINGS HAPPEN BOOK ONE

SHARON A. MITCHELL

ALSO BY DR. SHARON A. MITCHELL

PART I
MONDAY

CHAPTER 1

*J*ackson sipped his morning coffee - just the temperature he liked it, creamy and the best coffee beans Gevalia offered. At least Elizabeth got that right. He turned the newspaper to the next page. Behind his paper screen was the murmur of his wife's voice. You'd almost think she was there alone.

Well, time to get moving. He had stuff to do, a life to get on with and plans to make things even better. He let the paper flop onto his plate of congealing eggs. Straightening his suit, he stood and checked that his cuff links were properly seated.

Elizabeth placed a kiss on their son's forehead and rubbed noses with him. Four-year-old Timothy remained focused on plucking Cheerios off his highchair table.

Irked, Jackson thought he'd try once again. "Isn't he a little old to still be using a highchair? For God's sake, he's almost ready for school and could sit in a chair."

Elizabeth looked up, frowning. "I've explained before. He's much safer strapped into his highchair. He could fall off a chair and get hurt."

Jackson sighed. Turning, he picked up his briefcase in one hand and his suitcase in the other. That was another thing Elizabeth did right - she always had his case packed with exactly the items he'd need to wear during the week.

Elizabeth came to the doorway. She adjusted her husband's tie and brushed the lapels of his suit. Perfect, as always. She looked up at him. "Are you sure you can't come to the neurologist appointment with us this morning?"

"We've been through this. I have to work, you know that. Someone has to pay the bills and keep a roof over our heads." He didn't meet her eyes. "Besides, it'll be the same old, same old anyway."

"But things have changed. They're getting worse."

Of course they are, Jackson thought. And if you wouldn't baby him so much, he'd have a chance of being normal. He glanced over at his son who was oblivious to their conversation, the tension in the air or their very presence, he thought. "Anyway, gotta go." He leaned toward Elizabeth to place the obligatory peck on her cheek.

Behind Elizabeth, a bumping and rattling started as the highchair legs skittered across the floor. She rushed over to their son, wrapping her arms around his head. "He's having a seizure!"

Well again, of course he is, Jackson said to himself. When does he not? He loved his son, he really did, but for just a little while he'd like to have a normal boy, a boy he could play with, take places and be proud of. He shook his head. He was proud of his son, an appealing tike. When out in public, people commented on how good looking he was, but when they tried to engage him, Timothy's eyes slid away. Elizabeth would step in to explain their son's lack of interest, saying he was ill and not feeling well. Partially true; he was ill. That was just it. This was not what Jackson had signed on for. Still, the kid would probably be better if his mother would stop this over-protective bit. Every guy knew that when a baby entered your life, the mom's focus would be on the child for a while. Understandable. But should that baby remain the center of her universe for four whole years, with no end in sight?

He watched a few moments longer as the highchair shook with the violence of Timothy's spasms. Then the odor of urine filled the kitchen. Figures. Kid pissed himself again. If he would not be toilet-trained, he wished Elizabeth would keep the kid's diaper on. At least when he was home, rather than going through this farce of toilet training. He shook his head and went out the door. Outside, he said to the air, "Be back Friday night. See you then." Or not.

∾

ELIZABETH CRADLED TIMOTHY'S HEAD, protecting it from bruising and bumps on the back and arms of the highchair. Although the seizures rarely lasted more than a minute or so, they could seem to take forever when you held your writhing child in your arms, praying for it to be over, praying for him to be undamaged by this assault on his brain.

Finally, the thrashing stopped, and Timothy slumped to the side. The seizures took so much out of him. He'd sleep for the next hour, at least, and awaken groggy and disoriented. She liked to remain near, providing comfort and whatever security she could offer.

Unstrapping him from the highchair took a while because of the five-point harness and double locking system. Once, before all that was in place, a seizure had thrown him right out of the chair, adding a minor concussion on top of all his other problems.

With her nose that close, Elizabeth could smell the urine. Looking under the chair, she saw the puddle forming. She grimaced, knowing how much Jackson hated that. Well, so did she, and she was sure Timothy felt the same way. It was just that he had no control. None of them had control over this. Timothy actually smiled at her when she dressed him in his big boy underwear this morning. Was it just half an hour ago? She cherished moments like that, when he would look right at her and share his enjoyment. Even if he didn't say it, she knew he was proud to have that diaper off. So much for today's toilet training session.

Lifting a limp forty-pound child out of a snug-fitting highchair was no simple task, but Elizabeth honed this skill over the many times she had to do this on her own. Getting him into her arms, she felt the wet soaking into the sleeve of her new blouse. Another one for the dry cleaners.

She glanced up at the doorway toward her husband. Gone. Out of habit, she schooled her expression so her disappointment wouldn't show, then remembered that there was no one there to pretend for. Jackson was gone; Timothy was sleeping the sleep of the unconscious, as he always did after a major seizure.

It was Monday and Jackson was gone. Another long week of basically single parenting until Jackson returned home Friday.

CHAPTER 2

D r. Muller's office was familiar, sadly familiar. What Elizabeth wouldn't give to have never had reason to enter such a place. Or even if this visit was a one-shot deal. Or their last visit.

Set up for kids, there was a section in the corner with a low wall separating the waiting room chairs from the kids' play area. Meant to be easily climbable by the average child, a startling number of the small kids entering this office needed to be lifted over the barrier to sit in the ball pit or helped to reach for the toys. While some young patients obviously wanted their parents' help in getting to the play area, Timothy showed no such reaction. He appeared neutral to his surroundings, neither clinging to his mom, burying his head against her legs nor clambering to go play. Elizabeth assumed that he was more mature than other preschoolers, already above such things as a ball pit, and so self-possessed that he was content with his own thoughts. At least this meant he wouldn't be one of those kids who screamed when lifted away from the toys to have their turn with the doctor.

Instead, Timothy sat quietly beside his mother, playing with his hands. Jazz hands, she called them; he could twist them into such intriguing shapes and seemed content to do this for hours. Thankfully, Elizabeth thought that he had fewer seizures when quietly occupied. Maybe.

～

THE RECEPTIONIST CALLED Timothy's name. In the doorway to the hall stood a smiling Dr. Muller. Elizabeth stood, said her son's name softly. When there was no response, she gently took his upper arm and guided him off his chair toward the physician. Dr. Muller squatted to be closer to Timothy's height and held out his hand. "Hi, Timmy. It's good to see you again."

"Timothy," reminded Elizabeth. "His name is Timothy." She gave a soft nudge to her son's shoulder, hoping he would respond to the extended hand. She had practiced this with Timothy at home. While he would shake hands with her, he could not seem to generalize that action with anyone else.

The doctor straightened, unrebuffed and led the way to his office.

～

"SO, how has it been going, young man?" Dr. Muller directed his question to Timothy.

As always, his mom answered for him. "Not well, not well at all."

The neurologist tried again with Timothy. He called his name, waited then called again, watching for a shift in Timothy's attention, a glance his way or some recognition that he had heard his name called. Nothing.

"He's never comfortable in any place but home," Elizabeth explained. Then she started to describe that morning's seizure.

"Wait." Dr. Muller held up his hand. "I'll get the nurse in here to take Timothy away to play. Then we can talk."

"Oh, he won't go with anyone but me."

"I'd prefer not to talk about your son in front of him. If we had some privacy, you can speak more freely."

"That's not a problem. Timothy doesn't talk."

"I'm aware of that. But that doesn't mean that he isn't listening and understanding what we say."

"I only wish that were true. My husband and I talk all the time, and about our concerns over him and he never pays any attention."

"As you wish, Mrs. Whitmore. You are his guardian."

"Yes. As I was saying, the seizures are worse."

"Frequency? Intensity?" he asked.

"Yes, to both. And they're not just absence seizures, or at least we don't notice many of those anymore. Maybe they're still happening, but the major ones take up our attention. Remember those he used to have, the kind where his upper body would stiffen when he was lying down, and he'd sit up?"

"Jackknifing. Are those occurring more now?"

"They do, but it's not just those. Sometimes one arm will rise in the air, straight up, and stay that way for maybe half a minute. You can't bend his arm down when that's happening. He's clunked both Jackson and I in the face several times. At first Jackson got mad, thinking Timothy was doing it on purpose to be funny. But he's not - I swear he is not."

"How often is this happening?"

"Several times a day. And that's not all. Over the last week or two, he's having tonic-clonic seizures. I looked it up on

9

the internet. He seems to lose consciousness, then his body is twitching and moving. If I don't protect him, he hits his head. Hard. I try to keep him by me at all times, because he just drops to the ground when it happens. Once he got this huge bump on his forehead." She brushed Timothy's bangs back, showing the remnants of what was a nasty contusion. "What I need to know is when this will end."

Dr. Muller leaned back in his chair. "I know this isn't what you want to hear, but the honest answer is that I don't know. There's a chance never."

Elizabeth's body moved to the edge of her chair. "But before you called this Infantile Spasms. He's not an infant anymore. I thought that most kids grew out of this."

"West Syndrome," he began.

"But Jackson told me it wasn't West Syndrome."

"Mr. Whitmore did not want it to be West Syndrome." He sighed. "West Syndrome, although we sometimes don't know why it occurs, is a genetic disorder passed down from men to their sons."

"Jackson did not have seizures. Ever. I asked his mother."

"It can be recessive in a man, but still passed on to his son."

"That would mean…".

"Yes, I'm afraid that that's how your husband saw it, that if Timothy had West Syndrome, then the fault or blame lay with the father. There is no blame; it sometimes just happens."

"This is something babies get. I think we first noticed it when Timothy was about six-months-old. It's been three and a half years. Shouldn't he be growing out of it by now? It's getting worse and the seizures are changing."

"I understand. Since he first started having them, we've noticed abnormal EEG patterns. They were consistent with what we often see in West Syndrome. But they do seem to be changing. I think he might be developing a different variety of seizure disorder."

"Okay, that might be good, one you can do something about."

Dr. Muller shook his head. "I'm afraid that what we might be seeing is Lennox Gastaut. It's a rare form of epilepsy that begins in childhood."

"When does it go away?"

"It doesn't, or at least it rarely goes away."

"We can treat it, can't we?"

"We have medications that can help to keep it under some degree of control."

"He's already on anti-epileptic meds!"

"Yes, and he'll remain on some, but we'll tweak the doses, the timing and the exact meds until we find the optimum level of control with as few side effects as possible."

"Side effects?"

"We'll aim for a balance between dampening down the seizure action without overly sedating Timmy."

"Timothy." Elizabeth's voice rose. "It's Timothy. If we had wanted him called Timmy or Tim or some other variation, we would have named him that. We chose Timothy. It's a strong and solid name."

"Sorry." Dr. Muller glanced at the child. "Timothy, I didn't mean to get your name wrong."

The child seemed not to care either way. He fixated on the play of his hands in the sunbeam coming through the south-facing window.

∼

ELIZABETH TOOK a minute to absorb this news before composing herself. She grasped her son's hands, pulling them tightly to her lap. "What about his development? There was some question about that when you thought it was Infantile Spasms."

"You're right. There is often some degree of cognitive impairment with IS. But, when the child was meeting all development milestones previous to the onset of the seizures, there is a greater chance of development closer to typical."

"Closer." Elizabeth held on to that word. It meant good things. Sort of. "He seems fine now. I mean, just look at what he can do with his hands. He has more dexterity than do kids a year older than him. He can pick up the tiniest speck that I can hardly even see. But he knows it's there and goes after it."

Dr. Muller nodded.

"And he's far more content than most four-year-olds. He hardly needs any entertaining; he can amuse himself for long stretches where other kids plague their parents."

Again, Dr. Muller nodded, encouraging Elizabeth to continue. When she didn't, he asked the one question she did not want to discuss. "How is his speech?"

She looked away. "It's not there. Or, hardly at all."

"Hardly? That you would say that is encouraging. What words does he say? Momma? Daddy? Please? Me? Does he respond to his name? Go get the item you ask for?"

"No, none of those. Not once that we've ever heard. But when he says something, he can go on and on for sentences." Her voice became more enthused. "He can recite long speeches from some of his videos. He loves them and watches them over and over. And he's so smart he can run our DVD player all by himself. And he can find the things he wants to watch from You Tube on the iPad".

They both watched Timothy wave and contort his hands in the air, smiling as he did so.

"He's a beautiful child," Elizabeth whispered.

"Yes, he is a good-looking boy. Mrs. Whitmore, I wonder if there is something else we're seeing here."

"This Lennox-Gastaut?"

"Well, that and possibly something else as well."

"Something you can cure? Something that will go away?"

"I'm afraid not. We are likely talking about a lifelong condition. Conditions, to be exact."

∼

ELIZABETH PUSHED BACK her chair and reached for her son. She swept him into her arms. "Thank you, Dr. Muller. Anything further will have to wait until my husband is with us. He was really not pleased about the possibility of West Syndrome, and I doubt he will like the sounds of what you are insinuating now." She took several steps toward the door. "We'll call to make an appointment when Jackson can be here."

"Just a minute, please." Dr. Muller held up a piece of paper. "Here are your prescriptions for the new medications. You remember how we weaned him gradually off the current medication by going from three times a day to two, then one, then giving one day of rest before beginning the new one. The valproic acid was not giving as much control as we'd like, so we'll see what a combination of Lamictal and Clobazam will do. Begin with the Lamictal first, just one before bed then by this weekend, add one Clobazam first thing in the morning. We'll see what that does."

"We'll see? Aren't you supposed to *know*?"

"I wish I did, but medicine is not an exact science. Everyone's metabolism handles compounds differently. We'll need to play around with this until we find the best combination to give him some relief."

Clutching her son tightly, Elizabeth fled, prescriptions in hand.

Behind her, the receptionist called. "Mrs. Whitmore, don't you want to make your next appointment? Dr. Muller said he wanted to see you in two weeks."

"Later. I'll call you later when I know my husband's schedule. I want him here the next time."

CHAPTER 3

*A*fter securing Timothy in his car seat, Elizabeth sat behind the steering wheel, hands in the ten o'clock and two o'clock position, clenching and unclenching her fists. Okay, breathe, she told herself. In through the nose and out through the mouth. Calming breaths. She glanced in the rearview mirror at her son. Timothy was content, playing with his fingers, two of which found their way into his mouth. Elizabeth grimaced. She always cleaned his hands immediately after leaving a doctor's office. You never know what germs were floating around such places and Timothy could not afford to get any sicker than he was. Upset at the possible negative prognosis Dr. Muller hinted at, she had completely forgotten about cleansers when she fled his office.

Why did she have to do this alone? Why couldn't Jackson have taken even just an hour off work to go with her? Part of her brain knew that he was already halfway across the State by now and had to travel for his job, but still…. This felt too much like single parenting, something she had not signed on for. She wasn't one of those strong, independent women; she needed a man to rely on. A man like her dad had been would be ideal. But those were rare commodities, and it wasn't fair to Jackson to compare him to her pretty much perfect dad. Well, he would still be perfect if he hadn't ended up dead, leaving her alone.

I'm not alone, she reminded herself. I have a beautiful son and a loving husband. We're fine.

～

ELIZABETH UNCRUMPLED the papers still locked between her fingers. She spread them out - yes, the prescriptions were still readable. And yes, she knew the routine of weaning Timothy off one medication, while gradually increasing the dose of a new one, recording side effects, and efficacies. She could do this. She had to.

～

SHE MADE the drive to the pharmacy on autopilot. Great. Looked like Timothy was just falling asleep. He'd be cranky if she woke him. Sighing, she began loosening the straps on his car seat.

"Come on, big guy. We have to go see Mr. Rexton." A groggy Timothy leaned on his mom, the back of his head pressing into her neck. She hefted him up a little higher and with one arm firmly around his bottom, reached into the front seat for her purse, slinging it over her shoulder. Since she became a mother, there were no more clutch purses for her - only shoulder bags that would leave her hands free. This whole business was easier when Timothy was younger. Toting a forty-pound child was tougher than one might think. Who needed to go the gym when she did this all day?

~

Mr. Rexton's warm eyes greeted her. He always served Elizabeth himself rather than relying on his assistants. He took a special interest in Timothy. Elizabeth discovered that pharmacists held a wealth of knowledge and could help explain things she was too overwhelmed to ask her son's specialists, or didn't get the first time she heard them.

She handed over the new prescriptions. Sam Rexton raised his eyebrows. "Let's hope that these just might do the trick. How has the little tike been?"

"Obviously not well or well enough," Elizabeth replied, nodding at the prescriptions.

"Let me pull up his chart." After perusing the screen a minute, he asked, "Shall we go over the protocol for weaning him off of the valproic acid?" As they discussed the approach Dr. Muller laid out, Timothy stirred in her arms. It was one thing to hold a sleeping forty pounds, but another to keep a good grip on a squirming forty pounds. She slid him down her legs and steadied him until his feet seemed firmly planted, holding his right hand.

"We have a bit of a back-log right now, so it will take about twenty minutes for me to fill these. Do you want to wait?"

Timothy was pulling at her hand. "No, I think we'll come back. I have a bit of shopping to do then I'll fill the car with gas. We should be back within an hour or so."

The pharmacist pointed to the jar on the counter containing suckers. Elizabeth shook her head. "Still low carb so we're avoiding sweets. But thanks, anyway." Besides, such treats made such a sticky mess.

"See you soon," he told Timothy. "When you come back, I'll have a better treat waiting for you."

∾

SHE DIDN'T NEED MUCH, just a few things at the grocery store. Some nuts, cheese and avocados. They didn't last well so she liked to buy them fresh a few times a week. While it had at first seemed daunting, the ketogenic diet wasn't that difficult to maintain once she had firmly in mind which foods to have on hand. The worst part was eliminating breads. Sandwiches were a quick meal for a child, but they'd learned to make do. Mostly, she and Jackson stuck to the diet as well, and they'd each lost a few extra pounds. While it had helped them, she was not so sure that the diet was having any effect on their son's seizures. But, as Dr. Muller said, maybe they'd be worse without this low-carb diet. She grabbed her insulated bag out of the trunk, and they went to pick up their groceries. This would be a fast trip because she had a surprise in mind for Jackson so would need to make time for an extra stop. No, it wasn't his birthday or their anniversary; she just wanted to do something nice and keep it in the freezer for when he got home Friday. She had placed an order for a Dairy Queen Ice Cream cake - his favorite Reeses-Pieces kind and would pick it up after she got groceries, then gas, then Timothy's prescriptions. And Jackson thought that all a housewife did was sit at home watching soaps.

∾

JACKSON LIKED to tease that she was such a creature of habit. Maybe that was true, but she found it easier to get chores done when she kept to a schedule. She filled the car with gas every Monday. When she first got her driver's license, her dad had drilled it into her to never let her gas tank get below half full because you just never knew. Only driving around town she used little gas, certainly not like poor Jackson who put thousands of miles on his car each month. The life of a traveling salesman. Elizabeth often wondered if Frankfurt Electric knew just what a gem of an employee they had in Jackson. She wasn't sure his take-home pay he showed her reflected his real worth. Despite the long hours he worked, they'd have a hard time living off just his wage. Good thing her father had the forethought to prepare a trust fund for her and bought their home as a wedding gift.

~

ELIZABETH PULLED into the gas station, the same one she always went to. Sticking with the familiar made life easier - just one more thing that she didn't have to figure out during her day.

As she started the pump running, she watched her son's sleeping face through the side window. He looked so at peace. But she knew that even in his slumber a seizure could attack. Thankfully, there had been just one today.

When the nozzle clicked off, she placed it back on the pump, then shut her gas cap. She reached in the compartment in the driver's door for her hand sanitizer. You never knew who had last handled these gas pumps and what germs they might carry that she might pass on to Timothy. The seizures were far worse when he got sick.

After rubbing for the required thirty seconds, she replaced the sanitizer, grabbed her purse to head in to pay for her gas. Crossing the pavement, she felt the sun on her hair and wiped her forehead with the back of her arm.

She hated perspiring; it was not her thing. Goodness, it was a blistering afternoon.

Hot. She glanced back at her slumbering son. The temperature inside a closed car could rise quickly, and Timothy had already been in the car almost five minutes while she pumped the gas. Getting overheated was one condition that brought on seizures. Should she wake him up and carry him inside with her? He was such a dead weight when he didn't want to awaken. She'd just be a few seconds inside and he would be in plain sight all the time.

Elizabeth returned to the car, slid in and started the engine, cranking up the air conditioning. It was the right thing to do; it was already uncomfortably hot inside. In the rear-view mirror, she could see that Timothy hadn't stirred. That neurologist appointment this morning must have taken as much out of him as it did out of her.

"Just a few more minutes, baby, then we'll head home and relax." Leaving the engine running, and leaving the door unlocked so she could get back in, Elizabeth went to pay for her gas.

She timed it poorly, and there were two people ahead of her in line. But then it was finally her turn. "I'm on pump five, please." She placed her purse on the counter to rummage through to find her wallet. Her purse was cavernous. Who would have known you had to carry around so much stuff for one small child?

The gas station attendant repeated the price. "Yes, I just need to get my credit card," Elizabeth mumbled, face pointed into the cavern of her shoulder bag. Opening her wallet, the first thing she saw was the picture of her son, taken on his fourth birthday. It always warmed her heart, that picture. Timothy with his arms around his parents, all wearing silly party hats.

Pulling the wallet out, she glanced at the car where Timothy sat, oblivious to the world.

She froze like a mannequin posed in a catatonic position. She could not take in what her eyes were seeing.

What? Who was that? There was a man, and he was opening the driver's door. Wait! He was getting in. "Hey!"

Elizabeth took off, yelling. Whereas the gas station had been full when she pulled in, but now it was void of people - except for this strange man getting into her car.

The guy shut the door. She could see his hand go to the gear shift. He was going to take off!

She sprinted the last few steps, turning her ankle on the concrete lip, breaking off the heel of her shoe. The car crept forward. Her left hand grabbed for the rear door handle, latched on and pulled. The car was already moving and picking up speed. She threw herself inside, her torso sprawling atop Timothy's car seat, her legs dangling outside. As she attempted to right herself, her left shoe flew off as they bumped over the curb. She yanked her legs inside just as the car's momentum swung the door shut.

CHAPTER 4

"*H*ey! Stop! Are you crazy? This is my car!" Elizabeth worked at righting herself, checking to see that she had not squashed Timothy when she dove into the car. No, he was fine and still asleep. "Stop this car right now and get out!"

"Not gonna happen. I need a car."

"Well, you can't have this one."

"Could have fooled me, lady. I seem to be the one driving."

Her hand went to her chest as if that would stop her racing heart. More quietly she asked, "Why are you doing this to us? We haven't done anything to you. This is kidnapping. You'll go to prison."

"I'm not kidnapping anyone. What do you take me for? I started driving, and you slammed yourself into the car. While it was moving, even." He glanced in the rear-view mirror. "Right on that kid. What kind of mother does that?"

Elizabeth's head whipped from side to side, checking all the windows. Surely someone had noticed what was happening and called the police. Any second now, cops and rescuers would surround them. She just needed to buy some time. "Look, just slow down a bit and drive carefully. There's a child here. What is it you want from us?"

"I don't want nothing from you. I need a car. I didn't plan on you tagging along."

"But you were driving off with my son!"

"How'd I know someone would leave a kid sleeping all alone in a car?"

Elizabeth grimaced. He was right. "Look, just pull over and let us out, all right? You can have the car."

"Are you kidding? You can identify me and the car. How soon before you're screaming away to the police? You made your choice, so now you're coming with me." He thought a moment more. "Or you could jump out, the same way you jumped in, but I'll keep the kid as insurance that you'll keep your mouth shut."

"I'm not leaving without my son!"

"We could do this another way. You leave the kid on the street while you stay with me."

"I can't abandon my child on the street. Anything could happen to him." Anything *did* happen to him, she thought. And while under her care. Jackson called her an over-protective and hovering mother. And still this had happened. But it was her fault; she had done the unthinkable and left her son alone.

The initial panic was tamped down a bit now. Their lives were not in immediate danger, at least not at this moment. Although they were on the freeway heading south, at least this lunatic was not driving wildly. "Where are we going?"

～

"ARE you sure you gave me the right schedule? We can't find her." Impatience was in his voice.

"It's Monday, isn't it? You can absolutely count on her to be where she's supposed to be. The only deviation would be if the kid got sick. That happens, but she never keeps that information to herself. There would be calls for sure and there's been none."

"She's not where you said she'd be."

"Shit, man, she even follows the same route. Look, she was home for the morning, then had a one o'clock appointment with the neurologist. Maybe there was some hitch there, and she's running late because he overbooked his appointments again. Anyway, since his meds were running low, next she'd go to the drugstore. While the prescription's being filled, she'll go get groceries. Next, she'll fill the car with gas. She always does that Monday afternoons. If you just hung out there, you'll see her."

"We did. I got a guy there now and one at the pharmacy. I'm at her house. None of us have seen her. She's gone."

"Not possible. No one is more boringly the same than Elizabeth. Find her! That's what you're paid for."

∾

ELIZABETH RUBBED her son's knee. He slept peacefully, so the touch reassured her more than him. Only then did she realize that her hand still clutched the credit card she'd pulled from her purse. Thank god. She may need it. She hunched over slightly, slipping it inside her bra, out of site of the maniac who had kidnapped them.

Her purse! All her ID was inside it and she'd left it on the counter at the gas station. Relief washed over her. They'd know who she was, her address, her car registration information. Next of kin info was all over her cards, so they'd have called Jackson by now. Although there had been no other cars in the lot while she paid, surely the kid who worked there would have watched her run for the car and known she'd been car jacked. The place was likely swarming with cops even now. She just needed to sit tight for a bit longer then the rescuers would be here. Now, to keep this crazy man calm until then. Calm she could do. If nothing else, Mount Holyoke College had honed her skills at presenting as calm and self-assured. Act like a lady, she told herself. Decorum was everything.

∾

"Excuse me, sir." Sir? She winced. Maybe that was a bit over the top. She asked again, "Where are you taking us?"

"I'm not *taking* you anywhere. You chose to come along. Since you're here now, it can't hurt for you to know. Bathinghurst."

Bathinghurst was hours away, and it was just a little town. "Why Bathinghurst? Is that where you're from?" Maybe she could do a reverse Stockholm syndrome and get him to like her, to like them.

"My granny's place is there."

"Oh. Is she ill? Do you need to visit her?"

"She's dead." The car sped up. The tension in his voice was palpable.

Okay, wrong way to steer the conversation. But she had to go with it now. "I'm so sorry to hear that. Was it recent?"

"Eleven days ago, so they said."

"I guess you didn't get to go to the funeral then?"

"They wouldn't let me out."

CHAPTER 5

*R*eggie hunched sideways over the counter, mouth
hung open as he watched the woman. For a
classy-looking chick, she could sure move in those heels.
Oops, maybe not quite so classy - she nearly lost her balance
when her foot slipped off the concrete lip by the pumps.
Didn't slow her down much, though. Next, she grabbed the
door handle and did a nosedive into the back of the car. The
door cantered crazily for a few moments, then slammed shut
as the tires went over the curb.

Gone. Nothing left of her but the heel of one shoe. It lay
on its side abandoned by the pumps.

He pulled himself back, shaking his head. Nutsy lady.

Oh. It seemed that there was not only her heel left. Nope,
she had left him a treat. Open in front of him was her purse.
Glancing around to make sure no one noticed, he pulled her
bag behind the counter with him. He checked again, the
station still deserted. For once luck was with him. About
time he got a break.

Ducking down, he rummaged in the bag. What a load of
crap she carried. What the? Were those diapers? At least they

weren't used ones. He tossed them in the garbage can, or at least toward the garbage can. He'd clean them up later. His fingers made something rattle. Peering closer, he spied pill bottles. This really was his lucky day. Hopefully, she was some kind of hypochondriac housewife, stoned on Vicodin. The label said valproic acid. Never heard of that one. Shit, the other label said the same thing, just a different dose. He'd have to talk to someone to see if they'd do anything for him. The bottles went in the pouch of his hoodie.

Now to the good stuff. A cell phone. Yes! His never had any minutes left on it. He clicked the button for Safari and yep; the internet came right up. Now he could do some surfing. And would you look at that? She'd last been on Amazon and hadn't logged out. She spent $189.99 with free shipping. He brushed the Continue Shopping button, rewarded with the Amazon landing page and search bar. Could be useful, but where would he have stuff sent? He had no address anymore. Might be of some use, though. The iPhone went into the front pocket of his jeans, bumping alongside his useless burner one.

Ah, her wallet. He could see now why it took her so long to find it when she stood there. Why did women need to tote around so much crap? Who cared when you hit the jackpot? Lookee, lookee. A debit card, an American Express card and even better, cash. He yanked out the bills and waved them under his nose. Fresh. Looked like they just came from an ATM, all nicely stacked together. He counted them. Then counted them again to be sure. An even five hundred in twenty-dollar bills. Could it get any better? Well, yeah, there could be more, but five hundred cash all in one place was more than he'd had his hands on in well, almost forever. He fumbled the credit and debit cards and they fell to the floor. Good thing as a customer walked in. Bending, Reggie stuffed the cards inside the sole of his shoe.

After ringing up the gas purchase, he continued searching through the purse. A bunch of pictures, the kind no one but immediate family would find of any interest. Nothing else of use. He hesitated over her nail file but decided the handle wasn't secure enough to make much of a shiv. Having taken anything that would help him get by, he stashed her bag in the trash can under the counter. Just in time. The bell over the door tinkled as a guy came in to buy a cup of coffee.

"Hey," the guy said, taking a slurp from his coffee. He pulled his head back, wiping his lips. Reggie could have told him that the machines made it too hot to drink right away. But why spoil the fun? He liked watching people when they took that first sip.

The guy surveyed the array of candy bars then threw a Snickers and a bag of barbecued peanuts onto the counter, along with the large sized coffee. He reached into his pants for his wallet, pulling out a debit card. "Say, buddy, maybe you could help me with something else. I'm looking for my wife. She always gasses up here. Wonder if you've seen her - she'd be with a little kid, about four years old." From his wallet he pulled a picture of the lady who had left her purse.

"No man, sorry. Never seen her."

"She comes in here every Monday afternoon."

"I'm new here. I'm not that good at faces and we get a lot of 'em in here." To back up his statement, the door opened, bringing in two more customers. A third was about to grab the door handle.

"I'm trying to catch up with my wife. She's out running errands and not answering her cell phone. I hate when she does that. Can never reach her when I need her." He pulled out his own phone and pressed a button.

The iPhone in Reggie's pants vibrated. He rang up the purchase in the till, hoping the noise of the printing receipt would cover up the faint noise the phone made. No such luck, although why he would expect to get lucky, he didn't know. Life didn't spin for him that way.

"Do you need to get that?"

"Nah, I'm good, man. Not supposed to make personal calls while on the job."

The guy looked at him. Too closely for Reggie's liking, but let it go. Reggie kept an eye on him as the guy left the store. Pleased with his ability to multi-task, ringing up the next sale while watching the man. He got into a mud-colored sedan across the street, but didn't drive off. He sat there watching the station. Reggie swallowed.

It was a while before the stream of customers slowed. From the back closet where employees stored their personal stuff along with the stinky mops and cleaning supplies, Reggie pulled out his duffle bag, slinging it over one shoulder. Perching on the stool behind the counter, he pretended he was looking through it for his lunch. Checking to see that no one was watching, he stashed the lady's purse into his duffle. He'd dispose of it later.

When he had time to wander toward the front window, the sight made him nervous. Yep the guy was still sitting out there in his car. Who does that? He sure as hell wasn't her husband, at least he looked nothing like the guy in all the photos of her and a kid. Maybe he was an ex. No way did Reggie want to get mixed up in that shit. He jumped as the phone in his pocket vibrated again.

~

"No boss, there's no sign of her yet. Maybe we got here too late." He listened a moment. *"Yeah, well, she might stick to her routine, but there's been no sign of her in the two hours that I've been here."* He stared through the gas station window as he listened. There was no sign of her at the pharmacy or her house either.

"*There's something about that guy, the punk who works at the station. I showed him her picture, but he said he'd never seen her. He was jittery but could have been jacked up on something - looks that type. But when I dialed her cell number, his phone vibrated in his pocket. It was faint, but you could tell by his face he felt it. Could be nothing, though. Kids these days are on their phones all the time, so maybe it was just a coincidence. Still, I've dialed it several times in the last hour; I'm not sure, but I think he might have jumped a couple times right after I sent the call.*"

CHAPTER 6

Five o'clock dragged on, but finally arrived. Quitting time for Reggie. Sometimes he liked to sneak out early, but that was tougher to do when his boss hung around. Sometimes Reggie thought that Mr. Wilson arrived right around that time to check that Reggie was staying for his full shift. What did it matter? His replacement always came twenty minutes early, anyway.

He looped the strap of his duffle over one shoulder. "See ya, Mr. Wilson." Couldn't hurt to be sociable, could it?

Old Wilson raised a hand in one shooing motion. "And be on time tomorrow," was his reminder.

Reggie plastered on his most winning grin and waved. "Asshole," he said under his breath.

∼

He had no definite target in mind as he started off. Yeah, likely he could spend another night same place as last. He was couch surfing, had been ever since he got evicted from his place for not paying his rent. He would have paid it, for sure, just as soon as he got enough money together. Wasn't his fault that his job paid crap. Crap was about all those digs were worth, anyway, a one-room place with a hot plate, decades old fridge, saggy couch and a shared bathroom no one had ever cleaned. Well, good riddance. He'd find something better just as soon as he got his next paycheck. For now, he shared with various friends and acquaintances the pleasure of his company each night. Better than sleeping in the park he was walking through.

It was quiet here, away from the traffic and any prying eyes. Next to the bandstand was a garbage can. He dropped his duffle and pulled the purse from it. Dumping the contents onto the parched grass, he checked again, making sure that he wasn't throwing out anything of use to him. The light wasn't so good. He chucked the purse into the trash can but kept hold of the wallet. He'd check it under a streetlight before throwing it into some dumpster. There was a strip mall in the next block with several dumpsters out back.

～

THE ALLEY STANK. He didn't know whether it was urine, old food, or some other putrid combo, but it was not the place to linger. How many cards did that woman own? She seemed to have every kind of store rewards card ever invented and it took time to figure out each one to see if there was any advantage to keeping it.

He looked up as footsteps approached. Difficult to tell in the dusk, but it looked like someone dumpster diving. Well, he could have this wallet in just a few minutes. He bent his head to rifle through a few more cards, angling them toward the light coming from the store's back window to see better.

One of his arms was yanked up sharply between his shoulder blades. "Where is she?"

"Hey, man, whatcha doing? You got the wrong guy. I'm just minding my own business."

"Where is she, punk?"

Reggie angled his head until one eye could see his assailant. It was the guy from the gas station, the one who hung out in that car for hours. With one swipe of his foot, the guy took Reggie's legs out from under him. The grip on his arm kept him from falling too hard, but almost wrenched his elbow off. He groaned as the guy released his arm, and he hit the pavement. The dirty, stinking, puddled pavement. He tried to pull his arm under him to nurse the injured joint. Was it dislocated? Felt like it. Then thoughts of that pain fled as a knee punched into his back, pinning him in place as the assailant grabbed Reggie's other arm, ensuring that he could not move. He wouldn't have, anyway. Reggie considered himself more a lover than a fighter, especially when the other guy had fifty pounds on him and a nasty look in his eye. Reggie preferred to talk his way out of fights.

"Tell. Me. Where. She Is." He shook Reggie. "And don't pretend you don't know who I'm talking about. The woman in the picture I showed you."

"Okay, okay, ease up. Yeah, she was in this afternoon." The pressure on his arm increased. "But she left. She ran out without paying for her gas. Didn't want to say nothing because I'd get in trouble with the boss for letting a customer stiff him for gas."

The knee pressed harder and Reggie groaned. "Doesn't really sound like something she'd do. Wanna rethink your story?"

"Seriously, man, that's what she did. She was paying, pulling out her wallet, then she just ran out the door. A car was driving out, and she opened the back door and jumped in."

"And?"

"Not really jumped in, sort of dove. Not real graceful for a classy kind of lady."

"Then what happened?"

"That's the last I saw of her."

A second knee joined the first and Reggie groaned. Throw the guy a bone, his brain told him. "Here, look." He tried pointing his chin toward the fallen wallet. "She left this behind."

"And you were just taking what you needed."

"A guy's got to live, and she took off without it."

The pressure shifted. As the guy bent to retrieve the wallet, Reggie rolled over and slumped against the dumpster. Now he could see his attacker, but the guy seemed to have lost interest in him.

"I'll take this," the guy said as he pocketed the wallet.

Reggie cradled his arms, not sure which one ached more. He listened to footsteps retreat down the alleyway. Reggie closed his eyes. Then the steps came back. His hair was grabbed in a fist, his head pulled forward, then slammed into the side of the dumpster.

It was who knows how much later when Reggie woke up. A light rain dampened everything, including the ground around him, his clothing, and his skin. The rain felt sticky on the back of his head, or maybe thicker. Shit. That wet wasn't just rain.

Gingerly, he tried to get onto his knees. Bracing against the dumpster, he was able to make it to his feet, although somewhat unsteadily. He took several steps before realizing that something else felt off. He'd lost a shoe. As a kid his mom had hated how he wore his shoes, sticking his toes in, but resting his heel on the backs of the shoes. Wrecked the shoes, she said, but it made them easier to get on and off. Now that it was full dark, he couldn't see the other shoe, anyway. Well, worse things had happened in his life, in fact, on this particular day. He checked behind the dumpster and yeah, his duffle was still there. That asshole had not thought to look back there, but Reggie was not born yesterday. He knew better than to leave all his worldly possessions out in plain view. Slinging the strap over one shoulder, he started off. Every few feet he switched shoulders, unsure which hurt the least. Despite his pain, he smirked. That asshole thought he was born yesterday. Didn't realize that Reggie kept one of the lady's credit cards hidden in his shoe.

~

"CALL HER." *The woman wound her arms around his shoulders and played with the hair at the nape of his neck.*

"I don't really feel like it now."

"Call old Lizzie and get it over with. Then we can have the evening to ourselves. The whole night to ourselves."

"You know that Elizabeth hates being called Lizzie."

Her smile wasn't friendly. "I know." She brought her lips to his.

~

"NO ANSWER. *That's odd. She's always home at this time, making dinner. She thinks that Timothy does better when he's on a schedule."*

"Maybe she took him to McDonald's or something for supper."

"No, she's got him on this ketogenic diet that's supposed to be helpful with epilepsy."

"I hope you don't expect me to cook special for him."

"It's not a diet where you need to do a lot of special things. It's mainly a low carb thing. Since she started it, we both lost some weight and felt good." His hands clasped her tush. "Might do you some good, too."

She jerked away from him. "I thought you liked my curves rather than that broomstick wifey of yours."

He pulled her back to him. "I most certainly do." He showed her how much. "I'll try calling her again, then we can concentrate on us."

~

"STILL NO ANSWER. Odd, but I left a message, so she'll know that I called. Now, on to us."

~

AFTER DINNER, Jackson's second Monday night message said, "Elizabeth, it's me. This is the fourth time I've tried phoning you, but you don't answer. I was wondering how Timothy's appointment went this afternoon, but I'll take it that no news is good news. Well, I guess that's it. I'll talk to you tomorrow evening."

~

STRANGE that she didn't pick up or at least call back after his first message. She was kind of needy that way and liked him to call every night that he was away. At least every night, often more.

Seeing the doctor was stressful for her - stressful for all of them, really. Worn out, she was probably soaking in the tub. Once the kid was in bed and asleep, she liked to pour a bubble bath, light candles, have a glass of merlot and read her Kindle in the tub. She could lie there for hours, getting all pruny. but she said it was relaxing. If she had her music on, she might not even hear the phone.

Or the phone might still be on vibrate. She tried to remember to turn it off during the medical appointments, so she missed none of the discussion. Plus, she'd consider her phone going off rude while *the doctor was talking, and Elizabeth would go a long way not to offend.*

Well, that covered his ass. Since he'd left two messages, he proved that he'd tried calling her. Now he could go out with a good conscience.

CHAPTER 7

*D*usk now. Too dark for inhabitants of other cars to see inside hers, to see a mother and small child trapped by some crazy man and speeding farther and farther from home. Elizabeth rested her head against the seat back. A roadside sign was coming into view out the passenger side window. She sat up. Bathinghurst showed as the third town they would come to. She sat up straighter. Didn't she recognize one of those other names? Yes, this was an area where Jackson sometimes traveled; she was sure he'd mentioned staying at a crummy hotel in one of those towns.

Maybe, just maybe, they would run across him or he'd recognize her car going by and race after them. It seemed an off chance, but then again what were the odds of getting car jacked in broad daylight within miles of home?

It was close to supper time. Jackson always called by then to see how they were getting along without him and they'd chat for a while. When he didn't reach her, he'd try again then get worried. Yes, he would send out the alarm. All she needed to do was wait. They'd be rescued soon.

~

SHE MUST HAVE DOZED off because Timothy's cry woke her. Great. This was one of those times when he woke up grizzling. Well, she felt that way herself. She reached over a hand to rub his chest, his hair. He turned, holding out his arms to her. Normally she would take him into her arms, soothing him, snuggling him until he was fully awake and ready to greet his world. But she could not take him out of his car seat when they were in a moving vehicle, especially with this strange guy at the wheel. Timothy's wails grew more frenzied; he was working himself up. This was not good.

"Shut that kid up!" came from the front seat.

"I can't. He's upset."

"Lady, you wanna see upset, you let him continue that squawking. Either you shut him up or I will."

"He just woke up. He's tired and hungry."

"So, feed him, shove something in his mouth."

She thought quickly. She always carried snacks for him in her purse, but she'd left that back at the gas station. Ah, groceries. "If you'd pull over and stop, I could get something out of the trunk to feed Timothy."

"Not gonna happen, lady. We're not stopping. Now, make that kid shut up."

Elizabeth undid her seat belt. She cringed at breaking the law in this way and had visions of being tossed about in a crashing car. She squeezed her body in front of her son's car seat and edged to the other side. Timothy's howls lessened somewhat, probably wondering what his mother was up to. Reaching over his seat, she yanked on the strap that released the split seat back. Hopefully, she could get it folded down enough to reach into the hatchback trunk to grab one of her bags of groceries and find something for Timothy. Pressing her weight on her one remaining shoe, her ankle twisted, and her weight collapsed onto Timothy's legs. He roared his complaint; he wasn't really hurt, she knew, just startled, hungry and out of sorts.

"Laaadyyyy," the warning growl came from the front seat.

"I'm trying, I'm trying." She stretched again, ignoring the fact that her butt was in the air and her dress had ridden up dangerously. The seat backs were high and anyway, his eyes supposedly faced the road, didn't they?

There. Her fingertips snagged the handle of one of the insulated grocery bags. Hopefully, this was the right one. Inching it toward her, she settled back on the other side of Timothy, unzipping the bag. Yes! There was some cheese. That should hold him over until she could get him a proper meal.

The cheese came tightly wrapped in plastic. Safe and hygienic, but difficult to get into. If only she had her nail file from her purse. She tried using her fingernails, only to lose one gel tip. Darn. She didn't have a manicure appointment until the next weekend. Without thinking, she said, "You don't have a knife on you, do you?" Jackson always carried a tiny penknife on his key chain.

Silence.

Elizabeth thought of what she had just asked.

"If I did, do you think I'd hand it over to you, lady? What kind of idiot do you take me for? As my granny used to say, 'I'm not as green as I am cabbage-looking.'"

Took Elizabeth a minute to puzzle that one out, but she thought she got it. What she didn't get though was if he was actually carrying a knife. If so, would he use it?

Timothy started up again, so she used her teeth to saw her way into the cheese block. Then, tearing the opening the rest of the way, she broke off a chunk and handed it to her son. Timothy looked at it suspiciously before hunger won out. She never gave him pieces like that; she always cut them into bite-sized portions and put them on his tray in front of him.

Elizabeth rested her head against the side of his car seat. At least the cheese quieted him down. Her stomach growled. She wondered when they could expect to get supper and what it would be like. Was he planning to feed them? Timmy needed to keep to a strict schedule. When his meals and his life were all out of whack, his seizures were worse. The gnawing in her stomach increased, so she tore off a chunk of cheese for herself. It crossed her mind to ask their kidnapper if he wanted some, but she stifled her in-born politeness, wrapping the plastic around the cheese and replacing it into the bag. She zipped the bag, hoping to keep at least some of the coolness. She didn't know how long this food would have to last them.

~

It was fully dark now, and the miles raced by. Timothy played with his hands, holding them up in the light of passing cars, giggling as the headlight beams flashed by, showing the patterns of his twisting fingers. At least he was quiet, giving Elizabeth time to plan.

Plan what, she thought. So far, her plans revolved around Jackson realizing they were in trouble and sending out the cavalry to rescue them. Or come himself. In the meantime, there seemed little she could do except try to keep Timothy happy, sit and wait.

But they wouldn't be on this highway forever. Couldn't be. At some point they must have to drive through a town, even if just to get to the turnoff to Bathinghurst. Maybe she could attract someone's attention and they'd call the cops. Who was she kidding? She had had no luck getting passersby to notice their plight when it was broad daylight. No, Jackson would be on this. Any minute now.

◇

Timothy sat bolt upright, jack-knifing into an acute angle, his torso rigid, arms banging the back of the front seat, stiff legs beating against the driver's seat.

"Hey! Make that kid stop kicking my seat. Now!" He turned to glance over his right shoulder. "Why is he punching the ceiling? He's going to break the dome light." His head swiveled between the front windshield and the boy strapped into the car seat.

Thank god he was strapped in. Elizabeth didn't know how she would have held him otherwise. Out of habit, she automatically began counting the seconds in her head. Although they felt like they went on forever, most seizures lasted only seconds, maybe up to half a minute at most, although he had had some that persisted much longer. When that happened he needed to get to a hospital immediately. She prayed that this wouldn't be one of those times. What if this nutcase wouldn't take them? On the other hand, what if he did take them? Then they'd be free of him.

The driver yelled and Timothy thumped. Nice, Elizabeth thought. Does the guy really think what he's doing is helping?

Trying to be heard over both their noises, she tried explaining. "He's having a seizure." Louder, she said, "A seizure."

"Well, tell him to stop."

She looked at the idiot. "It's a seizure," she enunciated carefully. "That means involuntary movements. Involuntary, as in he has no control over them. It's a brain thing, his brain is misfiring causing the seizure."

"You mean there's something *wrong* with him?"

She gritted her teeth. "That's one way to put it. Timothy has some health issues."

"Ya think?" He shook his head. "How did I get mixed up with a woman and a spaz kid?"

~

ELIZABETH FOCUSED on comforting her son. The tension was leaving his little body. This was *not* the time for a lesson in political correctness or sensitivity training. It was probably a lost cause with someone like this guy, anyway.

Her nose wrinkled. Oh, no, oh no. It happened sometimes with a seizure - loss of bladder and bowel control. Please, please, why now? Automatically she reached for her purse where she always kept wipes, diapers, and spare clothing. Her hand came up with air. Right, she'd left her purse at the gas station. Now what? She hated leaving Timothy wet and dirty.

CHAPTER 8

*I*t took almost five minutes before the car's atmosphere became saturated with the odor of body fluids. Luck was not with her and the smell did not just remain in the back seat.

"What the hell is that stink?" He turned to glare at Timothy. "Is that what I think it is? Did that kid piss himself? Shit himself?" He punched at the dashboard, increasing the air flow aimed at his face. Warm, muggy air came in. He fiddled some more. "What's happened to the air conditioning on this thing? It was working before."

Elizabeth's shoulders slumped. Not now. Please, not now. "It's broken. Or at least it's intermittent. It works fine for a while then quits. I have an appointment to get it looked at Wednesday morning."

The man gagged and thumbed the button to roll down his window. Quickly all four windows were fully down, bringing in the moist night air along with the scent of oil and tarmac.

The force of the wind through the back window took Timothy's breath away. He took several gasps, then opened his mouth to scream, but a strangled wheeze came out. Elizabeth tried blocking the breeze with her hands and arms. She did not want his asthma to start up as well now. "Please, close the windows. He's having trouble breathing. Please!" Some desperation in her tone must have gotten through because the rear windows slowly raised. "The rest, please. I've got to get his breathing under control." He complied, and the quiet in the car broken only by harsh breaths of a little boy crying.

"God, I'm gonna puke." The driver's window went down again. He stuck his head partway out of the window. "That smell. What the hell did you feed that kid?"

Elizabeth held Timothy's hands, staring into his face, willing him to breathe easily, breathe with her, in time to the squeezes on his hands. Sometimes it worked. Maybe this time. At least it wasn't getting worse. His puffer was in her purse. Of course it was.

∾

THEY DROVE THROUGH A TOWN NOW, streetlights on, cars passing by. Russell pulled into the parking lot of a strip mall, away from the lights and other shoppers. Putting the car into park, he opened his door and got out, hanging his head over the door frame and taking deep breaths. "How can you stand to be in there with him? Talk about gagging a maggot."

Elizabeth glared at him. Yeah, it wasn't pretty, but this was her son they were talking about and he was sick. Some aspects of parenting were just not pretty.

"We gotta do something here." Russell looked around. "There are people here. We could dump the kid, and someone will find him. Hell, keep him strapped into his car seat then he can't get away."

"Good idea. Just leave us here and you can get on your way."

"Oh, no, lady. You're coming with me. I'm not having you hollering your head off about me. You jumped in, now you're going the full ride with me. The kid, though, he's optional. Ditch him."

"My son stays with me." There was steel in her voice.

Russell paced around the car. What a mess. He needed to get going, and he needed to be rid of these problems. But first, he could not, just could not get back in that car with that stench. For a kid who wouldn't even reach his waist, he could sure cut one. Okay, when babies did that, someone changed them. Not that he had any personal experience with it, but that's what happened on television.

Breathing through his teeth, he crouched a little, aiming his words inside toward the back seat. "Can't you change his diaper or something?"

"I would if I had one."

"What kind of a mother does not carry diapers?"

"One who got snatched out of her regular life."

"So, what do you suggest we do?"

"Go buy him some clothes. And some wipes."

Wipes? He didn't want to know.

Elizabeth liked this idea. "You can go into the mall right there and buy him some clothes. Nothing special, just some pants and underwear and wipes. Maybe a package of diapers, too, size 5."

Russell just looked at her. Had she lost her mind? Maybe she sucked in too many fumes. "You want me to waltz into the mall, leaving you and the kid alone here. Ain't gonna happen."

"What would you suggest?"

Russell paced some more. And then more. "Look, here's

what we're doing. Keep that kid strapped into his straight jacket. You go in and buy what you need to. I will give you eight minutes. If you're not back by then, the kid and I take off."

"You can't do that!" Elizabeth tried to put some reasonableness into her voice. "You don't want to be in here with him and the smell. You don't know how to look after him. Let me take him into the store with me, then we'll be right back."

"You'll scream your bloody head off as soon as you get in there with him. The kid stays with me. He's my insurance policy that you'll behave yourself." He produced something from his pocket. "Here's that knife you were asking about. I'll be watching you through those windows. One wrong move, you talk to anyone, you disappear from my sight and the kid gets this."

"Loosen his seat belt." Elizabeth's hands moved toward her son's chest. "No, not that one, the one holding his chair to the car. If I have to throw him out, I don't want to have to touch him."

Elizabeth weighed her options. Unless Jackson came tearing up right now, she was on her own with this.

"Or we ditch the kid right here. You can even put him under one of the streetlights."

That swayed her mind. She didn't doubt that he would do as he said, all of what he said. The stare in his eyes did not waver. "At least pull the car up nearer to the store so I can see you. And," she added, "you can see me so you'll know I'm not 'screaming my head off'."

A bit more pacing and a couple deep breaths and all the windows again went down before Russell got back behind the steering wheel. He audibly breathed through his mouth, even though he'd pulled his t-shirt up over his nose. Like a bandit, Elizabeth thought. Putting the car into gear, he found a parking spot that was still sort of isolated but nearer to the store.

Elizabeth protested that it would be hard to walk in with just one shoe when Russell asked, "Do you want it to be four minutes?"

She started opening the rear passenger door but stopped. "I don't have…" her voice trailed off. She was about to say she didn't have any money, but then remember the credit card she'd stuffed inside her bra. If she used that, there would be a trail that Jackson or the police could follow. "Look, this mall looks fairly crowded. It will take me time to find a children's clothing store, and I might have to wait at the till. There is no way I can be in and out in eight minutes."

Russell pointed. "You're going right there." Not far away there was a storefront with lots of windows, racks of clothing and milling bodies. The sign over the door said Value Village.

"Value Village? But that's used stuff. We donate old clothes to them." Her lip curled the way Russell's had when Timothy dropped his load.

"Is your kid too good for second-hand clothes? Believe me, lady, nothing could be worse than what he's wearing now. This is it. Either you go in there or we just ditch the kid. That's simplest anyway."

Placing a kiss to Timothy's temple and squeezing his hand, she said, "Mommy will be right back." She couldn't bring herself to say more. She limped her way across the parking lot, the sole of one foot shredding its pantyhose when she scraped it on a loose piece of gravel. Well, it would have been even harder to walk if the heel of this shoe hadn't broken off. As she entered the store, she stumbled a bit. The shoe was not meant to be worn minus its heel. She kicked it off, walking into the store. Her snagged, running pantyhose offered little protection.

At least the place was laid out sensibly, with signs pointing to the children's clothing racks, clothing arrayed in sizes. Her hand hesitated before touching some size four-five jeans, but a glance out the windows had her sucking it up. She grabbed two pairs, just in case. Both looked like they might work. Oh, god. He needed underwear. Yes, they sold some, but the thought of putting someone else's old gitch on her little boy gave her shudders. Did they even wash this stuff before they sold it? Sterilize it? Okay, there were three pairs. Who knew when she'd have another chance to get some? What was she saying? Rescue would arrive any minute now, of course it would. Jackson would save them.

Now, diapers. Did they carry diapers? Didn't look like it. Or wipes. But they had towels and face cloths and scarves. Snatching up an assortment, she padded toward the till. The side of one foot landed in something wet. She looked down. She'd landed in a small, yellowish puddle. It was near the children's clothing section. No, it wasn't, was it? God, she couldn't think about that now. She tried wiping her foot on the stained, dusty linoleum. Didn't work. Looking around, she didn't think anyone was watching her. Balancing on one foot, she lifted the dripping one toward the clothing rack and used some hanging shirts to wipe her foot dry. What would her mother have said?

From this angle, she spied the back wall where angled shelves held shoes. Used shoes. Shoes someone had sweated into. How could that be worse than what she'd stepped into? There were women's heels, but heels had not worked out for her earlier today. Tennis shoes were likely a better bet, especially if she had to carry Timothy and run. But they used sneakers and tennis shoes in sports. Sweaty sports. She took a heavy breath in through her nose, held it a second, then let it out through her mouth.

"Got the monthlies, honey? They take me like that, too," a

voice said to her right. A heavy-set woman with graying, corkscrew, disordered hair looked at her with kindly eyes. Elizabeth glanced over her shoulder. She was sure that Russell was staring at her, watching to see if she gave him away. If she opened her mouth, he'd take off with Timothy before she could get there. Then he'd probably dump him out on some highway. Alone. In the dark.

She gave a half-smile and shook her head. Her hand grabbed the first pair of shoes in front of her and she hustled to the till. She wished she knew how much time she'd taken, but she had not worn a watch in years, relying on her phone for such things.

She threw first one shoe, then the other, onto the floor in front of her. Cringing, she thrust her right toes into a shoe. They slid in easily, her heel coming to rest on the back side of the shoe which slid under her sole as if it had been doing it for years. Great, just great. She'd grabbed a pair where a kid had been walking on the back of the shoes. At least that made getting them on easy. She shuffled to the till, the shoe sliding sideways on her foot. How do you keep these things on?

No line-up, thank god. Placing her purchases on the counter, she pointed down. "I'm buying these shoes also, please."

The woman didn't look up from her till, just held out her hand. "Ticket."

What?

"The ticket off those shoes so I can ring it up."

Oh. She tore the orange label from the laces and handed it to the woman.

"That'll be $11.47."

"Uh, do you take Mastercard?"

"Right here, ma'am." She pointed at the machine and didn't blink an eye when Elizabeth reached inside her shirt to retrieve the credit card from her bra. She tapped the receiver and heard the reassuring blip.

"May I have these things in two separate bags, please?" She'd need something to store Timothy's soiled clothes. With a half-smile and a thank you, she grabbed the bags and ran toward the door. As she started down the curb, she had to backtrack a few steps when one shoe came off, but it only cost her a couple seconds. Then she was outside her car with all its doors open and the guy pacing along the passenger side.

~

HE REMAINED OUTSIDE, eyes averted as Elizabeth did her thing. Taking her son out of his car seat was always awkward, but more so now as she tried to keep his soiled clothing away from her body. Yeah, like that worked. She felt the dampness along her side but didn't dare look down at what may have leached onto her clothing. Where a third of the back seat was still down, giving access to the rear hatch made a convenient change table surface. She pushed Timothy's head and shoulders into the hatch, smiling, trying to make a game of it. For once she was thankful for his semi-dopey state which often came with the sequella of a seizure. At least it made changing him easier.

Rooting through the bags, she brought out the scarves and face cloths she'd purchased and did the best she could at cleaning her child without water or wipes. And, yeah, it turned her stomach too, but she was his mother. In the back of her mind, she knew that one day this would not be an issue - he'd be fully toilet-trained, and the seizure episodes would be a thing of the past. Both things would come true, she just knew it.

Dumping out the "new" clothes, she used an empty plastic

bag to hold the soiled garments. She double knotted the opening tightly closed, hoping it would contain the smell.

She was grateful that her brain had worked enough to think to buy Timothy an extra pair of pants. With all that cheese he'd consumed, and being off his schedule, this could all happen again. Could be a plus or minus. Could be an opportunity for them to escape or could enrage the guy to do them harm.

CHAPTER 9

$\mathcal{U}$nder the guy's watchful eye, Elizabeth placed the plastic bag with the soiled clothing and cloths in a garbage can. She hated to give up her son's OshKosh overalls. They were so cute, and she'd become quite good at removing stains.

Back on the road. If only it was daylight, she might have better luck at getting another driver to notice her and do something.

A new scent filled the car. Well, a semi-new odor. It had been there previously, just over-ridden by the other. Maybe he wouldn't notice.

As they sat at a red light, it became more apparent. "You're shitting me, right?" That came from the front seat.

Well, no, not exactly came from the sick part of Elizabeth's mind. Keeping a neutral tone, she said, "He has wet himself. Sometimes happens when he's had a seizure. He loses control."

The knobs and buttons on the dashboard went nuts as he jerked them back and forth, trying to get the air conditioning to bring in a fresh breeze.

"Change him!"

Elizabeth hesitated. He didn't know what was in the bags she'd carried out from the store. If she could get him to let them go shopping, maybe they could get someone to help them. "I can't. What am I supposed to change him into?"

The steering received a hard punch for that. Then another one.

In the next block, signs of another mall were visible - a smaller one, but still one with stores and people and another chance for rescue.

~

HE PULLED over to the curb. "Unhook his car seat," he instructed. We'll ditch the kid."

"No!" She thought fast. "Do you want to add child abandonment to the list of your crimes? He's little. He's sick. He stays with me." She tried the door handle, but the child-proof locks wouldn't let her open it. "Leave us both here. We won't tell, and you'll be long gone. You'll be safe and won't be bothered by us anymore. Keep the car."

"Gee, thanks, lady. I've *got* the car already." His fingers drummed the dash.

"I've an idea. Look, why don't we go into that mall, all three of us." She so did not want to leave Timothy alone with him again. "If anyone notices us, they'll think we're a family out shopping."

Shit. How could this have gone so wrong? Boost a car, then get to Granny's house where he'd be safe. He'd feel better there. It was home. Then this broad and this kid had to complicate his life. Granny used to rail against city people who dumped their unwanted pets on their road - just opened their door and threw the animal out, assuming someone else would look after them. What would Granny say if he did the same thing to this kid? Shit. He put the car back into gear, signaling to turn into the mall parking lot.

∽

BEFORE SHUTTING OFF THE CAR, the man opened all the windows a couple inches. Hopefully, that would air the thing out while still letting no one get their hand in to jack the car.

"Here's how we'll work this," he started. "We'll stick together - all the time. You will never be out of my sight. You know what I have in my pocket here and I'll use it on the kid if you try anything. I could cut him and disappear before anyone knows what's happening." He saw Elizabeth pale. "Now don't panic lady or pass out on me. I don't plan to hurt your precious kid as long as you do what you're supposed to do." Although why she was so stuck on this brat was news to him. He wasn't much of a kid. "He's not a runner, is he? Not going to take off on us when we get inside, is he?"

"No, no, he's good in the stores. Stays right with me." She pressed Timothy's head to her leg. "He's really no trouble."

"Riiiight. No trouble." He put his hand on the back of Timothy's neck and gave a small shove. He kept his hand there as the boy moved forward.

Elizabeth took her son's hand. "You don't need to do that. I'll keep hold of him."

The man's hand remained where it was. "Remember, we're just one big happy family. So smile." The grin he pasted on his face resembled one of those scary clown things.

As the automatic mall doors opened for them, the man pulled Elizabeth and Timmy to the side. "Wait. How we gonna pay for this? You got any money on you?"

Her brain couldn't think of a quick way out. "I have my credit card."

His eyes widened impossibly, and he loomed over her. He

spoke slowly and distinctly. "You telling me you used your credit card at that last place?"

Elizabeth stared back at him. She nodded.

"Christ." His palm struck his forehead. Okay, okay, gotta think. He paced in a circle, keeping the boy within easy reach. "How often do you shop there?"

"Never!"

"I meant Value Village anywhere."

"Never! I've never been in a place like that before. We've dropped something off but just at their outside door where they take donations."

That was not so bad. Even if they traced her credit card, it would show an unusual purchase for her so it could be identity theft or some such thing. "Did you give your PIN number?" She shook her head. But they would not use it again within the same town. He herded them back to the car.

As he unlocked the door and entered the car, the stale, sickly acidic/sweet scent of urine assaulted him. His stomach lurched. He could not, absolutely could not ride in a car with that smell and that kid. He got back out and looked at Elizabeth where she stood cradling her son's head. "You seem like a together-type, apart from your kid. Do you keep money stashed in your car? You know for emergencies when you don't have your purse. My Granny used to do that."

Possibilities whizzed through Elizabeth's mind, but nothing stuck. Her priority was keeping Timothy safe, and this whack job might hurt him or leave him stranded all alone somewhere. She nodded. "In the glove box I keep a bit of money."

The guy grabbed Timothy's arm and held it in the air. "Get it."

"I can hold him," Elizabeth said.

The guy gripped the child's arm more firmly and Timothy squirmed to get away.

"All right, I'm getting it." Elizabeth opened the passenger door and pulled a white envelope from the bottom of the glove box. She meant to take out a bit of the cash and give it to the guy.

He snatched it from her hand, letting go of Timothy. There was two hundred dollars there. Not a fortune but enough to by some clothes, some diapers and something to eat.

BACK IN THE ENTRANCE DOORS, Walmart was the most prominent store at this end of the mall. Hand back on Timothy's scruff, the man pushed him in that direction. Elizabeth hurried to take her son's hand.

"Now, we're making this quick. And remember we're a tight family." He moved closer, holding Elizabeth's upper arm with his other hand.

Oh, she'd remember his presence, all right. Not likely to forget what he was doing to them. She scanned the overhead signs for the children's department. Although she usually shopped for quality, this time she knew that she might need to make this bit of money last, so she looked for stuff that would fit that was on sale or cheap. Polyester. Synthetics. She wondered how they would do on Timothy's sensitive skin, but likely they'd only be worn a couple hours, then rescuers would be at hand. As her arm became laden with items, a salesclerk brought over a basket and handed it to the man with a smile. "Hi. Might as well put this guy to work. Isn't that why we bring our husbands shopping, to carry our purchases?" She gave Timothy a grin.

Husband? This woman actually thought that she'd married a greasy, stringy-haired oaf like this? She plastered on what she hoped was an appropriate look and passed the shopping basket on to the man. He dropped her arm to take it. Elizabeth smiled at the woman, then turned her back to end the conversation. No telling what this crazy guy might do if someone started asking them nosy questions.

Two shirts, two pairs of jeans, the same of socks and underwear, to better make that a package of four just in case. A hoodie and a pair of pajamas. Surely help would come long before it was time for bed, but she wanted Timothy to be comfortable just in case.

On to the diaper section for first wipes, then a large box of forty-eight size five diapers. No, that was excessive. She usually bought that size, but a small box of just a dozen should do any eventualities before they were back home.

Then the man shepherded them back to the kids' clothing. He grabbed a cap and put it on Timothy's head. Timothy took it off and looked at it, then grinned. It had the emblem of the Toronto Blue Jays. He knew it from watching games with his dad. Elizabeth doubted he got much out of the games, but a bit of bonding time with his father couldn't hurt. It was one of the rare times Jackson seemed to want to spend extended time with his son. Timothy put the hat back on his head, slightly at an angle. Then he took it off and offered it to his mom. She bent to pick him up so he could put it on her head. At least that guy's hands weren't on him now.

The salesclerk who had given them the basket returned. "You know, we have the identical hats in adult sizes. Over there," she pointed.

"Thank you." Those were the first polite words Elizabeth heard the guy utter. So, he had some civilized parts. Maybe she could use those to their advantage.

The adult hats were near the sportswear racks. "Find us each one," he told Elizabeth.

It was hard to separate out the hats with Timothy in her

arms. The man reached for Timothy, yanking him from Elizabeth's arms. She gave a cry of distress. Timothy arched back, whether sensing her alarm or if it was one of those times when he just didn't feel like being touched, she didn't know, but this guy was obviously not used to holding children. Timothy's arching pushed his upper body out and away, leaving his midriff touching the man. Two wet spots appeared, one along the guy's shirt sleeve and another along his torso. He jumped back with a look of horror. Timothy tumbled from his arms, his head knocking into hangers on the rack, his fall cushioned by the clothes raining down around him. Seeing that he wasn't seriously hurt, Elizabeth waited for the scream. You never knew how Timothy would react to things - sometimes with what looked like abject terror. At other times he'd giggle.

This time it was neither. His eyes rolled up into his head and his body began to tremble.

The pesky saleslady came racing up. "What's wrong? Did he fall and bump his head? Did you drop him?" She looked accusingly at the man who stood there helplessly.

Elizabeth turned Timothy onto his side in the recovery position. The shaking had mostly stopped now. With her eyes glued to her child, she explained. "He had a seizure. He'll be all right now, it was just a small one."

"Should I call 911?"

"No!" came out forcefully from the man.

"No," more softly from Elizabeth. "Thank you, but we're all right. This happens fairly often, and we know what to do." She indicated the obvious stain at the crotch of Timothy's pants and the dampening spot on the carpet under him. "I'm sorry about this. Is there some place where I could change him?"

The woman led them back to the kids' clothing area and

pointed at the change rooms. "You can take him in there. Looks like you'll need to use some of those clothes you were buying. Tell me which ones you want, and I'll cut the tags off for you. Wouldn't want them to scratch the poor little tyke." She looked expectantly at the man. When his blank stare didn't offer any action, she sighed and turned to Elizabeth. "Sometimes it's all up to us, isn't it? May I help you?"

Elizabeth nodded. She picked Timothy up in her arms and carried him to the change room the clerk had unlocked. She nodded her thanks at the clothing the woman handed her, along with an empty plastic bag for the soiled garments.

The man stood uncertainly outside the closed, and locked door. "You can go in with them, if you want," the clerk said.

Elizabeth's muffled voice hurriedly said, "No!" Then more softly, "There isn't much room in here. He's coming around now. We'll just be a minute."

Soon she opened the door and emerged with Timothy perched on her hip. His one hand grasped the Blue Jays cap resting on his head. He beamed when the man placed a similar hat on his own head. Spying the third one in the basket, Timothy reached for it and placed it on his mom's head, covering one eye.

"What a lovely family. You have a nice night now."

～

As they neared the tills, Elizabeth mentally tallied all that they had bought and if the total was under the two-hundred-dollar mark. Yes, by a long shot, she thought. Why did she not buy more? Checking out with not enough money to pay for the goods would draw attention to them, maybe good attention as in store security or a rent-a-cop. That could only be positive, couldn't it?

She noted the drool on her son's face. She thought she'd

wiped that off in the dressing room. Her forehead wrinkled. His drooling increased when he was having lots of seizure activity. There had been at least three since this afternoon, three that she knew about. Some absence seizures were swift and silent, hardly discernible unless you were looking right at Timothy when they occurred. In the car's dark interior, she'd have no way of telling.

"Look, he's ill. He needs his seizure medication. This is really important."

"So, give it to him, especially if it makes him stop pissing his pants."

"I can't. I don't have any with me."

"You're some kind of mother, aren't you? Shouldn't you carry stuff like that when you have a defective kid?"

She glared at him. "I keep some of his meds in my purse. I had to leave it behind when you stole my kid!"

His grip on her arm hurt. "Keep your voice down." The threat was oh so there in his voice.

She looked around. This was Walmart. No one seemed to be paying them any attention; they were used to stranger sights in this place.

She looked at the signage. "There's a pharmacy over there. I could probably get some of his pills there."

"Are they over-the-counter meds?"

Was this guy crazy? Oh, yeah, he probably was. "No, they are anti-epileptics. Seizure meds."

"No way. You'd need to give his name to get them. Unless something like Tylenol will do, he's going cold turkey and we're out of here."

Elizabeth worked out the number of hours since she had last given Timothy his valproic acid. Yes, she was supposed to wean him off the med before starting the new one, but abruptly cutting him off? Dr. Muller had warned her they could not start and stop these meds all at once. They needed to ease up to the proper dose and gradually taper off if they were discontinuing one. He'd given her so much info and she had spent hours, days, months researching this stuff online. Why could she not wipe from her mind the warnings associated with rapid cessation of some of these meds? Was valproic acid one of the dangerous ones?

CHAPTER 10

"*What game are you playing, buddy?*"

"*What? Is this you? Where are they?*"

"*Did you hire someone to double-cross us? See who could get to her first? Try to undercut my price?*"

"*No! Hell, I wouldn't do that. I had a hard enough time finding you, let alone finding two of you. So, where are they? You were supposed to call me to come get the kid. He's not part of this.*"

"*Same question I was about to ask you. They are not where you said they'd be. Either you had someone else lined up for this job, or you don't know this chick as well as you thought you did. She's gone.*"

"*Can't be. One of your men has them, and just didn't check in with you yet.*"

"*Me and my boys don't work that way. We've been watching her house since this afternoon and there is no sign of them there, or at any of the spots she's supposed to be at. They're gone.*"

"*Shit!*"

CHAPTER 11

*T*imothy consumed almost the entire block of cheese by the time they pulled into a pot-holed, weedy driveway. There were no neighboring lights for several miles after they'd driven through the hamlet of Bathinghurst and out the other side.

There was the tick of the cooling engine after it shut off. The guy sat with his hands on the steering wheel in a perfect ten-two position, staring at the house. Silence inside the vehicle; the child was again asleep.

The dome light felt harsh as the driver's side door opened. The car shifted as the guy got out. She could hear the night sounds - may be an owl in the distance, crickets for sure, and maybe were those frogs? She was a city girl through and through.

"You're not staying out here. I need to watch you. Get in here." The voice was not welcoming. What choice did she have? It didn't look as if Jackson or anyone else was striding to her rescue. Yet, she reminded herself, yet.

She unstrapped Timothy from his car seat and wrapped his boneless body over one shoulder. He was out. Was this just regular little boy sleep after a long drive or something to do with the seizures he'd had today or with the lack of medications regulating his system?

There was the rasping of metal on metal. "Going to have to put some graphite in this lock," he muttered. But he got it.

The stale smell of musty air rushed out at them. The place must have been shut up for weeks, Elizabeth thought. Stale air and dust and something else. Camphor? Some kind of rub? Jackson sometimes used something like that when he'd over done it playing racquetball. Sometimes his competitiveness got the best of him.

The guy flipped on the switch. Nothing. He flicked it down again and tried another one. He made his way in the dark to a table lamp and turned it on. Still nothing. "Damn solicitor must have turned off the power. Thought he was supposed to be looking after the place until I got here."

Elizabeth's ears perked up at that. Somebody knew who this guy was and that he'd be here. Maybe that somebody would come by and get her and Timothy out of here.

There were noises unfamiliar to Elizabeth. Sort of rasping then what might have been the lighting of a match. Then there was light - faintish, flickering light.

"Oil lamp. She kept them all over the place. The power here goes out regularly. Granny prepared for this." When he was a kid, sometimes these lamps were all they had for weeks until she got enough money to pay the power bill.

The flickering flames lent a homey feel to the room, somewhat at odds to the smell. What was that smell, Elizabeth wondered - something between an unused attic closet opened just once a year and those aromas that wafted from rooms in a nursing home, a combo of musk and camphor?

As he lit two other lamps, she could see more of this room, a living room. Along the back of every chair were doilies, the kind she'd seen in museums. The guy noticed her look. "Granny made them, each one by hand. She washed them regularly and starched them, too. See these on the end tables?" He pointed to the brown wood or faux wood that held a circular thing with raised, fluted, edges. In the center was a candy bowl. At least she thought what it held were candies. A closer look revealed cherry pits, stems and long-ago cherry remnants. Note to self - keep Timothy away from this area. They wouldn't be here long enough for him to explore, anyway.

Through an arched doorway she could see a galley-style kitchen. The guy opened a cupboard and removed a glass. There was the sound of water sputtering from a seldom-used faucet before a steady stream flowed.

"Make us some food, will ya?"

Took a second for her to realize he was talking to her. What was she, his maid? Oh yeah, according to that store clerk, she was his wife. Yuck.

"I'm holding Timothy and he's asleep."

"Well, put him down." The guy half turned, then pointed to the couch.

That couch looked like it had seen more than half a century of butts. How much crud was in those cushions? What had spilled there over the years? She could not set her son on that filthy upholstery.

"Or wake him up or drop him for all I care. I need some food. Now!"

There were some towels in the bags in the car, ones she'd bought at Value Village. She cringed at laying Timothy's sweet face on one of them, but it was better than that questionable couch. And she had groceries in the trunk, stuff Timothy could eat. She started for the door.

"Where do you think you're going?" In a flash, he was between her and the door. She explained that she was going for her grocery bags. "Not without me, you're not. You and I, lady, are joined at the hip." He seemed not to notice the innuendo, but she did. Oh, did she ever. New worries entered her mind.

Elizabeth grabbed the Value Village bag on her way in, but her hands were too full of sleeping boy to manage the grocery bags as well. "Would you mind?" she asked. He hefted the two zipped bags from the trunk.

Using one hand and her teeth, Elizabeth spread out a bath towel on the couch and settled Timothy.

"Good idea," the guy said. Protect the couch in case the kid decides to take a whizz in his pants again. Shouldn't he be past that stage? He looks pretty big."

Elizabeth's glare was his only answer. Keeping him in the corner of her eye, she backed toward the kitchen doorway, making sure she could see Timothy at all times. She was *not* leaving him in a room alone with this stranger. No worries; he followed her into the kitchen.

She cringed to see her grocery bags on that cupboard. But where was he going to place them? The floor would be worse, and that kitchen hadn't seen a washcloth in weeks. Months, maybe. As she moved to unzip a bag, something sticky on the floor gripped the sole of her shoe. Her bare heel slid off the back of the shoe, sinking into the semi-dried ooze. The stuff was dark red, with tiny, light brown bits. Seeds? Jam? Don't think about it now, she told herself.

Although her insulated bags offered some protection, they were probably at their end of their usefulness in chilling her Safeway purchases. These things needed to get into a refrigerator, anyway. She opened the door, and her head drew back. How long does something need to rot before it gave off a puke-worthy stench in a fridge? She took a breath over her shoulder, sneaking a peek at Timothy, before turning her nose into the fridge again. That dirty feet smell assaulted her again. That greenish orb might once have been a cabbage. Now much of it was mush, oozing around the wire mesh of the shelves, some parts clinging as if to a trellis, other bits releasing their essence onto the foods and shelves below.

She swallowed the stuff that rose into the back of her throat. Okay, it wasn't all a disaster. There were spots that looked clean, sort of. She could nestle her things in those areas. But someone was going to have to do a serious cleaning job in this thing.

Another aroma invaded her space, this one no less unpleasant, but different. It got closer and something brushed her shoulder. Elizabeth jumped, fumbling with the carton of eggs she held in her hand. The fridge door opened wider as the guy poked his head in.

"Shit! Granny would have a fit. Looks like no one cleaned up after she died. The lawyer was supposed to be taking care of the place." He looked closer. "God, what is that stuff?" He backed away, his index finger under his nose. He opened a back door, letting in the outside air. "You better get busy with that." He pointed in the general direction of the fridge.

She stood there, at first not getting it. Ding, ding, get on the clue bus. "Me?"

"If we're going to stay here, we'll need to eat, and we can't use a fridge that looks like that."

"I'm not staying here!"

He approached her.

"I mean, look, you've got what you wanted. You're here. So now you can let us go. We won't tell. Please, I just want to go home."

He laughed. "Like that Walmart lady said, we're a family now."

CHAPTER 12

"*H*ow do you think I can cook something when there's no power?"

That froze him. His eyes got larger and his body angled toward a door, a door Elizabeth had not yet noticed as the shadows from the oil lamp were hazy in that corner.

"Check the box." His voice was different somehow - more robotic and the pitch wasn't the same.

"What?"

He seemed to pull himself out of it, whatever 'it' was. "Go. Check the fuse box. In the basement?"

"Why can't you do it?"

More of the whites of his eyes were showing. "I cannot go down there. I haven't been bad."

Well, in whose opinion? What was wrong with this guy? While she tried to puzzle out what was happening, he grabbed her shoulder and shoved her toward that closed door. "Hey!" Elizabeth was not used to being handled roughly. The men in her life guarded her with care, the way you would a fine piece of porcelain china.

"Touch it," he ordered.

What did he mean? His eyes glued to the rusting metal doorknob.

Fearful of increasing his ire, Elizabeth rested one finger on the knob and looked at him. When his stare continued, she wrapped her fingers around it.

He nodded. "Now go check the fuse box."

"What's a fuse box?"

That got his attention. "Where were you born lady? The fuse box, the panel box hanging on the wall." His voice rose with each syllable.

Okaaaay. The door creaked as she turned the knob and pulled on it. "What do you mean, check it? What am I supposed to do?" Daddy always had people to do things like this.

If he were a rolling-his-eyes type of guy, she was sure that's what he'd be doing now. Yeah, it might be a "duh" moment for him, but she honestly didn't know what he was talking about.

"Go to the box. It's straight ahead at the bottom of the stairs. There's a lever on the left. Check that it's up. If not, then pull it up. Maybe the power is just turned off."

Elizabeth glanced over at Timothy. He seemed content at the moment, watching the flickering light from the oil lamp perched on the counter. It was too far away for him to grab. She started onto the first step. "It's dark down here."

"It always is."

"How am I supposed to see any lever?"

The guy moved a lamp from the table to the top of the stairs. The glow didn't spread very far, but enough that Elizabeth could now see most of the stairs. None of the treads seemed broken. She clung to the handrail just in case. She came back up two steps. "I'll just take this lamp with me, then I can see."

"No!" The lamp was snatched from the floor and held

high in his hands. "No lights allowed when you're down there." His voice changed again. "You have a job to do and that is to think about what you have done."

Whoa. What was that about? She didn't like the look on his face and checked over her shoulder for Timothy. Yeah, he was still in the same position, not too close to this nut case. Better get this over with so she could be with her son. Tentatively testing each step before putting her weight on it, Elizabeth made her way down. As her toe touched the second to last tread, something brushed the side of her face, something soft and clingy. She drew back and gave a yelp.

"Silence! Silence when you are in the cellar!"

She brushed the cobweb from her face and took a deep breath. You can do this, she told herself.

The floor was not concrete like she expected, but seemed to be dirt, hard-packed earth. Trying not to think of all the creepy crawly things that might be in here, she shuffled her feet and put her hands in front, feeling for whatever might be in front of her. Her hands brushed rough, cool cinder blocks. She looked back up the stairs to see if the guy would guide her to where he wanted her to go, but he was looking at his feet.

Raising her hands along the blocks, her fingertips brushed something cold and metal. Bringing her other hand up, she traced the outline. There was a fat, cloth-covered wire going into it at the bottom. Left, he had said, or at least she thought so. Dragging a tentative finger along the left edge, she found what must be a lever. It was a piece of thin metal lying along the edge. It curved near the bottom and broadened out in a curl, with a hole in the middle of the bulbous part. She put her index finger in that hole. What did she know about electricity? Only that it could be dangerous. Where was an electrician when you needed one?

From the kitchen came the sound of a tiny voice -

Timothy in singing mode. Sounded like something from his favorite Minions show. She needed to get back to him. She took in a big breath and let her shoulders sag back down. Just do it, she told herself. Her finger tried to pull on the lever. It didn't budge, putting forth more resistance than she would have thought. Keeping that finger in the hole, she wrapped her whole fist around the lever and pulled. Through the basement doorway lights flickered on, then off, and then returned to their on position, illuminating the stairway in a puddle of light. She didn't like what she saw and turned to charge up the stairs. Misjudging the backless shoes, her foot slipped out, her sole landing firmly on the hard-packed earth. Ewww! Oh, gross! What might have scampered across this floor that her bare foot was now touching? Balancing, she pushed her toes back into the shoe and continued her progress up the stairs more cautiously.

Timothy had not budged, but the guy had. He no longer blocked the path into the kitchen but had retired to the living room. There was a hum coming from the refrigerator now. No wonder things had rotted away in there. She hugged her son, using just her arms. Her hands needed a good washing before she felt she could touch him. She turned on the hot water tap. There was a trickle, then a spurt of brackish water before the stream settled down, gradually clearing. The water wasn't hot but at least looked like water. Under the sink she found a container of dish soap. Not so gentle on hands, but it would do the trick. It'd do until their rescuers arrived. That had to be soon. Jackson would arrange it.

CHAPTER 13

The man pushed past Elizabeth to peer into the fridge, holding his breath as he did so. He pulled out an opened package of bologna, a big package. "Here," he thrust it at her. "Make us something from this."

Elizabeth took the meat to prevent it from contacting her nose. Gingerly, she pried open the wrapping. Along one side of the meat was a greenish color, faint in places, a definite green in others. "It's gone bad," she told him, and looked for a trash can to dispose of it.

He snatched the meat from her hand. He looked at it more closely. "It's not bad, only a bit along one side. Just cut it off." He looked her up and down. "What, has Mrs. High and Mighty never eaten stuff that is just a bit off?" He set it back in the fridge and closed the door. "Clean this place up."

~

IT TAKES FAR LONGER to cook a meal, even a simple meal when you first have to clean an entire kitchen. Well, not the entire thing - Elizabeth started with just the fridge, counters,

73

and the utensils she'd need to scramble some eggs. Just. After using tongs and a ladle to scoop out the rotting messes from the fridge, she understood the term 'gag a maggot'. She thought it a disservice to maggots. Now the fridge was, if not pristine, at least usable. There was even a box of baking soda in a cupboard she used to help freshen the space a bit. Bit was the operative word.

She didn't stop with the kitchen table either. She did the table sides and legs then the chairs. If she and Timothy were going to touch things in here, even if only for a few hours, she was first going to get rid of some germs and creepy crawlies. What she wouldn't give for the rubber gloves stashed beneath her own kitchen sink.

A bottle of ammonia from under the sink helped cleanse the countertops and suggested that this kitchen might have been better cared for once upon a time. Although the pots were filmy, there were no obvious chunks of dried food residue on them. After a thorough washing, she felt safe using them.

"Darn." Elizabeth struggled to shave a carrot into thin strips. "These are the dullest knives I've ever seen."

"That's because I haven't been here to sharpen them for Granny. That was my job." He watched her struggle for a minute. "What are you doing that for?"

"I have to have hard items like carrots cut into small pieces for Timothy so that he doesn't choke on them if he has a seizure."

"That kid's a lot of work, isn't he?" He pulled a knife from the sheath attached to his belt. "Here, I'll do it." Backing away from the glinting knife, Elizabeth let the man have at it.

Raised by parents who'd protested the Vietnam war back in the day, she'd only seen such knives in movies. They were not the sort of things civilized people handled.

∽

SHE MADE a meal of scrambled eggs, bread, and peanut butter. Toast would have been better, but she was unsure how to ensure that the toaster was clean and didn't want to take the time to look. Whether it was the aroma of the cheesy eggs or his empty stomach, Timothy awoke with a vengeance. Rarely did he awaken easily, stunningly. It was like switching states didn't sit well with him, and he needed to share his protests with the world. It would get better in time, she hoped. But that future was not there yet.

She went to cuddle him and ease him into full consciousness. The guy sat watching her shush and soothe and rock her little boy. "Why do you coddle him?" he asked.

"I don't." Who was this man to criticize how she mothered her son?

"Yeah, you do. Look at him. You're treating him like a baby, and he must be what, five?"

"Four. He's only four years old."

"And still in diapers or pissing himself?"

Frustrated that she felt the need to defend her child to this guy, she tried to explain. Evoking some sympathy could not hurt. "He's ill. He has a seizure disorder. It's affected some of his development, so there are some delays. And most people, adults as well, lose bladder and bowel control when they have a seizure. It's an involuntary spasm and they can't help it."

Her rocking, rather than soothing, now seemed to stifle Timothy, and he struggled to get to his feet.

"See? Even he thinks you're on him too much. Let the kid go."

She did. It stung, but she did. Timothy followed his nose and stuck his head around the kitchen doorway. She rose and held out her hand to him. "Come get washed up. Supper is ready."

The guy must have assumed that this included him because he took a place at the table. He picked up a knife and spoon and turned them over and over in his hands. "Not seen these in a long time. Reminds me of my childhood. These are what Granny and I used every day."

He seemed a little softer when he spoke of his grandmother. Maybe getting him talking about her would be a way to build some rapport. She hoped that if they had some actual conversation, maybe found some mutual ground, that he might go easier on her and Timothy, maybe even just let them go.

"How long did you live with her?"

"Most of my life, at least until I grew up, and it was time to be a man. Then things changed. Instead of Granny looking after me, I looked after her. Only fair - she supported me until I was 16 and old enough to leave school. Then it was my turn to support her."

Sixteen? "When did you move away?"

Oops. Wrong question.

He glowered at her. "I never moved away. They *took* me away."

Dare she ask who? Why? Maybe better to find more neutral ground. She concentrated on her eggs. Try some rapport-building, she thought. "I lived in the same house also, right until I left home." That didn't bring any answering comment or question. She tried again. "What was your Granny's name?" There, that should be safe.

"Emily Rose, although her friends called her Em. The neighbors called her Miss Emily."

"Are you close to the other families around here?"

"When I was a kid, we were. Granny stayed friends with

some. I thought I liked them, and they liked me, but they called them on me, and it all went wrong from there."

"Them? Called who?"

"The people who came and took me away."

She didn't want to touch that one, at least not now. "What about your parents? Did they live here with you?"

"I never had parents."

"You must have had a mother."

"Granny said some whore birthed me, then took off. Granny disowned her. No one knew who my father was. No one ever came around looking."

How to put a pleasant spin on this. "So, it was just you and your Granny. The two of you sound close."

"We were. She was good to me, strict but good. 'Spare the rod and spoil the child' she always said. 'Bring up a child in the way he should go and when he is old, he shall not depart from it', or something like that. She made me what I am today."

Hmm, thought Elizabeth. Maybe that last bit should be chiseled on her tombstone.

His head came up, and he looked directly at her. "Granny would twitch my behind at my rudeness." He stuck his right hand across the table, into Elizabeth's face. "My name is Russell Rose Allen. Pleased to meet you."

How bizarre. She extended her hand. "Hello, Russell. I'm…"

"Russell *Rose*. That name connected me to Granny, made me hers." His grip on her hand tightened. Silence. "Say it." Her hand was in a vice.

She tried to keep the hesitation from her voice. "Hello, Russell Rose. I, I'm Elizabeth Whitmore." She could not bring herself to say she was in any way pleased to meet him. She clasped his hand in one brief squeeze, then pulled it back.

This time he let her. She nodded at the child. "This is our son, Timothy, I mean ours, my husband and me, our son." Thank god Timothy looked up from his plate in time to see the big hand coming toward him. He dropped his fork and put his tiny fingers into the big man's paw. Elizabeth gritted her teeth to keep from snatching her son's hand away from this guy, this Russell Rose. She bent to retrieve Timothy's fork from the floor, washing it off at the sink before returning it to him.

"We make polite conversation at the supper table," Russell Rose informed her. "How was your day?"

∾

FLICKERING *candlelight glinted off champagne flutes. Overhead the chandeliers cast muted auras onto the diners. In the background the string quartet was unobtrusive, but just pleasantly there.*

"To us, darling." Their glasses gave that satisfying clink that only came from leaded crystal.

"To our new beginning."

"Excuse me, sir, ma'am. Here are your entrees." He set the shrimp scampi with linguini on one side of the table, then went around to deposit the platter of island duck with mulberry mustard.

"Soon, this will be us all the time." She ran her fingertip over the back of his hand.

A quick look up to see if she was for real. "Well, not all the time. This is a special occasion. We're celebrating." Picking up his fork, he added, "This is a bit much for every day, especially with a child."

"I am so looking forward to seeing your darling little boy again." She hid the lower half of her face in her napkin.

CHAPTER 14

*T*he small child sobbed, clinging to the woman's leg.

"Get your filthy hands off me, you dirty little boy. You know what you've done and what happens now."

"I'm sorry, I didn't mean to. It slipped."

"Sorry doesn't cut it, you know that. In life you must take care, look after your things. Now, clean that mess up."

He scampered to do her bidding. Maybe if he did a really, really good job she would be pleased with him and that would be the end of it. Jam was not easy to gather up from the floor. Each time he tried to close his fist around gobs of it, some squished through his fingers, making new blemishes on the floor. He heard the click of the television going on. That should help. If she got wrapped up in her show, she might not realize how much time he was taking to get the kitchen floor cleaned. And maybe she might forget about punishing him, just this one time.

～

THE SMALL CHILD perched on the bottom step, one hand clinging to the railing over his head, the other wiping his nose on his sleeve. He *tried keeping his crying silent. If she heard him, she'd make him stay there that much longer. He didn't have a strong sense of time, but sometimes while huddled down here in the basement, he would hear the television go off, steps shuffling in house slippers to the bathroom, then the creak of a bed sagging. Then, nothing. Nothing at all for a long, long time.*

⁓

RUSSELL ROSE SCOWLED AT TIMOTHY. "Has no one taught you no manners?" He waited. Timothy stared off into near distance. "Pick up your plate." When no action followed his demand, he wrapped his hand around Timothy's and placed in on the side of the child's plate. "Now bring it to the sink." Elizabeth would never have counted on it, but her son complied. Russell Rose turned to her. "He must be used to you waiting on him, serving him, doing everything for him. That's not fair to women, you know. They work hard and deserve some help. Granny would never have stood for that sort of disrespect from a child."

"He's just four!"

"I was doing far more than that little chore by his age." Teachable moment over, he left, saying, "He'll learn. Spare the rod and spoil the child." The television clicked on.

⁓

THROUGH THE WINDOW over the kitchen sink, only her own reflection looked back at her. Not that of Jackson or of any other rescuer. Outside it was silent, and she meant silent. No sound of any cars passing by, no honking, no sirens, no voices raised as pedestrians walked by. Just nothing. With one eye on Russell, pardon, Russell *Rose,* she corrected herself, she tip-toed toward the rear door. Did it squeak? She couldn't remember what had happened when Russell Rose opened it earlier, but she had glimpsed that it led into a backyard.

Hand on the knob, she waited, waited until the start of canned laughter from the TV show. She'd have maybe two seconds, possibly three, she thought. Timing it perfectly, she twisted the handle and opened the door just a couple inches. Now she could see. It was all dark, no streetlights. She didn't know when she had ever seen a night so black.

And it wasn't silent after all. The inky outdoors seemed full of sounds, noises she could not identify. Dared she venture outside in this? Could she take Timothy and run? Run to where?

If only amongst her domestic skills was the ability to hot wire a car. Was that even really a thing? Seemed so in movies, or maybe that was just old movies. How did you hot wire something that didn't have a key to insert? Hers was a push-button start that worked, as long as the keys were within several feet of the car. She checked back at Timothy. Still occupying himself silently with his hands. Russell Rose was prone on the couch, half-lidded eyes on the TV. Was there a chance that the keys in his pocket were close enough to the car to allow it to start? Mentally she tried pacing off the distance. Maybe fifteen feet. Not likely.

What if she waited until he fell asleep then dug the keys out of the front of his pants? God, she'd have to touch him. What if he awoke? What would he think she was doing? Her mind pulled back from the possibilities. Good to have a Plan B but that one was more like Plan Z.

She eased the left side of her body out the door. The air smelled differently here. Maybe softer, if that was possible. In the not so far distance, something made a noise. An animal? A bird? She was so out of her depth here. If only Daddy was here. He'd done some wilderness stuff with his buddies. He'd know what to do. What was she thinking - if he were here, she would never have been in such a predicament? It would not have been allowed.

But neither of the men in her life had appeared to save her. Daddy was gone, but where was her husband? She might have to do this on her own. No, it was probably better to sit tight until help came. Didn't they say that when you were lost in the woods or your car broke down to stay put and help would find you?

She looked at her watch. Almost eight. Timothy's bedtime. Was it worth thinking about venturing out on their own at this time of night? A faint snore came from Russell, er Russell Rose. She needed to remember that if they were to stay on his good side.

Okay, she'd take just a quick look. Softly, she called, "Timothy." No response. She sighed. "Timothy." The water dripping from the tap held more interest for him. She went to take his hand, turning his head away from the water, and put her finger to her lips. "Shh. We're going to take a peek outside. But, quiet; Russell Rose is sleeping, and we don't want to wake him up." Timothy followed her willingly enough until she pulled him through the still open door. Then his feet planted firmly on the top step. "I know, buddy. It's dark out here, isn't it? But it's just a pleasant temperature, not too hot anymore." Here she was, lying to her kid. Sure, he had a hoodie on, but her arms raised goosebumps already. "Come on, this will be fun." Again, with the lying thing.

Venturing out a few steps, the tall grass snagged their footsteps. Although the grass and weeds were up to her shins, it was tougher going for a guy of Timothy's height. That whiny sound started in his throat. She swung him up into her arms, perching him on one hip. Better to have him up here, anyway. Who knew what might lurk in these weeds? She grabbed hold of her imagination and firmly shifted her thoughts away from that direction. If they could get out of this yard, then they could start down the road that had led them to this house. Surely there were neighbors around who would help them.

She kept her left shoulder parallel with the house, expecting to come to the corner any second. She did, but that corner firmly butted against a fence, a picket fence that ended about a foot over her head. Nothing to put her foot onto, nothing to help her climb over it. Not going to happen.

Retracing her steps, she sought the other side of the building. Same thing happened. The house ended with the fence. Feeling around, she could find no gate, no latch, no anything except a solid barrier.

Well, every yard had an exit. Wouldn't you think that was the law or something? The hand not clutching her son felt along the wooden fence, careful to not miss anything that her eyes couldn't pick up in the dim light that came out from the kitchen doorway. Concentrating on the side fence, Timothy's leg and her hand connected with the fence in front of them. That was one way to find the corner. "You're all right, son," she assured herself more than him. Following the right angle, she felt along the fence, certain she'd come across a gate any second. Her biggest worry was that it might lock or that it might make a horrid noise when she opened it, alerting Russell Rose to their flight.

She reached the next corner, certain she had missed no opening. It had to be along this third wall, then. Why hadn't she started in that direction the first time?

It was a small yard and didn't take that many steps until she found the last corner. What? Had she gotten turned around and doubled back on herself? No, she might not have any woodsman skills, but she at least knew that much. She had kept her right hand on the fence the whole time. Could she have missed it? Not felt high enough?

She shifted Timothy to her other hip. His head nestled into her shoulder. At least if he dozed, she knew he would be quiet, but he became such a dead weight when he slept in her arms. Okay, try this again. Slowly, slower than the first time, she circled the fenced yard, her left hand reaching high and low every six or so inches. She would *not* miss the gate this time.

Brick. She had reached the brick facing of the house. Again. How could it be that she had not found the exit from this yard? A breeze came up, and she wrapped her arms around Timothy, trying to keep them both warm. The breeze became a gust, sending a dried plant skittering by. Then, the light went out as the wind shut the kitchen door. Not slammed, really, but firmly shut for sure.

In her head, she said a bad word, one that would appall her mother. Ladies did not speak like that. Well, she didn't speak it, just thought it.

She wished that she was like so many young women these days, and carried a mobile phone in her back pocket, even if it broke the line of their pants. Keeping hers in her purse was a dumb idea; she always had trouble digging it out, anyway. If she had it here now, she could call Jackson, and they'd be home in no time.

It was hard to see in the yard now. If she could not find the gate with the faint light, she had no hope of locating it now. Best get back in before Timothy got chilled.

She turned the doorknob, tugged, meeting resistance. She tried harder, thinking the door mechanism might be old and rusty. The knob would only turn part way, then nothing. This would take more strength. She shifted her sleeping burden to her left side so could go use her dominant hand on the door. No way! Rattling had no effect, neither did pushing with her shoulder. It would not open. A wise person, a thinking ahead-type person, would have checked to make sure that they unlocked the door before venturing out. But the door had been open, and she didn't think any further than that. It was Daddy who was the planner; he was meticulous in how he went about things. Elizabeth and her mom didn't have to because he took care of all the pesky details in their lives. Now Jackson did that for her. How could she be expected to consider everything that could happen? She snuggled her slumbering child closer, hunching around him in the cool night air.

CHAPTER 15

Odd that Mrs. Whitmore had not returned to pick up her son's medication. She had said she'd be back within an hour. That was not unusual; standing there with a small child, waiting for a prescription was no picnic for anyone, even though Timothy was a well-behaved child, and good at amusing himself.

Mr. Rexton thought about the last few times he saw Timothy. As with all kids, he tried to engage the child in conversation. But Timothy had never uttered a word to him. He brought his computer to life, wanting to check the child's date of birth. Maybe he was just large for his age, making the pharmacist assume he was older and should possess more skills.

No, the child was four. Most four-year-olds, even shy ones, responded to his ways. If nothing else, his supplies of suckers won them over. At the least they'd give a hi, bye, thank you or a smile. He'd been gifted with none of these things from Timothy, not even a wave when they left. Yet, Mrs. Whitmore was the epitome of courteousness.

Where was she?

According to the doctor's orders, he was to reduce his current meds, then over the next few days gradually build up his dose of the new one. He needed the new medication on hand in case the reduction of moderating chemicals in his system caused a spike in the seizures. Mrs. Whitmore was diligent about her son's meds. Always.

Although it was doubtful she had forgotten, these things happen in busy lives. He'd call and just let her know that the prescription was ready for pickup.

No answer at either her cell or home number. He left messages on each. Too bad he didn't have the dad's number on file. Well, he was open until ten tonight in case either of them dropped by.

❦

THE DOOR DIDN'T fit tight. There was a hint of heated air leaking from its bottom. Elizabeth shifted position, so that that small draft of warmth was on Timothy's back, then curled her body around his front. Although the goal was to keep him warm, it helped her as well. Somehow, he slept through it all. Seizures often wore him out.

How long had they been out here? Afraid of waking him, she didn't want to move her arm to check her watch. It seemed like hours, but who knew. She was so out of her element. Only once had she slept outside, and that was using the term "outside" generously. The ritzy cabin they were in had brightly polished, pale logs that glowed in the firelight. Each of the four bedrooms contained a queen-sized bed, plush rugs and an ensuite bathroom. This was roughing it for her Girl Scout troop, the only one Daddy allowed her to join, but it contributed toward earning her badge.

But this, here right now was truly outside. Never before could she recall being exposed to the noises of the night. Oh, sure, she knew the city noises; they were natural and expected. But that cabin she'd slept in, with its foot-thick logs and triple-pane windows, muffled any outside noises. For a short while they all sat outside around a campfire but the crackling of burning wood, the stories and giggles had drowned out the ambient noises.

Who knew that the great outdoors was such a noisy place? Her senses became attuned to each individual sound, her brain straining to identify them, but the data was just not in her memory banks. What was innocent and what should legitimately raise her hackles? All she knew was that she should cling to her little boy.

～

DISORIENTED, she raised her head. How could she have nodded off? Shivering she focused her ears on what might have woken her. It was inside! There was rustling and banging and muttering and footsteps that were coming closer.

Quickly she scooted herself and her son away from the door. It opened outward and she could not risk Timothy being struck by the door. Sitting up with him in her arms, she waited. Only seconds later, Russell Rose's booted feet tramped down onto the step beside her.

"What the hell do you think you're doing? I told you we are joined now. Did you think you could get away?" His laugh was not a cheerying sound, just the opposite. "Did you try to find an escape route out of this yard? Good luck with that." His grin, oh, his grin was so not nice.

"We came out for some air. It was stuffy in the kitchen after I washed the dishes. Timothy needed to play a bit, and we didn't want to wake you up."

"Wake me up? I wasn't sleeping, just resting my eyes."

Hmm, well. She continued, "Then the door slammed shut and we couldn't get back in."

He watched her, just watched. In the dim light it was difficult to read his expression, not that she was any good at predicting what was in his mind, anyway.

For her son, she'd beg if she had to. "May we come back inside? We're getting chilled out here."

He reached for her arm and roughly hauled her to her feet. She struggled to keep her grip on her son. Checking, she saw that he was sleeping through all this. He was really out. She tugged her arm free and Russell Rose let her go. She doubted he was helping her up, more like making sure she couldn't get away.

"We used to have a dog. Granny said that dogs need space to roam outside so she had the fence made. It kept him safe and he couldn't get out. I used to play with him....". His voice trailed off.

Unsure how to respond to that, Elizabeth gave a half smile, but he wasn't looking at her. She stood there with Timothy draped across her forearms. Not possible that he had gained weight in the last several hours, but it felt like it. "Is there someplace I can put him down?"

Her question seemed to snap Russell Rose out of his reverie. He pointed at the kitchen floor. "Be my guest."

Although she had washed that floor, this was not what she meant. "A bed. Where can I put him to sleep?"

Apparently sleeping arrangements had not occurred to him. She wondered just how much of a planner she was. She was used to men who worked out all the details in advance. That was the way to get ahead and to plan a smooth life for your family.

Since Russell Rose appeared lost in his own thoughts, she started down the hall, turning into the first room she came to. She fumbled for the switch; there was no light switch.

The plate covering was a tarnished brass metal, and in the center were two black buttons. The bottom one protruded more, so she pushed the top one. The ceiling light came on, but the dim watt didn't cast out the shadows in the corners of the room. It illuminated the bed, though. She laid her son on the crocheted counterpane. She straightened, shaking out her arms; either Timothy was getting heavier or she was getting weaker. Most days she didn't spend this much time carrying him.

Doilies were everywhere. This woman had really liked to crochet. There was a smell or rather smells in here, apart from the dust and mustiness. Camphor. And something musky, much stronger than when they had first entered the living room. She brushed Timothy's hair from his forehead. He looked so peaceful in his slumber, as if he had not a care in the world.

"What are you doing in here?"

"Just putting Timothy to bed." Why? Isn't it obvious?

"Out! Out!" He pointed into the hallway. "Have you any idea what Granny would say? Dirty little boys cannot be in her bed. Do you know what happens to dirty little boys who don't do what they're told?"

Scooping Timothy into her arms, she backed up until her knees touched the edge of the bed. How could she get out of the room without brushing close to this guy?

He ran his hands over his head, then his fists clenched both sides of his hair. "There. Take my room. Just get him out of here before Granny sees. You won't like what she'll do."

Turning her back to Russell Rose, Elizabeth carried her son through the narrow doorway, trying to shake off the creepy feeling of being in such proximity to this nutcase. They had to get away from him.

Beside the bathroom was another door. Hard to tell if it had once been a little boy's room as there were no toys, no books or any memorabilia around. When she had left home, her parents preserved her bedroom for her.

She rested Timothy on one hip while she pulled back the covers and sniffed. Not great, but the best they would get for now. She tried to not allow her gaze to linger on the yellowed spots in the middle of the pillowcase. She told herself that the smell was from disuse, not a lack of proximity to laundry soap. She removed his shoes and pulled up the covers to his neck, careful that they didn't touch his chin; he hated that. She briefly thought of the pajamas she had picked for him, but decided it was too risky trying to retrieve them.

Checking the door, she saw that they were alone, thank god. As quietly as her ill-fitting shoes would allow, she tip-toed to the door. No, he wasn't lurking there. She went into the hall, shutting the bedroom door behind her. She really needed to pee but wanted to be able to hear if Russell Rose opened the door to get to her son. She'd only be gone half a minute.

That done and sorely missing a toothbrush and a change of clothing, she kicked off her shoes and climbed into bed beside Timothy. Whoa, this would not work. She moved him over, just a bit, but the edge of the bed was so close on his side as well. What was with this bed? The only time she had seen one this narrow was her first semester at college. She'd stayed in a dorm and her parents thought it would be fine because they paid the extra to ensure that she had a private room. Well, it was all hers, but in total it was smaller than her closet at home.

When her daddy had seen it and the cot, they called a bed, he had immediately moved her before she could spend another night Within half a day he'd found her a lovely apartment - small by his standards, but cozy. The second bedroom was just eight by ten, but fine for an office. Daddy said that it was not good to work and sleep in the same room; you needed physical separation if you were going to turn your mind off to go to sleep.

She smiled, remembering all the little ways that he took care of her. A tear slid down her cheek. If only he was here to help her now. But he wasn't coming. He never would again.

Laying on her side, she cradled Timothy to her. This was the only way one of them wouldn't end up on the floor. Her eyes leaked some more. No. No, no, no, she could not allow herself to cry. What if she woke up Timothy? What if he felt her distress?

Taking a deep, wavering breath, she closed her eyes. Her hand went to her earrings, identical emerald sets daddy bought for her and her mother. Elizabeth could hear Mother's voice in her head, telling her to stop fidgeting, but it soothed her, feeling the smooth stone between her fingers, knowing that it was her mother's favorite gem. Jackson was away, so it was taking him longer than she'd expected to find them. Daddy might not be around, but her husband was. He'd come for them soon. Surrounding herself with people she could count on comforted her.

She pulled her son, her beautiful, trusting son closer to her side. If Jackson didn't come, was she on her own to save her child? Could she?

PART II
TUESDAY

CHAPTER 16

*T*uesday morning, a twinge of guilt had Jackson phoning Elizabeth about the time she was usually getting Timothy's breakfast. No answer. Well, life with Timothy was not an exact science, what with the seizures happening whenever. The two of them probably got caught up in something, but he'd connect with them later. He needed to demonstrate his loyalty.

~

HE TRIED AGAIN at supper time. When there was no answer, alarm bells rang in his head. If Plan A was in effect, he should have had a call to come get his son. He scrolled through his phone's history and no, there was nothing he missed.

~

MARGE AND KEN across the road were their emergency contact on the street; they had a spare key to their place.

Jackson phoned them. "I know that she's probably just

busy. You know what life is like with a kid, especially *our* kid, but would you mind going over to check that everything's all right? I'd really appreciate it although I expect Elizabeth to be a bit embarrassed when she learns that she hasn't been returning my messages." He hung on a minute while Marge went to find the key.

Ken took his phone with him to the front window and opened the drapes. "It's all dark over there, Jackson. Doesn't look like she's home. Her car's not in the drive, but maybe she pulled into the garage. Still, there are no signs of life. I'll go check and call you back in ten minutes."

~

It was Marge calling him back. "Jackson, there's no one home. I know that Elizabeth and I are not terribly close but whenever we've been over there in the evening, the kitchen is immaculate."

Yeah, Elizabeth was anal about that. Although she might leave breakfast or lunch dishes in the sink (but never both), she could not rest until the supper dishes were at least tucked in the dishwasher and the kitchen put to rights. "Are you saying it's not clean now?" It was almost eight o'clock.

"No, it has not been cleaned up. And the food on the dishes is dry, like it's not from this evening's meal. Jackson, I'm not sure, but it almost looks like she cooked eggs. There's the dirty pan, two plates, two sets of cutlery, some toast crumbs and two mugs with what might have been coffee in them."

Two? His ire flared. *Two?* Who did Elizabeth have over for a *morning* meal? Was she stepping out on him, doing someone else while he was away working? Is that the thanks he got for slaving for his family?

"Jackson? Jackson, are you there?" That was Ken on the phone now.

He raked a hand down his face. Okay, think. "Did you check Timothy's room?" Although why on earth would Elizabeth put him to bed and then leave? That was not like her. But then, given those dishes, maybe he didn't know her as well as he thought.

"Yes, that is the first thing Marge did after there was no answer when we called and turned on the lights. There are rumpled sheets, but no Timothy. Marge peeked into your room, but it was empty too."

Elizabeth made the bed as soon as she was out of it in the morning. No news there. But she often did not remake Timothy's until after their son's afternoon nap. She was weird about beds. Before putting Timothy into his bed at night, she always made his bed. Made no sense and she'd laugh about it herself, but she did it anyway.

"Ken, did you poke your head into the garage to see if her car was there?"

"I did and, it was empty."

Marge came back on. "When did you last talk to her?"

"Monday before I left for work. I tried calling her a couple times that night and twice today, but she doesn't answer and hasn't returned my calls." This was sounding bad, even to him.

"Maybe she's lonely while you're gone. Did she talk about going away for a quick trip? Maybe visiting some relatives? An old girlfriend?"

"She doesn't have any relatives, at least not any that aren't really distant. Since Timothy's been born, she's been so busy with all his medical stuff and sort of lost touch with her friends she used to hang out with before we married." This sounded bad.

"Look, buddy, we're here for you. Anything you want us

to do, just tell us. But I think you might wanna consider calling the police. Don't mean to be an alarmist, but just in case, you know?"

One hand pulled the hair at the nape of his neck. If Elizabeth was here, she'd gently release his hand and smooth down those short hairs. She liked to soothe him when stresses got to him.

Well, he knew this was coming. "Thanks, guys. Thanks so much for your help. I'll hang up now and call the cops. It's probably nothing and I'm wasting their time, but I just don't know where she is. On the other hand, she'll probably kill me for embarrassing her by involving the police, but dammit, I don't know where she is with my son."

"Will you guys be around in case the cops want to ask you what you found in the house? Or to let them in if they want to look around our place?" He listened. "Thanks. You're the best. I'll be in touch. And give me a ring, will you, if you see her drive up. Thanks."

◠

"ALL RIGHT, sir, we'll head over to your house to check things out. We'd appreciate you texting us those pictures of your wife and son right away. Do we have your permission to enter and search the house? This will just be a cursory look, but we can check to see if there are any messages or notes."

"Definitely, I'd appreciate it. This is not like her. I left a couple messages that she hasn't returned. Thanks, officer. I'll wait to hear from you. Probably she's in bed sleeping by now and will be ticked at me for involving you."

◠

"Mr. Whitmore? I'm afraid it didn't turn out as you had hoped. There is no sign of either your wife or son at your house. The neighbors who let us in say they haven't seen her, although they're both gone during the day. So far, when we canvassed the street, we can't find anyone else who has seen them either but not everyone was home. We listened to two messages from you, one from the pharmacist saying a prescription is ready, but there aren't any others on your answering machine.

"Usually, we wait forty-eight hours before filing a missing person's report for an adult, but since there's a child involved, we can do some preliminary work. How long before you'll get here?"

"It's about a four-hour drive."

Silence. "We thought you'd be on your way already."

"I was sure this would all be a misunderstanding, and you'd find her at home all embarrassed."

"Please head straight to the station when you arrive."

~

Brendan James turned to his partner. "Jake, if you were away and hadn't talked to your wife and kid in over a day, wouldn't you be a little more uptight than this guy is?'

"Yeah, I'd be all over this if it was my family. In half a day I'd start to worry, but if we didn't talk before bed the first night, I'd be on the highway back here to find out what was wrong."

"It'll be after one in the morning before he gets here. That makes it Wednesday, and he has had no contact with his family since Monday morning. Let's tell the Chief what's going on and do a little digging."

CHAPTER 17

*T*he park had been perfect that day last month - just the right sun, temperature, and wind. He didn't spend much time in environments like this; he was far too preoccupied with making a living, being seen in the right places, and planning for the future. Exactly why no one he knew would think to look for him here.

The child walked between their hands, periodically swinging his legs as they raised his arms up into the air. Yeah, his laughter was nice to hear. It wasn't often they had moments like this, moments when the mother let their son out of her sight.

While he sat on a park bench indulgently watching, the woman played with the child. For an initial meeting, it was not going badly. She was gentle with him and maybe a little stand-offish at first. That was okay; so was the kid. The man liked that - better a kid who kept his own council than one who was overly clingy. That would not do.

The woman looked up at him more often than she gazed at the child. It felt good to be the center of someone's universe; it felt right. It had been a long time since he had had that comforting feeling.

Perhaps she didn't know any modern games, so she reverted to what she remembered from her childhood. That was all right; the kid didn't seem to care. Ring-around-the-rosy was fine with the child, it was the woman who seemed to tire of it first. She switched it up, using the same actions to a new rhyme. While now she looked into the child's face as she chanted, the man knew that the words were meant for him. "Daddy and Barbie sitting in a tree, k-i-s-s-i-n-g...". That was fine, kind of cute in a way. She was trying so hard, and it wasn't like the kid was going to tell anyone.

The woman and child seemed to be warming up to each other now. Just as well, as they'd be together permanently soon.

❧

"THANKFULLY, she's not one of those cash-only purists. Makes our job easier."

Jackson smirked. "No, she's anal about collecting points, saving for a trip we'll take one day. She puts everything she can on plastic. She goes over her credit card and bank statements online almost every night to make sure everything's kosher."

"*Her* statements?"

"Yeah, we have separate personal accounts, but I put money into the one for our household expenses." He rubbed his face. "Could I get some coffee? It's been a rough night. Long drive."

He looked no worse than either of the detectives who had also not seen a bed in over twenty-four hours.

"We thought we'd see you around one this morning."

"I caught a few winks before setting out, you know. Wouldn't do to get myself in a crash on the way here, on top of everything else. Elizabeth would kill me if I did that."

"We've had time to look into her recent spending.

Monday it looks like she bought groceries at a Safeway on Dumont."

"That's where she always shops."

"Spent $89.37."

Jackson shrugged. "She handles that stuff, so I don't know if that's usual or not."

"Pulling her credit card statements for the past few months, that's a little shy but not out of line with what she spends there. Then she spent almost nine bucks at a gas station."

"Let me see that. That's not much to spend on gas. She always fills up on Mondays." Jackson looked at the details. "Yes, that's the station where she goes. It's in between the grocery store and our house."

"A small amount like this usually means the person bought junk food. Would she have paid cash for the gas?"

"Never, not Elizabeth. And she would not buy junk food. She always was something of a health food nut, but way more so since our kid has been on this special diet. And she would not eat junk in front of him. There must be some mistake. Maybe the attendant rang her gas purchase in wrong."

"Could be," agreed Brendan James. "Jake, let's swing by there a little later and ask the manager if there was some discrepancy between the till and the gas gallons used that day."

Detective James continued. "Then she withdrew four hundred dollars from an ATM in the same strip mall as Safeway."

"She withdraws that amount about once a month, so we have some cash in the house in case it's needed. You know, the cookie jar thing. She refills it when it's getting low."

"Yes, we found withdrawals of this amount over the past

few months. So that is not out of the ordinary." Brendan continued. "The next morning, Tuesday now, she again went to Safeway. Looks like she must have been there right when they opened at eight o'clock, but this is a different Safeway."

"A different Safeway? She always goes to the same one - says it makes shopping faster because she knows exactly where everything is, no hunting around. And she'd never go to a store at that time of day. She'd still be getting Timothy up and dressed. Plus, she's not really a morning person. Neither is he. She likes to do errands later, like after lunch."

"Well, her debit card was used to purchase fourteen dollars and thirty-five cents worth. For that amount, she could have just tapped it, no pin required. Might if she was in a hurry."

~

"TELL US AGAIN, Mr. Whitmore, your wife's itinerary for Monday."

"Again. Okay. She would have been home in the morning after I left. Like I said, neither of them is that perky first thing in the morning, so I'm pretty sure they would have stayed home then.

"Not sure, but I think she mentioned something about Timothy's prescription needing renewing, so she probably went to the drug store sometime, probably in the afternoon." He looked down and sighed. "He needs a lot of meds and can't be without them." He shook his head. "The other thing she does on Mondays is get the groceries for me."

"For you?"

"Well, for all of us – me and Timothy and her, you know. It's kind of like Elizabeth's contribution to the family while I'm out working to support us." He gave them a knowing look. "Oh, and she fills her car up with gas on Mondays. There might be other, petty stuff, but not much. She sticks pretty close to home with Timothy. Except when she takes him to those endless appointments."

"Sounds like she's a creature of habit. You seem to know her well."

"Oh, I know her all right. There are no surprises with Elizabeth."

Thinking of his own extended family, Jake asked, "No play groups? Stopping off at a friend's house? A relative's?"

"No, I doubt it. She doesn't really have friends, close ones anyway. Since Timothy's been born, our world has sort of narrowed. A kid is a lot of work."

"So I've heard," said Jake. "My brother-and sister-in-law have their hands full with their two."

⁓

BRENDAN WATCHED his partner's attempt at bonding, then took charge. "To sum this up, Mr. Whitmore, you think your wife and son would have been at home for the morning," he checked his notes. "Then they might have stopped at the drug store, the one owned by," he checked his book again, "a pharmacist name Rexton."

Jackson nodded. "I don't really know him, but I think I've heard her say that name."

"Not necessarily in this order. She would have gone to the Safeway on Dumont, then the gas station over on Regency. Have I got that right?"

"Yeah. She sometimes goes to a dry cleaner in the same strip mall as Safeway, but I don't know if that was in her plan for this week or not. She looks after my shirts and suits so that I don't have to pay attention to details like that.

Sometimes when my car needs servicing, we switch vehicles, and she takes mine in, but that was done last week."

"Sounds like you rely on your wife for many things."

"Not really. I'd say it was the other way around. She does the household stuff, but I do everything else."

～

REVIEWING THEIR NOTES, Brendan asked Jake, "How can a woman and child just be gone?"

CHAPTER 18

*D*isoriented, Elizabeth didn't know where she was. The patting on her cheek came again, and she opened her eyes to greet Timothy's smiling face. He was up standing by the side of the bed. She raised herself up on her elbows. Did her son actually dress himself? Naw, he never did that. She flopped back down as it all came back to her. Where they were. Why both she and Timothy had slept in their clothes. Why she felt like she could smell herself. And why she heard voices.

Voices? Was help here?

She listened some more closely. There seemed to be only one male voice but there was almost a conversational cadence to the tones. Was that Russell Rose? Talking to himself? Well, she did that the odd time too, especially when Jackson was gone all week and talking only to a toddler got to her.

But Russell Rose's speech didn't sound like the talking aloud she did. This sounded animated. She listened more. Or agitated. Oh, god. Could they just hide in here? Maybe he'd forgot about them.

But Timothy was dancing around, one hand holding between his legs. Of all the times to remember and want to act on his toilet training.

The cot creaked as she drew back the covers, putting her feet on the chilly floor. Feeling around for her slippers, all she came up with were the worn sneakers with the broken back. Not difficult to slip on, at least. She bent to put her son's shoes on him, but he was having none of it. His jumping increased; he would not wait.

Placing one hand around her son's, she tentatively edged open the bedroom door. It was only about four feet to the bathroom - maybe they could make it unseen. While she considered the odds, Timothy broke free and dashed to the bathroom. Just steps ahead of her, he shut the door behind him, blocking her way. She looked toward the living room to see if Russell Rose was coming, but his pacing back and forth didn't diminish, nor did he look up from his monologue. As he turned to take his pacing away from her, she risked the two steps toward that room to look. No, there was no one else there. Russell Rose was talking to himself.

Both relief and disappointment flushed through her system - relief that he didn't have an accomplice that would place them in even more danger and disappointment that the help Jackson organized had not yet arrived. But now that it was daylight, they would be easier to spot. Wouldn't they?

～

THE TOILET flushed and Elizabeth winced. Even that didn't interrupt the guy's pacing.

The bathroom door handle turned. Well, at least Timothy had remembered to flush, even if there had been no sound of handwashing. Before he could come out, she pushed her way into the bathroom, then turned and locked them in. First, she washed her son's hands, then searched for a washcloth. There was one, just one in a bottom drawer. Since it was still folded, she assumed that it was clean. Didn't bear thinking about it in any other way. She shed Timothy's clothing and most of her own. Not willing to risk a bath or shower, at least she could wipe them off. She wrinkled her nose as she put back on the same clothing that she had both worn yesterday and slept in. When had she last done that - like, never?

The bathroom knob turned, and she froze. Even Timothy seemed to know to hold still and silent. It jiggled again, then harder. Would he break it down? Given the state of this old house, it wouldn't be too hard. She needed that door intact for at least the sense of privacy it gave her.

She opened her mouth, but what she wanted to say didn't come out. Her throat and tongue were dry. She tried again, "Just a minute, please. We'll be right out."

Silence. Had he forgotten that they were there? Oh, if only that was true, but what an opportunity she had missed for them to sneak away. She'd need to be more alert, if only to keep them safe until help arrived. He seemed to give up trying to enter the bathroom. Weird.

For once she was pleased that Timothy did not talk. She waited in silence a minute more, and then the pacing started up again, accompanied by Russell Rose's monologue.

She opened the door enough to peer out. When his back turned, she hustled Timothy back into the bedroom they had shared. Sitting on the bed, she wondered, now what?

Well, this was ridiculous. They couldn't sit in here all day. She needed to get some food into her son. Her stomach rumbled. And herself. She could sit in here and imagine all sorts of things. Was it better to just hunker down and remain out of sight, or should she risk him seeing them and getting who knows what ideas?

Timothy whined. Oh, she hated that sound on the best of days, but it did not help now, not at all. "Hush, son, it'll be all right." He fidgeted and even his fingers didn't seem to interest him today. She needed to get him some food. But keep him hidden in here or take him with her into the kitchen?

Timothy took her hand and pulled her toward the door. Guess that settled it. Keeping her little boy firmly to her side, the side that was farthest from the pacing man, she went down the hall and into the kitchen. Behind her, the pacing stopped as did the man's speech but there was nothing further.

As quietly as she could she reached into a bottom cupboard to withdraw a frying pan. With her mind more on the guy in the living room than Timothy, she didn't see her son reaching for two pans himself until it was too late. He clanged them together over and over, raising his voice in a yell over top of the din.

Footsteps charged into the kitchen. Russell Rose stood there with his hands over his ears, holding his head and yelling, "Stop!" He swiveled back and forth from the waist up, repeated that same word over and over. His distress appeared real. She understood. Timothy had banged pots once when she had a migraine.

"Hush, son." She put her hands over Timothy's then removed the pots from his grip. Setting them on the counter as quietly as she could, she picked up Timothy, holding him tightly against her chest. His arms and legs went around her, his head buried in her neck, turned away from Russell Rose.

Russell Rose's yells slowed then stopped. In their place was sobbing. What was wrong with this man? Was he in pain? He might be their kidnapper and enemy but, well, look at him. He didn't appear so threatening now, just hurting.

She let Timothy slide down her body, but still kept him between her and the cupboard.

"Russell," she called. "Russell Rose? Are you all right?"

No response.

She tried more firmly this time. "Russell Rose, go sit down. Now!"

What? It worked. He pulled out the nearest kitchen chair and sank into it. Hardly ever in her life had she raised her voice. Issuing an order felt kind of good.

Now what?

She gave Timothy a wooden spoon and a plastic spatula to play with. At least they were quieter when banged together. "I'll make us some tea." Not sure anyone was listening, but she said it anyway. The thought of the Stockholm Syndrome flowed through her mind. Rather than trying to make Russell Rose feel something for her and Timothy, was she feeling sympathetic toward him? Never. She was just acting as one would toward any other human being in distress.

They ate a breakfast of fried eggs, toast and tea in near silence. The only words spoken came from Elizabeth as she encouraged Timothy to eat. Although he mechanically moved his fork between his plate and mouth, Russell made no sound nor looked their way. Abruptly, he pushed back his chair and went to the living room. There he lay on his back on the couch with one arm across his eyes. No television, no talking, no sound.

Clanking the dishes as little as she could, Elizabeth washed up and tidied the kitchen. She noted their stocks and saw that she could make maybe one more meal out of eggs, then they were down to bread, milk and cheese. In her other grocery bag, she had some almond butter, some honey, crackers and fresh vegetables. But she'd not had time to bring them in.

～

EVENTUALLY FAINT SNORES came from the direction of Russell Rose. Was this their chance? Taking Timothy's hand, she opened the back door. She needed to check in the daylight to see if he had been telling the truth when he said there was no way out of the backyard. That just didn't seem possible. Who would build a fence like that? This time she was wise enough to stuff a dish towel between the door and frame and make sure that the locking bolt remained safely tucked away.

Now that it was light, she could investigate the yard. Checking the ground, she saw nothing she could use to protect them. Just as well. She could not see herself using a weapon against another human being. All her life she'd been taught that words and compromise, not violence were the way to resolve conflict. Daddy would say that she needed to dig deep and try harder with Russell Rose. Oh, if only Daddy was here.

The sunshine and gentle breeze refreshed her, after so many hours in that stuffy little house. Even Timothy seemed to take bigger breaths out here. Tugging away from her hand, he ran a few steps in front of her. She let him go; if Russell Rose was right, then Timothy could not go far.

And it seemed he was correct. In the bright sunlight it was easy to examine the fence, pretty well every inch of it. It was solid with no door or gate or even a visible weakness in the barrier. It was too tall for her to see over, but straining to hear, there were no sounds of human occupation. Hollering for help from neighbors would most likely just bring Russell Rose out to them. What if he locked them out here? They'd be trapped, way worse trapped than they currently were.

Catching up with Timothy, she led him back into the kitchen, shutting the door quietly after removing the dish cloth. Snoring still came from the other room.

The front door led outside to where they left the car, and to the road they came in on. If she could get out there, maybe she could find the spare key. When it was brand new, Daddy had bought her this little magnetic tin. He had an extra key to her car made, placed it in the tin, then told her where he hid it. Why did she not pay more attention? She and Jackson had laughed about it - if they ever locked themselves out of a vehicle, their plan was to call AAA. What had Daddy said? Something about the wheel and a well?

She'd find it - she had to. And, if she couldn't so they could drive away, at least they could start walking down the rutty road they had driven in on. Surely, they'd find help. Or maybe meet the rescuers coming to find them.

But the only way to get to the car was to cross the living room where Russell Rose lay sleeping. How deeply did he sleep?

She'd make better time and be quieter if she was on her own. Could she stash Timothy in the bedroom and hope that he'd stay in there, safe and alone, until she returned with help?

No, she could not do that and risk the possibility of her little boy alone at the mercy of that man. She kneeled in front of Timothy. "Shh, we're going to play a game. We don't want to wake Russell Rose. We are going to tiptoe ever so quietly across that room, then go out the door. It will be nice out and you'll like it." She took his hand, then let out a big breath. Putting her index finger to her mouth, she made eye contact with Timothy, reinforcing the need for silence. He giggled. Sigh. She should *not* have told him this was a game. He might not talk, but he understood well enough and took whatever he heard at face value. Nuances were lost on him. But he's only four, she reminded herself.

They started across the living room toward the front door.

CHAPTER 19

"No, you can't come."

"But the place will be ours soon. And I want to spend the night with you."

"How would that look? The house might be under observation. For sure the neighbors will be watching."

"They won't know I'm there if you drive into your garage. I'll duck down; they won't see me."

Possibly. What her hands were doing led to other possibilities. He caved.

~

"Bit bland, isn't it?" She turned around in the living room, inspected the dining room and then the kitchen. "Could do with some fixing up, don't you think?"

His response was noncommittal as he looked through the accumulated mail. Not much here. He wondered if there was more in the box outside. No use advertising to the neighbors that he was home, in case they hadn't seen him turn into his driveway.

"I want to see the master bedroom again."

He waved toward the stairwell. "Knock yourself out." He didn't much care what the place looked like as long as it was clean and comfortable and reflective of his social status, which was upwardly mobile and rising all the time. At least, that was the goal, along with doing that rising without having to work quite so hard.

~

REMEMBERING that it had creaked when they first entered, Elizabeth grasped the knob and lifted the door at the same time as she turned the knob. That trick had worked with the door to the swim cabana behind her parents' house. It worked this time, too. Funny how little details stuck in your mind including the fact that the door to this house creaked. At the time it had stuck in her brain as fitting with a haunted house movie.

She glanced back, but Russell Rose didn't stir. Again, motioning to Timothy for silence they left the threshold, shutting the door gently behind them. The sun struck her eyes, making her bring her other hand up to shield them. Timothy already started down the rickety wooden steps. She hurried after him, worried that one would break under his weight, only after realizing that there was a far greater chance of her crashing through one.

In front of Timothy, a grasshopper jumped. He followed, his little hands outstretched, tracing its erratic movement. That would keep him occupied for a few minutes while she searched out the hidden key.

Her footsteps halted. The car! It was gone. Was it stolen? How ridiculous - obviously there was no one around here to steal anything. A warped part of her brain giggled - a stolen car getting stolen. She clamped down on that, could not afford to let any part of her brain go loosey-goosey on her now.

What the hell happened to her car? Oops. She never swore; it was a sign of possessing a small vocabulary and a small mind, not something ladies should do. But hell. Where was the damn thing? Had he moved it?

She checked the closest side of the house. Maybe he'd driven it where passersby could not see it. No, not there. The other side?

No, it was not visible there either, but about a hundred and fifty yards away stood an old building made of weathered boards, the type you'd see on ancient barns. The building listed decidedly to the left, as if leaning into the prevailing winds. Or, more likely, about to be taken out by prevailing winds.

How long would it take to walk there? It looked large enough to hide her car. Timothy was occupied with that grasshopper, or something grasshopperish.

She didn't know how much time she had. Investigate that shed to see if it held her car? What if it was locked? What if even she got in, she couldn't find that key? Or maybe if Russell Rose drove it in there, he left the key with it. A city person would never, ever do that, but a guy brought up around here? She looked around and could spot not a soul or even evidence that a person lived within miles of here.

That gave her pause. Her other option was to take Timothy and walk out on that road. It ended at Russell Rose's granny's house, so there was no debate about which direction to go. How far had they driven on it after turning off the highway? She had no clue. Between the dark and her fear, she didn't trust any of her perceptions. Plus, she had dozed off at some point during the drive here.

One or the other. She needed to decide now while Russell Rose still slept. But which one?

～

"We need to meet."

"I don't think we should be seen together."

"Not my favorite thing either, but I need to watch the look on your face while we discuss this."

"I'm kinda tied up for a while, you know. My wife and son are missing, and the police are meeting with me."

"Yeah, exactly why we need to talk."

"No. Next week, I might be able to fit it in."

"And I might be able to fit in just a little note to the police. Or through the Crime Tips line."

～

The bus station seemed busy enough, people hurrying on their way, wrapped up in their own business. A noisy, anonymous meeting place. And yes, the coffee was about as bad as you would imagine.

He sat alone on one side of the booth, facing two gentlemen he had never met face-to-face.

"So, here's the deal," said the larger of the two men. "You approached me to do a job. We agreed to take the job. When I give my word, I do what I say I'll do."

As the nervous man on the other side of the booth began to speak, the other held up his hand. "I ain't finished. In order for us to do my job, we needed certain information from you. You said you gave it to me. We find now that you lied." He waited a beat. "My partner and I here, we don't like liars, do we?"

Crossing his arms, his partner agreed.

"But I didn't lie to you. I told you her schedule exactly as I knew it. They do not deviate from their plans, unless the kid is in hospital."

"If you didn't lie, we see three other possibilities. The first, we *don't like very much. You didn't trust us to do the job, so you hired someone else. Maybe you hoped that one of us would get done what you wanted. Which one of us did you plan to pay, and which were you going to rip off?"*

"Neither, I swear!"

"Neither? So, you are saying that you set up two groups for this job, sort of two opposing forces, working without knowledge of the other?"

"No, that's not the neither I mean. I meant I didn't contact anyone but you. God knows I had enough difficulty finding you; don't know how I would unearth two of you in the same line of work." He tried to continue patiently. "What I'm trying to say is that I did not lie to you and I did not hire anyone but you."

"Here's door number three. You arranged for someone else to snatch just the kid. If that's what happened, you might be in a world of hurt. If you'd stuck with us, your kid might have been scared but safe. We don't do nothing bad to kids. But not every contractor has our, shall we say, ethics."

Jackson shook his head vehemently back and forth. "No, never. I want my son back safely."

"Then there's a fourth option. You don't know this chick as well as you think you do, and she has double-crossed you."

Uh-huh. He shook his head. "Not possible. She's a straight-shooter and always is up front about things, especially to me. And she's not smart enough to pull something over on me."

"I have news for you, buddy. She did."

CHAPTER 20

Timothy looked toward her, waving his arms, and smiling that cherubic expression, the one that would melt the heart of Ebenezer Scrooge or any Grinch, no matter what time of year. The expression that no one, but no one could resist. She wondered how anyone could exude so much charm without talking, but her son pulled it off.

She hated it when Jackson was too busy to spend time with their child and had vowed years ago to never be like that. Russell Rose was sleeping, and it would only take a few minutes to see what was delighting Timothy. Being rather a solitary little human being, he rarely wanted to share his enjoyment with another person. Kneeling in the grass beside him, she oohed and aahed over the leaping grasshoppers and the odd butterfly cavorting in the long grass. Timothy was right; they were rather magnificent. She gave him the name for each insect, at least the broad category name, and showed him how to cup his hands gently to capture one without harming it.

When he was again content to play alone, she rose to her feet, glancing down the road. Walk or car, car or walk?

The reality was that as much as she loved her son and would do anything for him, at four he could not walk far. He was too heavy for her to carry any significant distance, and she really had no idea how far they would have to walk to reach help. Besides, if she could not get the car started, the walking option was still open to them, other than having lost a bit of time.

Watching Timothy over her shoulder every couple of steps, she made her way to the side and behind the house to the rickety wooden building. There were two windows along this side, but they were at a height meant for someone six foot at least, not her five foot three. Checking behind the building, she saw two old metal drums, the five-gallon type. Pushing them onto their sides with her foot, she chose the one that appeared the least rusty and placed it under one window. Peering in through the dusty glass, she could see the faint shape of what might be a vehicle. Angling her head the other way, she shaded her eyes, she saw. Yes, it definitely looked like a car, but she could not swear that it was hers. How likely could it be anything else, she thought. And, even if it wasn't hers, a car was a car and would be faster than trying to walk or run away from here.

Timothy had not wandered far and still seemed content. He had looked a couple of times and waved to her. To him, this must seem like one of their usual trips to a park, just a different park. She had a bit more time, then.

Circling the building, she found no walk-in door. The only way in seemed to be through the double doors on the narrow end, near where the rear of the car would be. Thankfully, she could see no padlock or any other type of locking mechanism. The doors appeared to be held closed by a long piece of wood, maybe a twelve-foot two-by-four held in place by two wooden bracket sorts of things. On inspection, it seemed that the only thing she had to do was to lift the long piece of wood up and out of the brackets, then the doors should swing open on their hinges. Or she could wait for a nice, strong wind, she thought, and the whole place would blow over. No, that might make the car inoperable, and back to walking as the only option.

Grasping the wood in the middle, she heaved. Like *that* was going to work. The thing budged not a smidge. Okay, she'd start at one end and maybe push the piece through the brackets. No, that wasn't working either; it wedged in there too tightly.

Another quick look to check on Timothy, then back to the building. She needed a lever of some kind, something to pry on this board. A search of the building and surrounding area turned up nothing suitable, but she found a rock, several rocks in fact. Maybe if she could not push the bar, then she could bash it, either up or down on one end, breaking it free from the brackets.

She wiped her forehead with the back of her arm. She hated sweating; it was bad enough at the gym when others around her were doing the same and there was a purpose to it. But she did not exercise outdoors. Especially, she thought, when she had exactly one pair of clothes to wear and not one thing to change into.

But her sweating paid off. Perhaps those few nasty words helped as well. If her mother only heard the language she uttered. Well, she'd said even worse things in her head since yesterday.

With a creaking that made her cringe, the wooden bar started to lift. Just on one end, but it was starting to clear its bracket. The other end was edging out of its bracket as well. Slowly, ever so slowly, her pounding and creaking were working together. With a clatter, the bar released itself and fell to the ground. Elizabeth did the same but just for a second. She couldn't see Timothy!

Had the noise frightened him, and he'd taken off? Had it woken Russell Rose and he'd nabbed her son?

No, neither of those things. Timothy was just closer to the front steps than he had been, following a butterfly and not in her line of sight. She pointed to some purple flowering clover and guided him in that direction, picking some and tickling him under the chin with it. He giggled and did the same to her. Pointing out a butterfly, she directed his attention that way, hoping he'd stay in this vicinity for a while now.

Pulling the wooden bar back out of the way, she went to work on the doors. It was a joke to think that she could stand in the middle and swing open both doors. Not going to happen. Ever. Who would have thought they could be so heavy?

With little for a handle, there was little to grasp, but eventually she could open a crack large enough to get her hand through. Trying to push with that fist and pull with the other hand opened the door enough to get her foot and then her leg through. She could then use enough leverage to push on the door, so it was finally open at a ninety-degree angle to its partner.

It took a minute for her eyes to adjust to the darkness, even with the light that came in through the door. She'd chosen to start with the wrong door; the other one would have let in more sunlight but, as fitting for her luck, she'd picked the one that would block the sun's rays from entering the building.

But yes, this was her car. Never had she felt such affection for a vehicle as she did right this minute. It was hers and a part of her life, her normal, safe life, and it could return her and Timothy to that haven where they were safe and cared for.

Peering in the driver's side window, no keys were just

lying around in plain view. No, that would be too easy. As quietly as she could, she opened the door - not locked! Yes! Things were looking up. Where might he have put the keys? She would not even think about the possibility that they were even now in his pants pocket. She lowered the visor. No, not that. Checked the glove box. Nope. The center console. No. Under the driver's seat, then the passenger seat. No and no. Hanging in the ignition? Why hadn't she looked there first? But no, nothing that simple.

Okay, Plan B. Find where Daddy had hidden her spare key for her. That meant getting on the ground and feeling around under her car. Appetizing? I think not, she said, but then since this ordeal began, she had done things that were new to her, unappealing things, but she'd done them for the sake of herself and Timothy.

Timothy. She popped to her feet and went outside to check. Yes, he was where she had left him.

She searched the wheel wells and under the running boards and bumpers. She wondered if she raised the hood, then realized that was not smart. If she was locked out of her car, she could not lift the latch that allowed the hood to open. Her father would not have hidden the key there. She had a picture in her mind of the key's container. It was just a little thing, black and oblong with a lid that slid to the side to reveal the compartment where the key nestled and a magnet on the back of the box.

Jackson had thought the whole notion ridiculous. They had AAA. If locked out, they'd simply call, and someone would come and let them into their car. He had no intention of laying on his back in some street, feeling around for some stupid key that was supposed to be there but had probably fallen off years ago. As much as she trusted Daddy, she feared that Jackson was right. She could not find the thing.

But, while here, she might as well bring in the other bag of groceries, the one with the non-perishables. It looked like she was going to have to feed herself and her son another meal here in captivity.

Was that a door she heard slam?

CHAPTER 21

*D*etectives Brendan James and Jake Dean speculated with their captain.

"Tell me your early thoughts, guys."

Brendan began. "The usual suspect would be the husband. Statistically that would be accurate, but we have nothing pointing to him. He was out of town when she went missing and the neighbors don't describe their marriage as on the rocks - no open fighting or anything like that."

Jake agreed but didn't get good vibes from Mr. Whitmore. "For a guy with a sick kid, he didn't seem to know a lot about the medical side of things. He didn't mention that the kid had an appointment with a specialist that morning. "He looked at his partner. "Isn't that a thing that would stick in your mind?" He shook his head and continued. "Hubby was also slow in reporting them missing, at least in my opinion. And he took his time getting here. If that had been a wife and kids of mine, I'd have been on this a day sooner than he was."

"Not every marriage is paradise, remember. The bloom falls off the rose for some."

"I know, but still…. The other thing is that there are no

relatives or friends to have raised the alarm either. The parents on either side are dead, and both Elizabeth and Jackson were only children. Jackson spent time in the system after his parents passed on. Elizabeth's parents died in a plane crash a few years ago."

"The other trope is 'follow the money'. What have you got there?" Their captain looked between his two men.

"Still working on that. Should have access this morning to the rest of the wife's accounts. Seems that except for a joint household expenses account, they kept their finances separate."

"They both had jobs?"

"No sign that Mrs. Whitmore has worked outside the home since the birth of their child. We haven't had time to delve farther back than that yet." At the look from the captain, Brendan added, "But we will."

"We haven't had a call back from the messages we left for Jackson's employer yet, so we're headed over there today. Looks like he has a typical traveling salesman job, maybe less glamorous than he lets on, but we should know more later. Both their income tax records should be in this morning."

"So, here's what you've got so far. On Monday, a young mother did what her husband expected her to do - took their kid to a doctor's appointment, then went to a drugstore, the supermarket and got gas. We know that she had her kid with her during the first two stops, but no verification after that."

"Right."

"Then you got her on surveillance camera paying for gas, then leaping into her car as it was moving, driven by an UNSUB. No sign of the kid."

"Yeah, but we couldn't see on the tape if the boy was in the back seat of the car or not. The techies should have it cleaned up for us any time now."

"Are we ready to go public with this?"

~

No longer worrying about subterfuge, although why would she after all the racket she'd made getting into this building, she stretched into the trunk, reaching for the grocery bag. Thank god she'd zipped it closed so she could grab it without spilling food all over. Slamming the car door, she raced out of the building, not caring if the ancient wooden door swung slightly in the breeze.

Now she ran full tilt toward the front of the house. She couldn't see Timothy. Oh, she took too long searching the car and now look what had happened. Her principal job while they waited to be rescued was to look after her son, and she failed. What would Russell Rose do to him if she wasn't there?

Rounding the front corner, her right toe sank into a hole in the ground. She had not seen it; how could she when the grass and weeds in the unkept yard were almost knee high? Down she went.

Raising her upper body on her scratched arms, she looked for Timothy. There, there he was, but on the bottom step was Russell Rose. She could not get between them in time. Holding her breath, she watched.

Timothy wore an intense look. One arm was outstretched with his fist turned upward. He walked right up to Russell Rose. Stopping just a foot away, Timothy looked into Russell Rose's face and gave that signature cherubic smile, the one that won over strangers whenever he flashed it. Did Timothy know that they needed to get this guy on their side? No, doubtful. He was only four. The child held out his hand to Russell Rose and slowly opened his fingers, all the time watching the man in front of him.

Please, god, please god, prayed Elizabeth.

Disarmed, Russell Rose didn't know what to do. He

glanced over toward Elizabeth, with a surprised and a puzzled expression on his face. Probably he wondered why she was lying on the ground, Elizabeth thought. But he ignored her and turned his attention back to Timothy. Russell Rose lowered himself to the second-to-bottom step, seating himself just above Timothy.

He asked, "What you got there, buddy?" His voice didn't sound too menacing.

Elizabeth let go of that breath, and then held onto the next one as Russell Rose stretched out his big hand toward her son's tiny one. With his index finger, Russell Rose tentatively touched the grasshopper. It moved, although listing to one side. The lower part of one leg was missing. Either the kid had broken it off, or maybe the insect came that way and that was why the little boy could catch it. "Grasshopper," he said. "That's a grasshopper."

Timothy beamed at him. How could he? wondered his mom. This man was nothing like Timothy's dad or any other man he came in contact with. Russell Rose's hair was almost to his shoulders, unwashed and looked like it had not seen a comb in days and days. She raised a hand to her own. Someone could say the same about her.

Now that he'd shared his new toy with someone, Timothy lost interest. He turned away and thank god, Russell Rose let him. The man watched Timothy for several seconds as the child searched some more in the tall grass. Then he turned his attention to her.

"What kind of mother leaves her kid alone outside in a strange place?"

He was critical of *her*? Usually slow to anger, Elizabeth felt her ire rise. He, this man caused all their troubles. If not for him, she and Timothy would be safely home with their own things, eating proper meals she prepared in her tidy, organized kitchen, taking regular baths and showers, not stinking like this. She got up, ready to tell her kidnapper exactly what she thought of him. As she put her weight on her right foot, with a cry, she went down again.

While he might have just been kind to her son, his face showed no expression as he watched Elizabeth try to get to her feet, then limp toward Timothy. When she had made it the entire way, he pointed back the way she had come and asked, "Did you forget something?" There on the ground was her grocery bag. Yes, she had forgotten it. "Gotta watch out for gopher holes around here."

Gophers? Alarmed, she looked around the area where she and Timothy stood. She had no experience with gophers. Were they something they needed to be afraid of? There were no gophers in her yard, nor on the estate where she had grown up. Daddy would never have tolerated something digging holes in his manicured grass. He would have had the grounds keepers on that immediately.

"Never met such a city girl. Doncha know about gophers? They dig burrows into the ground. Horses break legs when they fall into them. People can too. Looks like you mighta sprained yours."

He continued. "Once had a dog. He was running behind the house with me. Good dog, he was. Then he caught his foot in a gopher hole and went down. I heard the bone snap even though I wasn't right beside him. Darndest thing. Never was any good after that. He tried his best, but he grew ornery and couldn't get around very well. Had to put him down, Granny said so."

"Put him down?"

Was this a conversation? Sort of like normal people might exchange? Kind of, although the subject was a little off. While he was in this mellow mood might be a good time to get him to see them as humans, people to have a rapport with, people he might feel sorry for and let go.

"Yeah," continued Russell Rose. "If you love something, you're responsible for it, Granny said. Sometimes you have to make tough decisions - life and death decisions." His face crumpled, and he squeezed his eyes tight shut.

Elizabeth stared and checked to see that Timothy was safe.

The sobs began welling from deep in Russell Rose's gut, spewing out with a mixture of semi-comprehensible words. "I should have been here. It was my responsibility," he wailed. "She would have wanted me to put her out of her pain, but I wasn't here." He collapsed on the step.

Gradually, he quieted, wiping his nose on his sleeve.

$\sim$

TIMOTHY, bless him, seemed to get it. When the man quieted, he came back to Russell Rose, again holding out his hand to him. This time, when he uncurled his fist, the wings of a moth or butterfly were visible. He moved closer, resting his arm on the man's leg. Bringing his other hand up to cup the creature, he grinned up at Russell Rose. As Elizabeth watched, Timothy's eyes rolled up toward his forehead until almost all that was visible were their whites. The tremor started along his left side and his knees buckled. Then the spasms shook his entire body as he dropped and lost consciousness.

"What! What's happening to him? What the hell is the kid doing?" Russell Rose backed up, as if this could be catchy.

Elizabeth was too busy turning Timothy onto his side in recovery position, brushing his hair from his forehead, murmuring what she hoped were reassuring words. She'd asked Dr. Muller if Timothy could understand what she said when he was having a seizure. The answer was unclear, doubtful, but if on some level he could hear, it would help. It would not hurt, and he smiled as he told her it might make *her* feel better. So, she did it. Although most of his seizures didn't last long, it felt like hours while she watched her little boy's body twist and jerk. She timed it because seizures lasting longer than a few minutes might require a trip to the hospital.

The scent of urine filled the air. Almost always he lost bladder control, and often bowel control as well when his body seized. As the tremors ceased and Timothy seemed to deflate, Elizabeth gathered him to her, rocking and soothing him.

The door slammed as Russell Rose made his getaway. If only she could do the same, Elizabeth thought. A tear, just one, trickled down her cheek as she pressed Timothy's head to her chest. When he was quiet, when they were both quiet, she rose with him in her arms and made her way back into the house. Timothy needed a bath and a change of clothes.

Russell Rose was there, in his pacing mode once again. He talked to himself as he walked back and forth, his speech becoming more agitated it seemed with each lap. Elizabeth ignored him and entered the bedroom where she had left the Value Village bag of clothing she had bought. Down to his last pair of underwear and jeans, she noticed. She carried her son, the clothes and a towel into the bathroom and locked the door. Propping Timothy up against a wall, she ran a bath, careful to get the temperature just right. No point in shocking his systems with either too hot or too cold a temperature and risking another seizure. She slumped against the wall beside the drowsy boy, pulling his head to her shoulder and running her fingers through his hair.

She hated when he was like this. Well, that was not exactly true. She enjoyed the cuddling part but hated that the seizures would make him dopey, sapping the personality out of her little boy. Just twenty minutes ago he seemed so well, and the real Timothy showed himself to Russell Rose. Then, this. She put her lips to his temple and murmured things that really had no meaning.

Elizabeth removed Timothy's clothing and as she lowered him into the tub, there was a pounding on the door. It leaped in its frame. Oh, for the love of....

CHAPTER 22

*A*fter their meeting with the husband at the bus station, the two men gathered in a bar, savoring a craft beer sample. Usually, the place was raucous but not so much this early in the day.

"Not bad, this one. But who in their right mind thought it would be a good idea to add lavender to beer?" He wiped his lips with the back of his hand and took a swig of a dark ale to drive out the lavender taste. "Ah, better."

"There's a lot of that not-in-right-mind stuff going around. What do you make of this job?"

"I'm not sure that husband has the brains to pull off a double-cross on us. My take is that he thinks he's hot stuff and that the world should bow to his will. And that he's better than everyone else. Don't know how that little wifey stands him."

"You don't think he's lying?"

"Nah. Not positive, but it's not looking that way. What I think has happened is that *she* pulled one over on him. He's so up his own ass that it would never occur to him that someone might plot against him."

"And the other lead?"

"I worked that punk in the alley over good the other night. Don't think he had anything else to offer. Too dumb to know anything anyway. He was just looking for a quick score. How the hell did he get her purse, though? He said she just left it there, on his counter. Doesn't make sense. You know how women cling to their purses."

"We got her wallet now. The cash is gone, but her American Express card's here."

"Guess the drinks are on her." They clinked glasses in a toast to Elizabeth.

~

ANGER SURGED THROUGH ELIZABETH. Couldn't they even have ten minutes of peace. This guy, this brute disrupted their lives, stolen them from all they knew and valued and would not even give her time to clean up her child. She put her shoulder against the door just in case it was about to be broken down and her face to the crack.

She screamed at Russell Rose to leave them alone, just leave them alone. A whimper came from the tub. God, she was frightening her son. She did not yell like that, ever. Taking a deep breath and consciously lowering her shoulders, she tried again, willing her voice to be calm.

"Russell Rose, look. We'll be out soon. Timothy had a seizure - you saw that. Now I need to give him a bath and fresh clothing." She waited but could hear only his heavy breathing. At least he'd stopped trying to break down the door.

"I thought you were leaving."

She looked at the door and her brow wrinkled. What? Never mind, she had too much to deal with right now. Timothy was her first concern.

. . .

WHY DID it seem like she was always placating males? Maybe because she was, she thought. Understandable that she would need to do that to Timothy. But to her kidnapper? She shook her head. And yes, she did it all the time at home, too, to Jackson. At least on the days that he was home.

Was that what life was like for all women? She couldn't ever remember her mother doing that with daddy. Daddy was so in charge, so confident that he didn't need it. Really, why should anyone be placated but a child? No one did that to her.

WHILE TIMOTHY PLAYED with the bar of soap, Elizabeth quickly rinsed out his underwear, jeans and the ones he'd worn yesterday. She wrung them out as best she could and hung them over the curtain rod. How she wished she had clothes of her own to do the same with. Never in her life had she worn clothes that she'd slept in all night. Come to think of it, she could not recall ever wearing the same clothes twice, not even as a child. Jackson always told her she needed to be open to new experiences. Well, this was new.

Timothy, dry, warm and smelling like a sweet little boy, tugged on the door handle. He seemed to recover from this seizure better than some, without the typical exhaustion. He didn't look like he needed a nap just yet.

Elizabeth wondered if this had anything to do with the fact that he had not had his medication. He'd missed last night's dose and this morning's. She'd worried that there would be a rampant increase in seizure activity, but so far there hadn't been a significant regression. Dr. Muller had directed them to decrease the valproic acid; she wondered what he'd say when he learned that they'd stopped it abruptly.

Squaring her shoulders, she tucked Timothy to her side and entered the living room. Russell Rose was on his back on the couch. The television was off, and the only sound was the ticking clock on the corner table. Russell Rose had one arm bent across his face and gave no notice that he was aware of their presence. Was he asleep?

Timothy pulled away from her and ran to the man. Standing close, he gently placed his hand on Russell Rose's forehead. Russell Rose startled, and half sat up. He looked at Timothy with an, "Oh, it's you," then settled back down.

Timothy brought his other hand up to stroke the man's cheek. Russell Rose's eyes met Elizabeth's.

"He thinks you're sick," she explained. "That's what I do to him when he's ill. You're laying down in the middle of the day, so he thinks you are sick, and he's trying to make you feel better."

Confusion was in Russell Rose's eyes as he watched the small boy. "Why would he do that? Why's he care?"

She shrugged. "That's just the way he is. He's kind. One of his nurses calls him an old soul."

He watched Timothy with something like wonder. Then he tentatively returned the child's smile.

THAT TICKING clock reminded Elizabeth just how much time had gone by since breakfast. She needed to get some food into Timothy quickly. His seizures were worse when his body was off of its schedule. Damn! She'd left the grocery bag outside. What to do, what to do?

Russell Rose reached for the remote and raised himself to a sitting position. Timothy remained by his side, one hand resting on the couch beside him. To Elizabeth's surprise, the remote flicked through channels until landing on Sesame Street. Russell Rose acted as if this was his intention all along. Timothy kneeled on the floor beside their abductor, placed his elbows on the coffee table and watched.

"Ah, I'll just grab my groceries from outside." Neither male appeared to have heard her.

The short walk took longer than it should have. Her ankle really hurt when she put weight on it. When she returned, Timothy and Russell Rose were both engrossed in Sesame Street. Timothy turned to the man with his engaging smile, his eyes bright. He loved those characters.

"Yeah, kid, that's the Count," said Russell Rose. To Elizabeth's astonishment, he began counting aloud. "One, two, three, four, five…. Hey!" He looked at Elizabeth, his eyes wide. His body backed away from Timothy. "What's wrong with him? Look! Look what he's doing!"

Dropping the grocery bag, Elizabeth hobbled over as swiftly as she could to get a better look at her son. Timothy still knelt, half-turned around toward Russell Rose. But that animated look replaced by a blank one. He eyes stared fixedly; his body moved not a muscle.

Her shoulders slumped. "He's having a seizure, an absence seizure. They never last long." As she said those last words Timothy blinked, seemed to take a second to re-orient himself, then turned back to the television.

"God save us," was all Russell Rose said. "This is one weird kid."

Like you should talk, thought Elizabeth. She could hear her mother chiding her in her head. But she really was not feeling charitable right this moment, not at Russell Rose and not with the world.

"Maybe some time alone in the basement would snap him out of it."

. . .

JACKSON COULD BE MOODY, especially after being gone all week, but she had seen no one whose moods flipped as quickly as those of Russell Rose. What was with that guy? He sounded furious when pounding on the bathroom door. Then ten minutes later he's laying comatose on the couch. Then, maybe in response to Timothy's touch, he's sitting quietly watching a children's show.

Lunch was not much, but she did what she could with the few foods at her disposal. She put Timothy down for a nap, then cleaned up the kitchen. All done, she thought about joining her son for a rest. She rarely slept during the daytime, but these last couple days had been exhausting. And she needed to while away the time somehow before help arrived.

What was that? That sound? It was not coming from the direction of Timothy's room. Quietly going to the doorway, she peeked into the living room. He was on the couch again, but this time face-down. His shoulders moved and that strange noise came from him. What the...? Was Russell Rose crying? Could her life get any more bizarre?

She sighed. Okay, she couldn't drive them away from here and she didn't think she could walk herself and Timothy to safety, so they were stuck in this guy's presence for at least a bit longer. If they had to co-exist with this guy it was best to figure him out. She took a few steps toward him, careful to remain out of arm's reach.

"Russell Rose?" Nothing. She tried again, just a little louder.

The sobs got louder as well.

She tried not to roll her eyes. Had she no compassion for someone in distress? She took a check of her emotions - ah, no. She felt no compassion for this person who caused all her current problems. Okay, Elizabeth, you can do this.

She went into the bathroom and returned with a spare

roll of toilet paper. She plunked it onto the coffee table with as much force as she thought reasonable to get his attention. "Here," she directed. "Sit up and blow your nose."

To her shock and dismay, he obeyed. Now what was she supposed to do? His eyes were brimming. Tears and snot mingled in his mustache and scraggly beard. He pushed hair back from his forehead. His leaking was disgusting. She raised, then banged down the toilet roll again. "Use it," she ordered.

He did. Maybe she was on to something. Maybe this was the way to handle this guy - be authoritative, not wimpy or cajoling. Tell him, order him around.

Well, she had tried that when he first stole her car and it hadn't worked, but maybe if she gauged his moods, she could use this to her advantage.

"What's wrong with you?" She wished she could pull back those words. She'd said them accusingly, aggressively. Not good to raise the hackles on the man who has you at his mercy. But he didn't retaliate, at least this time.

"I thought, thought you were leaving me," he said through sobs. The filthy, scarred hands covering his face muffled his words. "Everyone leaves me."

"We're still here, as you can see."

"I don't want to be alone. Don't ever leave me." He lowered his hands. Fierce eyes bored into hers.

CHAPTER 23

*A*fter leaving the bar, the two men went their separate ways. While one planned to watch the house, the other would trail Jackson. This was their last day of giving time to this project.

No matter how many places he parked his car on the Whitmore's street, the scenery wore thin. He'd swapped cars with his partner just to change it up in case any nosy neighbors got suspicious. It would be a long wait, so he stopped off at a convenience store to buy smokes. He did love his cigarillos.

Parking farther away this time, he surveyed the street. Calm place, boring as hell.

Twenty minutes later, that feeling came over him, that feeling you get when someone is staring at you. Without moving his head too much, he checked for anyone in his field of vision. Nothing unusual and no movement. Taking out his cell phone, he placed it in camera mode and held it beside his head, over his shoulder. There. Behind him about fifty feet was another car, one he didn't recognize from this street. He could make out the shadow of someone sitting behind the wheel, but that was about it. He snapped a couple of pictures, moving the phone slightly to take in various angles of the vehicle.

Time to get his acting gig on. Reaching for the clipboard he kept on the passenger seat, he exited the car. Pretending to read the papers on his board, he walked up the drive of the nearest house. From past surveillance, he knew that the people in that home left during the day. He knocked on the front door, keeping his head down and his ball cap tilted over his face. When no one answered, he made a show of looking at his watch, then knocking again. After waiting another two minutes, he returned to his car and drove off.

He called his partner. "We've got company."

~

AN ANGRY RUSSELL ROSE was frightening. A silent Russell Rose unnerving, a chatty one disarming, but a sobbing one was just plain bizarre.

The nice Elizabeth, the one raised by a mother to be kind, felt for Russell Rose. Well, felt a bit. Watching him twigged bits of her college psychology classes, but he was too multi-sided to figure out. Yet, figure him out she must if they were going to survive this thing. She'd been not too bad in drama in school; now was the time to channel her inner actress. Anything she could find out about this weirdo might help them get away.

She didn't want to go there. No, emotions were messy things. Better to suck it up and keep it in. But she needed to use whatever was at her disposal. Prying into Russell Rose's psyche seemed to be the only weapon she had right now.

Bracing herself, she began. "Have you been alone much?"

That brought on another bout of weeping. She hoped that

he didn't awaken Timothy, although her son usually slept deeply once he was out.

The crying was of no use to her. She needed words. Trying her firm voice again, she gave an order. "Stop. Stop it right now. I can't help you if you don't tell me what's wrong. I need words." She was always telling Timothy to use his words; who knew she'd be saying the same thing to a grown man. Letting go of her actress persona, she tried channeling her inner Freud. "Start at the beginning and tell me about you and your Granny."

It seemed to take forever, but slowly, a phrase at a time, a picture emerged. Elizabeth wished she had the kind of clipboard you saw in pictures of Freud. At least she could doodle as Russell Rose gave away bits and pieces of his story.

His mother was bad - a hussy. She left him with Granny, only returning for short bursts when he was quite young. When she was around, things were fun. She made him laugh, but her visits were whirlwind and interspersed with screaming matches with Granny. Then she was gone, and silence rained down on the house, a silence broken only by the tread of Granny's lace-up shoes and her television shows.

As much fun as his mother's visits were, Russell Rose dreaded when she left. The silence was hard, especially from the basement. Every time his mother left, he spent time in the basement. Granny said it was because he was bad spawn and needed punishment. See what he had done to his mother? She used to be a good girl.

He was never sure exactly what he had done wrong. He tried to figure it out so he could not do it the next time, but he always got it wrong. He was too noisy. He laughed too much. But mom teased him and played games with him and for just a couple days the air seemed lighter. She cuddled him and said that she loved him. Russell Rose looked up at Elizabeth from where she stood on the other side of the coffee table. "No one has ever said that to me." He seemed to be living in his own head for several minutes. "But she was bad. Evil, even, Granny said. Up to no good."

Apparently, she had not always been that way. Oh, there were some signs. As a small child she had been willful at times, but Granny fixed that. Then she became a quiet, obedient child until the teen years struck. It took a while to come on, but then she started to not listen. Chores slipped, just a bit, and standards not always upheld. She would come home from school late with some excuse or other. Granny knew; she always saw through her. She was not born yesterday, Granny wasn't. She liked to say, "I'm not as green as I am cabbage-looking." She'd get annoyed when the young Russell Rose would protest that she looked nothing like a cabbage. He was just trying to be honest and helpful, but this usually earned him at best a clout on the head or at worst, time in the basement.

Some days Granny stood at the window watching as his mother left for school. Once out of the house, the slut would roll up the waistband of her skirt, baring more of her legs than was proper. Repeatedly Granny searched the house and found a stash of makeup. Although why the girl would want to paint herself up like that, Granny didn't know. She was not having any of it though, not in this house.

Then there were the Friday afternoons when she didn't come home from school, didn't come home at all until the early hours of Saturday morning. She would try to creep in quietly, but Granny always heard her. Who wouldn't when she stumbled over things and retched in the bathroom, leaving it stinking with her foul fumes? When Granny threw her down into the basement, her willful girl would say it was worth it for the fun she'd had.

Then, one Saturday, she didn't come home at all. Not for days, not for weeks. When she finally darkened

Granny's door again, her stomach entered first. Granny beat her, tried to beat the evil out of her. When she lay on the floor without moving, Granny dragged her and then tossed her down the basement stairs. She stayed there for days. When she crawled back up, knocking softly on the locked door, Granny had opened it and threw down a bucket with supplies. "Clean up your messes, you filthy creature."

What was Granny to do? This was her own flesh and blood. Now her girl was about to bring another life into this world, one created in sin. A bastard. A stubborn bastard because he remained inside her daughter and continued to grow.

The girl got a job waitressing. Good. She needed to earn her keep and not expect her mother to feed her and her bastard. The girl's feet swelled, her belly swelled as did her head with wild ideas. No, none of those fairy-tale things were going to happen to her. She had made her bed, literally, and now she must lie in it.

The baby was born right here. Russell Rose pointed toward the bedroom in which Elizabeth and Timothy had slept. Elizabeth shuddered inwardly at the thought. "Was your Granny a midwife," she asked?

"Nah, but she had been a wife."

Oh god, thought Elizabeth. That poor young woman.

"Granny said that the blood never came out of the mattress."

Elizabeth took a tentative step toward the bed where her son lay sleeping. No, there was no fresh stain under her little boy. Any remnants had long since dried up decades ago. Or maybe the mattress had been changed. Not likely, she thought.

"Such caterwauling, Granny said. She had never heard the likes of it. In her time you gave birth silently, bearing your pain as the burden of your sex." Russell Rose's expression of disgust likely mirrored that of his Granny, the old battle axe.

Russell Rose continued. "When I was about a month old, we left - mom and me. I don't remember any of it, but Granny says we came back with our tails between our legs when I was about a year old. Just walking and big enough to get into all kinds of things and make a real nuisance of myself."

Elizabeth tried to school her face, tried to not let her disgust for that nasty old woman show.

"It was a strain on Granny. So many mouths to feed, a baby underfoot, her routine disrupted and always the noise and busyness. It was too much, so mom left to find work and send home money." Russell Rose's face was earnest. "She did, too. At first money came every two weeks. Granny said it was only fitting as she had all the work and all the responsibility." He looked down at his hands. "I tried to be good. I tried to help, but it wore on her nerves. Sometimes she had to have a break."

"A break?"

"Yeah. Bingo is what she liked. She had a car back then and a couple nights a week she'd go to bingo."

"Did you go with her?"

He looked at Elizabeth as if she'd lost her mind. "No! That was Granny's thing. I was in the basement."

"She left you alone!"

"Not totally alone. Over time, I had sort of made friends with some mice and rats that came into the basement. If I kept food in my pockets and laid out just tiny bits at a time, they would come to me. Or some of them would. A couple even learned to eat out of my hand."

His story continued. His mother would reappear with no warning and stay for a few days, maybe a week or two even, then he would wake up one morning and she'd be gone. Over time he got so he would automatically head to the basement and shut himself down there. It was better that way - no falling down the stairs like when he was shoved. And he could fill his pockets with food so he'd have something to eat in the coming days. He even hid a blanket down there. He had to be careful about it in case Granny found it when she went down to use the washing machine. He hid it in a dark corner under some boxes of old books and china. Over the years the blanket had gotten many holes in it, holes made by the tiny teeth of nibbling rodents seeking to create a home for themselves.

Then, his mother just stopped coming, and he never saw his mother again. Granny said stuff like, "Good riddance" and, "The trash needed taking out" whenever he asked when she was coming again. Because it got Granny's ire up, he stopped asking; it was not worth spending days in the basement alone in the dark. He got hungry down there and scared. His mother was gone.

Despite herself, Elizabeth was getting into this tale of a poor, lonely boy. "Did you ever see anyone else? Did you go to school?"

He looked affronted. "Of course I went to school. Do I seem ignorant to you? It's the law of the land - every child must be in school."

Ignoring his question as rhetorical, she nodded agreement about the law. "Did you like school?"

"Sort of. Parts were okay, and I liked arithmetic, but I didn't like the kids. Or, they didn't like me. They were mean and made fun of me. I didn't dress like them. Granny said there was no money for new clothes; she rolled up the legs of my dead Grandpa's pants and tied them up with string. I rolled up the shirt sleeves myself. They were warm and serviceable, she said."

What must life have been like at school for this child?

"Then I was fourteen. That was school-leaving age. Granny said better to get out before the evil set in. I guess my mom was not so bad before she turned fourteen. Granny tried to protect me from turning out the way she did. She was good to me, always looking out for me, always responsible."

CHAPTER 24

"In the center, they talked about conversation skills. Conversations have a back and forth, you know."

Head tilted slightly to one side, Elizabeth nodded agreement. Where was he going with this?

"Did you have someone looking after you when you were growing up," he asked?

Elizabeth eased herself into the recliner, the one that had been his Granny's seat. As she put her hands on the armrest, she thought about the nasty old lady who had sat here year after year. She switched to another chair.

"Yes, I had a mother and a father to look after me. They did that very well."

"Lots to eat?"

Strange question. "Yes, having enough to eat was never a problem. And it was good, the cook was excellent. We had help in the house because it was a large place."

"So, your little boy has a Granny."

"No, not now. She passed away just before he was born."

Better no Granny than an evil crazy woman who had raised Russell Rose.

"A Grandad?"

She shook her head. "They both passed away at the same time. A plane crash."

"I've never been in a plane. Granny said that if mankind was meant to fly, they'd have been born with wings."

"I sometimes think it would have been better if they had not flown. Daddy had his own plane. He was flying, and they crashed in the foothills - some kind of freak wind gust." Those were dark days following the search for them when they didn't land at their expected destination. Then identifying the bodies. She had tried to get Jackson to do it for her, but he said he couldn't stomach the thought. The coroner had been kind, just showing her part of each of their faces. But it had been enough. It was her mother and father. Dental records, their wallets and of course since it was their plane all clinched it. There was no mistake; her parents were dead.

Russell Rose looked at her like she was from a different planet. Actually, they were mostly. Their lived experiences shared little in common. Except perhaps the need to connect with someone. Elizabeth realized that it had been some time since she had shared confidences with another human being. And who did she choose? She needed to give her head a shake. But she couldn't seem to stop herself now that she had started.

"Daddy was a good man, a good father. He looked after us well and we didn't need to worry about anything while I was growing up; he took care of it all." Really, he was still taking care of her even now with the trust fund that he had set up. Although she married and her parents knew Jackson well, Daddy set up a trust that was in her name and hers alone. He said it was best that way, and no one questioned Daddy. Well,

Jackson had, but it was Daddy's money and he said that I was his little girl to provide for in how he thought best. He had paid the down payment on their home and put the house solely in Elizabeth's name. That ticked off Jackson, but he liked the house and the upper-class neighborhood, so he got over it. The trust fund paid the mortgage payments easily; Elizabeth handled the utility and upkeep payments. Jackson liked to say that he provided for his family, and he did. He put a bit of money into their joint household account every month and some of their groceries and day-to-day living expenses came out of that.

It was the only account that they had jointly. Initially, she moved money from her trust each month into the shared account that Jackson said he'd handle. But they kept getting notices from the bank about their overdrawn account, and finally phone calls when the overdraft wasn't taken care of as Jackson said that he would. Elizabeth was not used to living that way, to having to worry about money and credit ratings. So, it was easier to separate out their money. She kept close track on her own investments and funds and their joint household account. When they first set it up, Jackson's contributions were sporadic, despite his assurances he'd get on it. When Daddy overheard one of their discussions on this, he insisted that Jackson sign on for automatic transfer of funds. No one went against Daddy, and Jackson caved. It was a wise decision, and they carried on better from then on. Sure, there was still the occasional letter or phone call about overdraft problems, but those were on accounts that Jackson managed on his own. Although it worried Elizabeth, she learned that she had to let go. Those accounts were Jackson's accounts, even if he swore that each time a letter arrived it was a clerical error.

She caught Russell Rose observing her. How long had she been inside her own head? This was not the way to win him over. He needed to feel sympathetic toward Timothy and her. Create a bond, she told herself. Share. Show a vulnerable side and build an alliance. The more she learned about him, the more leverage she might have to get them out of this mess.

BEHIND THE CLOSED bedroom door came the sound of a little voice singing. The barely decipherable words accompanied the tune from Sesame Street that morning.

"I thought you said he doesn't talk," said Russell Rose.

"He doesn't, mostly. He has said the odd word here and there, but nothing regular. But sometimes he sings something that he's heard. Or he might repeat some dialogue from a kid's movie that he's watched over and over."

"How can he sing or repeat stuff if he can't talk?"

"Good question." She wondered if that was part of what the neurologist wanted to talk about at their next appointment. "These seizures interfere with development, so he might be delayed in that area."

SUPPER WAS A QUIET AFFAIR, but no one complained about the meager rations. If they had to be here much longer, they would be in serious trouble. Elizabeth skills only stretched so far, and the food on hand stretched even less.

IN BED, Elizabeth cuddled her little boy. She did not want to cry, oh she so badly didn't. She feared that once she started, she could not plug the dam. Plus, she'd frighten Timothy. But what were they going to do? She had been sure that Jackson would have found them by now. This was their second night away. Even though her husband was not home, they talked on the phone most nights and he would have missed their call for two nights in a row now - unheard of for them. And she'd left her purse at the gas station. With the amount of identification in it, surely Jackson and the police were on their trail now.

If Daddy was alive, this wouldn't be happening. He and her mother had talked to her several times a day on the phone, even before Timothy's birth. They would have preferred that the young family permanently move into the suite they'd renovated for them, but Elizabeth and Jackson wanted a place of their own. So, Daddy bought the house for them. When Elizabeth protested that it was too much, he had relented partially. He put up the down payment, then increased her trust fund so that the monthly mortgage would easily come out of it without harming the principal. Daddy always thought things through and planned. He was so good about providing for her and her mother and keeping them safe. Her thoughts flowed to Jackson and how he differed from the man she had grown up with. No. Pushing those comparisons way down in the crannies of her brain, she would not allow herself to be disloyal to the father of her child. But the tears flowed. She rubbed her earring, trying to find some comfort in the gift daddy had bought for his girls.

~

HE PLANNED, had really planned to rise early, but there was a definite inducement to remain in bed longer. He didn't get into the shower until several hours later than he had hoped. Still, it was important not to look disheveled.

After they were both suited up in their usual styles, they left in the car. As the garage door rolled up, he reached over and pushed her head down below the dash. She may have forgotten, but he did *not want anyone to see him leaving with a woman in the passenger seat.*

Twenty minutes later, he pulled into the underground parking lot of the downtown mall and they exited the car. Together they took the escalator to the main floor and entered an electronics store. There he purchased two burner phones. They took a few minutes to exchange new numbers but said goodbye with a kiss and a promise to meet later.

PART III
WEDNESDAY

CHAPTER 25

he wheels didn't spring into motion immediately, but when a child was possibly at risk, things happened more quickly.

When they returned to the station, Brendan and Jake found print-outs waiting for them. These listed the details of the items purchased with Elizabeth's credit card.

The groceries from Safeway looked like pretty typical family shopping, but they'd show it to the husband just to make sure. The fourteen bucks from the convenience store went to junk food, as they'd suspected - a large soda, bags of Cheetos, a mega-sized O'Henry bar, and a package of beef jerky. Nasty stuff with all those preservatives, Jake thought. The Tuesday morning purchases at a second Safeway looked like takeout breakfast items - a sausage and egg English muffin, a coffee (Starbucks, no less) and an O'Henry bar, mega-size again this time.

New to the spending list was a six-pack of beer, a mickey of rum and some Clamato juice. At least one item leaned toward healthy.

Time to give Jackson a call.

A cheerful, male voice answered with a hello. There was a humming in the background.

"Mr. Whitmore?"

"That's me. What can I do you for?"

"Mr. Whitmore, this is Detective James."

Instantly, Jackson's voice changed. "Have you found them?" The buzzing in the background clicked off.

Was this guy shaving? Sounded just the way Brendan's razor did. "No, sir. But we'd like to talk to you about some information that we have discovered."

"Information?

Did the guy sound nervous? Wouldn't he be eager? Originally Brendan had planned to go over the purchases on the phone, but now he changed his mind. Better to watch the guy's reactions in person. Something was not sitting right.

"We'd like you to come to the station, sir. Now, please."

❧

A LITTLE OVER AN HOUR LATER, Jackson entered the station and asked to speak to Detective James and he couldn't remember the other guy's name.

Jake timed his entrance. They had a wager going. Based on the location of the family home and traffic that time of day, Brendan expected that they'd see Jackson in about twenty minutes. Jake thought it would be double that before they saw the guy. Neither had guessed it would take him three times that amount. Wouldn't a guy frantic about his wife and child be racing in here?

Jackson looked well put together. Maybe some guys were just natty. Brendan wanted to check something out, though. "Mr. Whitmore humor me a moment. This has nothing to do with your wife's case, but I like to keep my skills sharp. I'm trying to place that buzzing sound I could hear when I called you this morning."

"Buzzing? Oh, you must mean my razor. You called just after I'd gotten out of the shower and I was shaving." As an affable salesman, he knew it never hurt to flatter the client. "Not bad, not bad detecting at all. You're the kind of cop I'd like to have on my team."

"That works out then, because we *are* part of the team looking for your child and your wife."

Jackson immediately sobered, almost like he was schooling his expression to match the visage the situation called for. "What news do you have?" He shook his head. "This waiting is so hard. I wish I could *do* something to bring them home."

"It so happens that there is something you can help us with." He spread out the pages detailing the spending on the credit card. "We'd like you to look over this and tell us if they look like purchases your wife would normally make."

After a second, Jackson picked up the papers. "I don't know everything she buys. I'm not that kind of husband, you know, the kind who oversees his wife's spending. She's an independent woman, at least in some ways."

"Just a general overview, please, and let us know if anything jumps out at you as out of the ordinary."

"You should look at her past credit card statements, then you can see what she often picks up."

"We have, Mr. Whitmore. We already have. But right now, we want your opinion. After all, you are the person who knows her best, right?"

"Of course." He flipped over to the second page. "So far this all looks like stuff she'd buy at the grocery store." He read some more and pointed. "I already told you she does not eat junk food and definitely doesn't feed it to Timothy, so these things from a convenience store don't look right." He looked up. "Do you think someone stole her credit card? Should I be contacting someone about identity theft?"

Jake shared a look with Brendan. "You *are* talking to the right people. So far though, it looks like more than identity theft - maybe kidnapping or abduction if Elizabeth and Timothy can't be found."

"Or," continued Brendan, "she's taken off. Taken your son and left. Do you think that's a possibility?"

"No, no, not at all." Jackson shook his head. "That is not like Elizabeth, no way. She just would not do that."

That's the conclusion Brendan and Jake were rapidly reaching, too. A search of the house had turned up two full sets of luggage; Jackson identified them as his and hers. None of the pieces were missing, and they didn't own others. Always possible that the missus had bought more without her husband knowing. Jackson didn't think there was any clothing missing either, not in Elizabeth's closet or from their son's room. But what guy had a great handle on his wife's clothing stores? Still, in the master bath there were two toothbrushes, a woman's opened make-up bag, deodorant, and hair spray. Either she had bought new ones to take with her, or she was on an unplanned get-away.

"This doesn't look right," Jackson pointed. "I have never in my life seen Elizabeth drink beer. Wine, sure, champagne, and maybe the odd cocktail, but not beer. She gives a look like this when she even smells it." He raised his upper lip and made a face. "Not a woman's drink, she says."

Brendan returned the printouts to their folder. "Anything more on your answering machine at home, Mr. Whitmore?"

Cell phone chimes interrupted him. Jackson pulled his mobile from his pocket and pressed a button, but the ringing continued. Slightly flustered, he replaced that phone, pulling another one from his other pocket. "Sorry." He shut it off.

The detectives exchanged looks. Who carries two cell phones? Jake asked, "You carry two phones?"

"Yeah. One's my personal one, and one's for work. With Timothy gone, I'm afraid to be without my personal cell in case they try to call me on it."

Hmmm.

Returning to their previous line of questioning, Brendan repeated, "Your answering machine? Were there any messages?"

"God, I never even thought to listen. It's usually me leaving a message for her. I'm home so I didn't think to check."

Another look between the officers. "That's okay, Mr. Whitmore. We'll check for you."

"Can you get access to them?"

"Rest assured, we have the ability to get access to all records. And will."

DISCUSSING their take on the interview after Jackson left, Brendan glanced at the padded chair Jackson had used. Something glinted in the fluorescent light. Getting up to check, a grin split his face. "Well, look what he left us." Brendan held up one of the phones from Jackson's pocket.

~

THE POLICE DETECTIVES sat in their car, observing the gas station. So-so busy, on a semi-main street where traffic was light. The station was not a dive, but reasonably well-maintained, the place where someone might be on the ball.

Waiting for a lull in customers, they entered the building. Introducing himself to the kid behind the counter, Detective Brendan James showed his badge. "Were you working on

Monday?" Not too hard of a question, but there was a long pause, long enough to get his spider-senses tingling.

"I'm not sure."

"Not sure? That was two days ago." He looked at his partner. "Maybe we can find someone around here who has the staff schedule."

"No, that's right, I was here on Monday. I get mixed up sometimes 'cuz we work different shifts. When did you mean on Monday?"

"During the day, say the afternoon."

"Yeah, I was here for some of it, but Sam comes on at three."

Jake thought the kid was better at knowing other people's shifts than recalling his own. He pulled out a picture. "Have you seen this woman?" This was a photo Jackson emailed them, supposedly a recent one. It showed her playing with Timothy.

The kid's eyes glanced at the color photocopy. His eyes quickly slid to the right and away. "Nah, don't know her."

"Then look at this one, please." This time it was a photo of Elizabeth from the side, everything cropped out but for her face.

Same reaction from the kid. "We get lots of people in here, man, and I'm not good with faces. Don't pay much attention to the customers, just take their money and on to the next one." His eyes slid up and to the right. "Maybe you could ask Sam, though. He'll be in later."

"We'll bother you for just a few more minutes, Mr...."

"Bonning, Reggie Bonning. But, just Reggie is good."

"Thanks, Reggie." Brendan pointed to the far corner and then to the ceiling near the till. "Are those security cameras?"

Reggie's head came up fast. Damn, he'd forgotten about those things. Well, everyone knew that half of them were fake, just to fool people to think they were being recorded.

Old Mr. Wilton was too cheap to pay for the real thing. Even if it was real, cheapies reused the same tapes, erasing them every night. Probably what Wilton did when he was in there overnight, supposedly doing the books. "I dunno. That's not part of my job. They might be fake. Yeah, they probably are. I don't got nothing to do with them. I just take money." Then, to be helpful, he added, "And credit cards and debit cards, too." Best to look cooperative, he thought. He grew more confident. The cops seemed to think he was helpful, and he'd securely gotten rid of any evidence of that woman. He smiled to help them on their way.

"Is your boss around?"

Shit! At least he didn't have to lie about this. "Nah, he's never here this time of day." Then, being ever so helpful, "You never know when he'll drop by and when he does, he hides in his office doing stuff. He doesn't do much with the customers or get his hands dirty - leaves that stuff to us staff."

"If you see him, tell him we'll be by."

CHAPTER 26

*Y*ou might think that much of police work is now done with computers. While technology has certainly sped up some types of searches, others were still better done by hand. And some by foot. No computer could replace the cop's perception as he watched a potential witness or suspect.

Jake and Brendan began much the same as how Elizabeth began her day on Monday, in her neighborhood. They were searching for a few things. For sure they wanted to know of anyone who had seen her that day or any day since. They were also after impressions - impressions about this young mother, her family life, the activity around her home and about her husband. It was unfortunate that in this day of two-job families, there was often no one home in the daytime. Gone were the days of eagle eyes in each neighborhood, watching and only too willing to report on the comings and goings of each house.

No different here. Although there was no answer at most homes, there was the odd shift worker they roused from bed, one retired woman and one other young mother near the opposite end of the street, as well as cleaners and service people. They'd need to return this evening to try to catch the other homeowners but for now, they gathered information that helped build a better picture of this family.

They'd already met Ken and Marge, but this was an opportunity to talk to them individually. Marge was home but Ken was at work. During this second interview she seemed just as worried about Elizabeth. "This is so unlike her. She is dedicated to that child and a real homebody." The two women didn't talk often, maybe once a week; they both had busy lives. "When Elizabeth would talk about her days, it seemed that the only time she left the house was to do some household chore or to take Timothy to one of his appointments. Poor child."

"What were the appointments for?"

"Oh, you name it. He was a sickly child." A look of horror crossed her face. "I mean IS, he *is* a sickly child. I was trying to say that he was that way since birth, or almost." They waited expectantly. "We didn't know them well at first; she was pretty pregnant when they moved in. Then things seemed pretty normal for the first half year or so, then this seizure thing started up, or so Elizabeth said. There were trips to the emergency room at all hours. Ken drove her once when she had to hold on to Timothy and her husband was away." She shook her head. "But she got to be pretty independent - had to if you ask me."

"Why is that?"

"Well, this is just gossip. Or speculation, but as I see it, the sicker that wee child got, the more that husband was away. His job, you know, she said. As a salesman he had to be gone most of the week. He was trying to work his way up to better provide for his family. Hmph. He could have better provided by being here, if you ask me. Why, if that was my Ken and we had a child as sick as that, I would insist that he get another job so he was around to help." Jake nodded encouragingly. "But she never complained about him or her lot. A nice young woman, she is."

After getting from Marge the time that Ken should be home that evening, they moved on. Of those home, no one had noticed Elizabeth either leaving or coming home Monday, Tuesday or today.

When asked if there was anything out of the ordinary they had picked up on, both the retired teacher and the young mother mentioned seeing a car several times earlier during the week although they were not certain of the day. Theirs was a small side street and there wasn't a lot of traffic. Most of the cars were regulars or belonged to visitors who stayed for a few hours in the evening. What caught their attention about this car was that it parked during the day - sometimes in the afternoon, sometimes in the morning. It was too hard to tell if it remained once it was dark. But they never saw anyone get out of the car or go to a house. A man remained slumped down in the vehicle which faced the Whitmore's house. Neither woman could describe the car well other than to say that it was mid-sized and mud-colored, nothing special.

QUESTIONS of a more personal nature about the Whitmores brought strictly polite responses for the most part. But, like Marge across the street who had been more forthcoming about her opinions of the family, the young mum and the retired teacher had a bit more to say. Neither professed to know the couple well; they weren't that type of family to invite confidences. Mr. Whitmore was seldom home, especially during the week. When they'd first moved in, he would do the occasional spot of yard work on the weekend, more and more his wife took over those chores. After their child was born, a gardening service maintained their lot.

Mrs. Whitmore was out more, pushing the stroller, or walking with her son. She'd pass the time pleasantly with any neighbor she encountered but did not go out of her way to make their acquaintance. She didn't seem to arrange play dates for her son. She and Timothy often left in her car, and were gone for a few hours. The rumor on the street was that the child was ill and needed a lot of care. Elizabeth spent time in their yard with her son, but no one could recall seeing the father in such pursuits.

Returning that evening to catch the residents who had been at work during the day brought little more information. It seemed that no one on the street was close to the couple. Nor had anyone witnessed animosity between the couple, or at least that they were willing to say. No further information was gathered on the car that had been hanging around the street for a few days.

CHAPTER 27

*B*rendan called ahead, so Dr. Muller knew to expect the visit from the detectives. He came equipped with the required paperwork so that the neurologist could speak with them.

They confirmed Timothy's one-thirty appointment, and the receptionist was sure that she had seen him, and his mom leave the office that day alone. The only odd thing was that Mrs. Whitmore had said she would call to set the next appointment after she talked to her husband about his schedule. Elizabeth was one of those people who either made the next appointment as she was leaving, or else she'd call the next morning. A bit strange not to have heard from her yet.

Dr. Muller hadn't seemed surprised that the detectives got his name from the pharmacist. No, it was not the norm for a pediatric neurologist to know where patients got their prescriptions filled, but in cases like Timothy's, drug interactions were a constant worry and with the parents' consent, the doctor and druggist shared communications.

Dr. Muller was initially reluctant to cooperate with any more details. But when he learned that the pair was missing, his concern for Timothy over rode his professional ethics. For the good of the child, were the words he used.

He explained that Timothy had several diagnoses. The first was West Syndrome, also known as Infantile Spasms, first recognized when he was about six months old. A form of epilepsy, West Syndrome, can be quite severe. Often it either causes or goes along with a developmental disability. In Timothy's case, that was unclear; he met all developmental milestones at around the appropriate times, with the exception of language. While he appeared to understand what was said to him readily enough, he did not speak.

Well, that was not strictly true- he was not always a silent child. He made sounds and at times he repeated rhymes, jingles, or dialogue from shows he watched.

"What are you saying?" asked Jake.

"We're not sure." Dr. Muller laughed at himself. "How often do you hear *that* in medicine?" He clasped his hands together and leaned forward. "We have done no testing to either prove or rule it out, but we - no, I - have been wondering if I see an autism spectrum disorder here. Not sure his parents, or at least his mother, are ready to go there yet."

He pulled from his bottom drawer some sample medicines. "See these? These are just some meds that little Timothy has had to take. Right now, our priority is getting his seizures under control."

"How's that going?"

"Not well, obviously, because I just changed his meds again on Monday. What we've been doing, despite many changes to the protocol, has not been working. We've also changed his diagnosis - it's now Lennox-Gastaut, another form of epilepsy. It's a severe one, and one that does not go away. It's also one of the more difficult ones to control. And I use the word "control" loosely. With Lennox-Gastaut, the best we can hope for is to lessen the frequency and intensity of the seizures somewhat. We can't make them go away.

"For now, we're trying to gain some level of control through meds. There are surgeries, controversial surgeries, but they are fairly drastic."

"How drastic?"

"I'm not saying that this is the plan for Timothy. Talking in generalities about this questions, would you want someone drilling into your child's head?" Then, he added, "And with no guarantee of success?"

Jake could not imagine facing this possibility for your kid, or any kid.

"So, no surgery scheduled for now, but he takes pills."

"Correct. Fairly serious meds that you don't want to fool around with. Lucky for this child, he has a mother who is diligent about taking care of this. She watches for side effects and reports that along with efficacy to me."

"Efficacy?"

"If the medication is doing what we hope it will do."

"And does it for Timothy?"

"Not ideally, no, but then that would be more than we could hope for. What it does is decrease the frequency and perhaps the intensity."

"We need to know what to be prepared for when we locate the child." He shared a look with his partner. "Doctor, just how often would a kid like this have seizures? Monthly? Weekly? I've seen a couple seizures and they can be scary."

"Yes, they can, especially for a parent. With Lennox-Gastaut, we often talk about how many times an hour the individual seizes; not how many times in weeks or even days."

Both detectives just stared at him. "From what you know of Mrs. Whitmore, even if she is off somewhere with her son, will she still give him his medications?" asked Brendan.

"Can't see why she wouldn't. She understands the ramifications of uncontrolled seizures. We're talking about the possibility of brain damage, lowered cognition and even death." He looked back at his chart notes. "But I wouldn't think she would go off on a holiday just now. We were switching Timothy's meds, so beginning Monday she was weaning him off of one while gradually starting him on another. Until the new one is at full therapeutic dosage, the child is more vulnerable to seizures."

This time the detectives looked at each other. Brendan gave a small nod for Jake to explain. "She's gone, Dr. Muller. That's why we're here. Her husband has not spoken to her since before leaving for work Monday morning. No one else has seen her."

"But it's Wednesday afternoon now!"

"Yes, we are aware of that. Her husband called us Tuesday evening. So far, you and your receptionist may have been the last people to see them." He gave him a minute to digest that. "How was she when she left here?"

"All right. She is a determined woman, devoted to her son. His medical condition is trying at the best of times, but she manages as well as any parent could - probably better than most. I've met her husband just once; she attends the appointments alone, and I think she manages his medications and the monitoring on her own." He thought about it some more. "Look, it is tough, really, really tough to have a child with a chronic illness. All your hopes, your dreams for your child alter. When Timothy first received the diagnosis of West Syndrome, we all hoped that it would be something he would grow out of and the seizures would go away. It was encouraging that until they began about halfway through his first year of life that he was meeting all milestones as expected. Some kiddos with this diagnosis have a definite accompanying intellectual disability, but that was not clear with Timothy.

"Mrs. Whitmore was adjusting to the fact that seizures would likely be a part of her son's life now that the diagnosis changed from West to Lennox-Gastaut. That's a lot to take in and understandably, she was struggling. Any parent would. But then I noticed other things, maybe not big things but subtle signs that there might be something else going on as well."

"What sort of things?"

"Something about his manner. He was more compliant during tests and procedures than are most toddlers and preschoolers. Then, the lack of speech. He's nonverbal or rather minimally verbal would better describe Timothy because it's not that he has never spoken.

"In my line of work, I'm used to kids reacting to me strongly, either favorably, or they really, really dislike me. I like to think that that's because of the things I have to put them through, or they realize that I'm the one ordering the tests they have to endure. I'd rather think that than that they have an aversion to my personality." His little joke fell flat. "But it's different with Timothy. It's almost like he's indifferent to me or oblivious to my presence. Initially, I put it down to over-sedation from medications, but his response has lingered no matter the med he is on.

"It's a lot to take in for any parent, I know. So, although I tentatively raised the possibility of something besides Lennox-Gastaut, Mrs. Whitmore is not ready to consider anything else. I'm sure she will come around, but she's still reeling from the present circumstances. She said she will make their next appointment when her husband can accompany them. I'll try again then."

LEAVING their cards with Dr. Muller and his receptionist, the two detectives headed for their car.

"Damned if I'd let my wife go through that alone."

"Can you imagine the worry? Most parents go nuts when one of their kids has flu or chicken pox, and they know that it'll only last a few days. But with this, it hangs over their heads all the time and she keeps doing it. Alone."

Brendan agreed. "Does she sound like a woman who would take off on a whim?"

CHAPTER 28

*B*rendan's phone rang. "Thanks for getting back to me. Yes, we're investigating the disappearance of Mr. Whitmore's wife and son. It's routine that we look at the phone records of the victim and those around them." He listened to the usual commiserations. "Does Mr. Whitmore have a work cell phone?"

Hanging up, he turned to Jake. "Interesting. According to his boss, our friend Jackson does *not* have a work cell phone. The company pays for half of his mobile phone bill, expecting employees to use their personal device for work."

"So, what's with the other phone?" mused Jake.

～

JAKE PUNCHED the pharmacy's address into the GPS. They'd follow its directions, then, once familiar with the area, guess at the route Elizabeth might have taken. Although not definite about it, this was one place Jackson thought his family would have gone on Monday and Dr. Muller mentioned that he'd given Timothy a new prescription.

They presented their badges to the clerk in the drugstore, asking for Mr. Rexton. He was with a customer, so they observed the comings and goings behind the counter before he approached them. Again, showing their badges, they explained the reason for their presence. Presenting Elizabeth's picture, they asked if he had seen this woman.

"Often," he said. "She's a regular customer."

"How regular?"

He laughed. "Probably far more regular than she would like."

"When is the last time you saw her?"

"Monday afternoon."

"Do you always have such an excellent memory for your customers?"

"Sadly, no, but she is in here often, her and her little boy. But I remember specifically because she brought in a prescription to be filled, then didn't pick it up."

"Is that usual for her?"

"Not at all. She said she'd be back in half an hour. That's normal. Few people with a small child want to stand around waiting until I fill the prescription, especially when there are others in line ahead of her. What's not normal is that she didn't come back for it."

"Never happened before, eh?" asked Brendan.

"I wouldn't say never. A couple times her little guy has been really sick, so she sent her husband to pick up the pills that evening."

"Her husband didn't come by this time?"

"No. I'm sure because we're open until ten p.m. When she didn't come back by early evening, I phoned and left a message on her answering machine and on her cell phone. Would have on Mr. Whitmore's phone as well, but I didn't have his number."

"Any response to either of your messages."

He shook his head, and the creases in his brow deepened. "It was really important that her son have those meds, too."

"May I ask why?" Jake handed over the papers, granting Mr. Rexton permission to disclose medical information. "This could be really important." Then he added, "Dr. Muller has filled us in on Timothy's diagnosis - both of them and explained about the seizures."

Relieved that he wouldn't have to be the first person to share confidential information, another thought struck the pharmacist. "Look, if you are with Child Protection and investigating Mrs. Whitmore, I can't tell you when I've seen a mother take better care of her son. It can't be easy, you know, but she does it and without complaining. She just gets on with it, asking questions, learning all that she can to help her little boy."

"That's the impression we're getting of her from others, too. No, we're not here at the instigation of Child Protection Services. Mrs. Whitmore and her son are missing." He waited for that to sink in. "You may have been one of the last people to have seen them."

"Good god. What could have become of them? That's two days ago." He thought some more. I'm not sure... let me go check." He went behind the counter, tapping rapidly on a computer. "Just as I thought. He was almost out of his current medication. That's okay because the plan was to decrease it starting Monday, and gradually add this other one, slowly building up that dose as she eliminated the other one." He looked up at them, stricken. "But she didn't pick up the new one and unless she'd been skipping doses, she only had enough pills of the original prescription to last him until Tuesday night or Wednesday morning. That child cannot be without his meds. The seizures would be right out of control, far worse than they are now, and he'd be risking permanent damage."

This was even grimmer than the picture Dr. Muller had painted. They gave Mr. Rexton their cards. "Sir, probably better than us, you realize how important it is that we find Mrs. Whitmore and Timothy. Anything else you can think of, if you spot them, anything at all, please call one of us, anytime day or night."

They were almost out the door when he called out to them. "Could you wait just a minute, officers?" Rexton was on the phone, but they turned around, as though impatient to be off.

"I just called Dr. Muller and let him know how few pills Mrs. Whitmore had for Timothy. He's okayed this." He held out a small white pharmacy bag. "Here are two pills from each prescription. The child should have one immediately. Mrs. Whitmore will know which one. And, if she's not around, god help her, then call me." He handed Brendan a card. "That's my home number and personal cell on the back. I'll keep a phone by me at all times until I hear that they've been found. Call me, describe what's going on with the child, and I'll tell you which med to give him. Dr. Muller and I will keep in touch."

~

NEXT ON THEIR agenda was Safeway, the one Jackson said she always used. It was a large supermarket. Showing Elizabeth's picture around brought out some blank looks, but others said they'd seen her in there before. No one working right now could remember when she had last been in, other than to say that she was a regular. Nothing about Elizabeth's and Timothy's visit Monday rang any bells for the staff. The detectives wouldn't even have been sure she'd been there if she hadn't used her credit card for her purchases.

CHAPTER 29

"Okay, let's just head west," Brendan decided. "We know the general direction of her house and of the pharmacy. Just because Mr. Whitmore says that his wife always uses the same gas station does not mean that she did this time. Let's see if there's another station nearby that she might have used."

The first one they came to was the one they had visited yesterday. "Let's keep going and see if there's another one that could be a possibility."

The next one was a bit out of the way, past the turnoff she would likely take to drive home. They stopped anyway, showing their badges and pictures of Elizabeth and Timothy. They received only shaking heads from each employee and picked up no hint of subterfuge.

"Let's go back to that other one. I didn't like that punk; something off about him." Jake agreed.

Pushing his long hair from his eyes and lifting his head from his phone, Reggie startled to see the police officers again. He pulled his shoulders into his usual slouch and pretended he didn't recognize them.

Stepping behind the counter and invading Reggie's space, Jake flashed Elizabeth's picture once more. "Hey, Reggie. Have you seen this woman yet?" He stared at Reggie's face. The kid's face looked worse today. The bruising, while dark yesterday, was sporting brighter colors now. "Looks like that might hurt, man."

Reggie covered his cheek bone with the side of his fist. "Nah, it's nothing. Fell over. Little too much to drink, you know?"

"Yeah, could happen to anyone."

Brendan leaned over the counter. "Your boss turn up yet?"

A voice behind him said, "He's right here."

A rotund man with a Friar Tuck hairdo stood with his arms crossed. "May I help you, gentlemen?"

Showing his badge, Brendan asked if there was somewhere they could speak privately.

THE OFFICE WAS TINY, too tiny for three big men. Harold Wilton squeezed his girth into his chair, the desk cutting into his paunch. He introduced himself and held out his hand to the detectives. "What can I do for you?"

They showed him pictures of Elizabeth and Timothy. He shook his head. "Sorry, but I'm not out front very much. I'm only here part time and I'm usually stuck doing paperwork in here." He waved his hand around his closet-sized office.

Discouraged, Jake turned to inch back out the door.

"When did you say she might have been here?" When he learned it was just two days ago, he held up a finger. "We may be in luck. Our security tapes erase themselves every forty-eight hours. If she was here within that timeframe, we might have caught her." He typed away for a few minutes, glancing between his computer screen and a monitor high in the room's corner. "We only have a couple cameras, but if we're lucky…."

Brendan craned his neck. The monitor showed a grainy, black and white video of Reggie behind the till, then it began reversing in rapid motion, making Reggie look like a jerking puppet.

"Here we are. This begins around two o'clock Monday afternoon." He looked at Brendan. "How do you want to do this? Watch it all the way through; it's two full day's worth or fast forward, hoping to catch her?"

"The speed you're using right now should work. Let's rewind to the beginning again, but start with the outside camera. Here's what her car looks like." He placed the photocopied photo on the crowded desk between them. The image was not of Elizabeth's car exactly, but a manufacturer's rendition of her make, model, and color. "The earliest she could have gotten here would have been about two o'clock, considering what else she did that afternoon."

It was tedious, staring intently at the hazy, rapidly advanced images. Luckily, they had control over the speed and quickly found a pace at which they could recognize the cars in the lot, but faster than real time. Gradually dusk approached on the monitor, then the pictures took on a different quality as the exterior lights came on. No luck.

"Let's back up and try this again." Not what any of them wanted to hear, but Brendan was right. They could not afford to miss something. Harold started the video again, but this time at a slightly slower speed.

"There! Stop!" It was Jake, with his younger eyes and interest in cars who thought he spotted Elizabeth's car. Harold rewound the tape just a bit, now playing it in actual time. Brendan held the picture up, hoping to compare it to the car Jake had targeted. Yes! They were close enough to be a match. As they watched, the driver's door opened, and a woman exited. She reached into the door's pocket and pulled out a pair of gloves. Putting them on, she finally turned toward the pumps and they got a look at her face. Well, sort of.

Harold Wilton apologized for the quality of the tape. "The lenses need a good cleaning. It's on the roster of duties for the staff when they have down time, but I'm not sure how often it gets done." Rarely, by the looks of it, he thought.

It *could* be Elizabeth, but it was difficult to be sure. He pulled his notebook from his pocket, checking the description Dr. Muller's receptionist had given of what Elizabeth had been wearing when she attended Timothy's appointment. Doubtful, she had gone home to change after that. Unfortunately, the receptionist was not a clothes addict, so could only give a cursory description of what Elizabeth might have been wearing two days ago. She talked about how Elizabeth was always tidy and classy in her apparel, but not flashy. Refined. More pastels than bold colors. She thought the young mother had on pants and a sleeveless shirt with high-heeled shoes. She remembered the latter because that's what Mrs. Whitmore always had on her feet. The receptionist herself could not wear heels, turned her ankle in them, and they hurt the balls of her feet. She'd often wondered how mothers carried kids wearing those things.

The woman in the video had on pants and a tucked-in shirt without sleeves. Impossible to determine the colors since the footage was in black and white. Yep, those were high-heeled shoes on her feet. She didn't appear to have any difficulty walking in them.

After glancing into her back seat, the woman opened her gas door and cap, removed the nozzle from the pump, pushed a button and began filling her car. It all looked pretty normal so far.

They waited and waited, hardly blinking as it took the

four minutes to fuel up her car. They watched as she hung up the nozzle, screwed in her gas lid, then opened the driver's door. Taking off the gloves, she reached across the seat then backed out of the car, slinging her handbag over her shoulder.

"Did you see the size of the purse?" asked Jake. "My sister had to have one like that when her girls were little. You would not believe all the stuff she carried with her. She said it was a milestone when she could go back to a normal-sized handbag once the kids didn't require so much stuff."

As they watched, the young woman strode toward the glass windows, coming closer to the camera. Just as they anticipated getting a better look at her face, she raised her arm and wiped her forehead. Damn.

Then, when she was only a yard from the door, she turned around and headed back to her car. Climbing behind the wheel, she started the car, glanced again into the back seat, then started again toward the door to the station.

"Did she have keys in her hand as she came closer?" asked Brendan. No one was sure. "Can you replay that?" In the replay it was not clear. She could have dropped a set into her purse while in the car. Then she was out of view of the exterior camera.

Harold was busy on his computer, inputting the request to have the program switch to the interior camera. It took several minutes before he could find a time stamp that matched the one where they'd left off from the first recording.

The woman approached the counter; there was no one ahead of her and yes, there was Reggie perched on that high stool behind the counter.

"I thought he said he had never seen her before."

Harold explained, "It's Reggie. Not the sharpest knife in

the drawer. But he does come in for his shifts." Mostly, he thought.

The woman set her over-sized bag on the counter, then began digging through it for her wallet. Jake thought about how much easier it was to keep your wallet in your pants pocket. They couldn't see her expression as she peered into her bag, but then it looked like her hand pulled out, as if she had found what she was looking for.

Then, with something in her hand, she glanced over her shoulder, outside, toward her car. Like a still-motion shot, she froze. Her mouth opened, but there was no way to tell if she formed words. As they watched, her fingers let go of the wallet and, faster than you would think anyone could move in heels like that, she sprinted out of the store.

Both detectives turned to Harold. "I'm on it, I'm on it," he said as his sausage-like fingers moved over his keyboard. Soon, but not soon enough, the images on the monitor changed to the outside of the building.

At first they saw an arm reaching for the driver's door. Then more came into view - a short-sleeved shirt revealing biceps too bulky to belong to a woman. As the door opened, the side then back of a guy with longish hair came into view. While the length might be semi-fashionable, the stringiness was not. He got into the driver's seat, shut the door, and seemed to adjust the seat.

As he was entering the car, the woman came into the camera's view. Not slowing her pace, the woman ran over and across the first set of pumps to the second ones where she had parked. The front door had already closed when she went down. Either she stumbled over the curb or those heels tripped her up. Ah, yes, there on the ground was a broken-off heel. She barely went over before she was in motion again, her left hand reaching for the rear door handle. Brendan noted that. Reaching with her left - did that mean she was left-handed? Or was there something occupying her right so she couldn't use it?

With the rear door open now, the car started moving. Slowly at first, as the driver bent over, maybe still fiddling to make the seat accommodate his larger size. He must have gotten it right, because the car sped up. The woman took two steps toward her rolling car, hanging on to the door handle. When it didn't stop or slow up, she dove. Her upper body was in, face-downward, but her legs dangled, still outside from the knees down. As the driver turned to the right to get to the approach, the open door swung, clunking those legs. Harold winced. That must have hurt. The door swung back on its hinges, then as the vehicle turned another right onto the street, the momentum swung the door shut. They glimpsed feet being pulled in, but not before one shoe plopped onto the pavement.

"Pause it right there!" While Harold paused the film, with one mind, Jake and Brendan ran out of the office, outside and toward the curb. Semi-flattened in the gutter lay a taupe high-heeled shoe, size 7. Looked like more than a few tires ran over it. Into an evidence bag the shoe went. They both knew that it didn't offer any real clues, but if they found a body with one shoe, this might help identification. But they weren't going there just yet. It had only been two days.

At Brendan's request, Harold rewound the tape to the part where the male hand reached for the driver's door. "Damned cameras are supposed to catch all parts of the lot. Had never realized that they stopped just beside the far pumps," Harold complained. No matter how many times they watched that part of the video, it was not possible to tell if the man had exited the passenger seat to get behind the wheel or if he came from elsewhere. The interior of the car was too dim to see anything else.

"We'll need to take this film with us," said Brendan.

"But, it's the only one I have. It rewinds itself every forty-eight hours and…." He got it, really he did. What was his inconvenience when a woman's life could be at stake? "It's getting pretty grainy. Could stand replacing anyway."

With the tape in hand, Brendan and Jake left. Surely the techs at the department could clean up the images so they could see more. Even a couple profiles of the man would help.

As they drove away, Jake voiced what was in both of their minds. "But where's the kid?"

CHAPTER 30

"$\mathcal{M}$r. Whitmore, bear with us. Please tell us again your wife's schedule for Monday," said Detective Brendan James.

"Good lord, how many times have we been through this? Wouldn't your time be better spent out there looking for my son and my wife rather than dragging me down here again?"

Brendan just regarded him.

"All right, all right. I'm under a lot of pressure, you understand. I wouldn't exactly call what my wife had as a schedule. She was at home with our kid; schedules are for those people who work. But all right. When I left, she was feeding Timothy breakfast. Just as we were finishing our meal, he had a seizure. Again. I had to leave then, or I'd be late, so I'm not sure how long it lasted this time. Probably not long, because after the long ones she always took him to the hospital. I'm sure she would have called me if they were at emergency."

"We can check with the hospitals on your behalf if that's worrying you."

"Ah, yeah, thanks. The only thing she mentioned is that

Timothy was running low on pills, so she probably went to the drug store for a refill. Like I told you. Then, Elizabeth is a creature of habit, even more so since Timothy got sick. Mondays she gets groceries and fills the car with gas. It's almost a ritual with her, sort of like a control thing, I think." He thought a few seconds. "Or like following her father. She idolized that daddy of hers, and he had set days for taking care of chores. Said that way everything got done or some such notion."

"He had?"

"He died a few years ago. Plane crash along with his wife. Never cared much for the guy; kind of stuffy, if you know what I mean. He was a systems guy in his job and it carried over into his personal life. Too much so, if you ask me. Took all the spontaneity out of life, the fun. He was all about seriousness and responsibility. Elizabeth is a bit that way, but what do you expect, being raised in a house like that."

"Did she have any siblings? Any relatives she's close to?"

"No, an only child like me. But at one time she had a brother who died. No one ever talked about that. And there were no relatives that I ever met." Jake wrote that down.

"Okay, back to her schedule. Anything else come to mind?"

"No. I mean, what does a homemaker do to fill her time? Play with the kid, go to the park, maybe do a little house cleaning? I don't know; I'm away making a living."

Jake checked his notes. "Ever heard of a Dr. Muller?"

Jackson brushed a hand over his head. "Maybe. That kid has seen so many doctors that you wouldn't believe it. A Muller could have been one of them. His mother takes him to those appointments."

Running his finger down the page, Jake stopped about a third of the way down. "According to this, they had a one-

thirty appointment with a pediatric neurologist, Dr. Muller."
He looked up at Jackson. "Did you know about this?"

"Maybe, I don't know. Elizabeth talked about lots of
things. Sometimes she tried to involve me more in Timothy's
medical treatments, but what was I supposed to do?
Someone in the family has to work, and my job takes me out
of town almost every week. There was no way I could go to
the appointments. It was Elizabeth's role to keep track of
such things. She might have mentioned it, but there were so
many doctors and so many appointments I could never keep
them straight."

"A pediatric neurologist sounds like someone you'd get to
see only if the condition was serious."

"Yeah, she needed a referral before she took Timothy
there, I think."

"When we visited the pharmacist, he said she had just
come from the neurologist's and had a new prescription for
him."

"Sounds like it could be right. Those quacks were always
changing the kid's medications."

BRENDAN PULLED an evidence bag from his drawer. In it was
the heel of a shoe. "Does this look familiar to you? He handed
the bag to Jackson.

"Nah, never seen it before."

Bringing out a second bag, "How about this?" This one
held the shoe he'd found against the curb outside the gas
station.

"No. I pay little attention to women's shoes. Although this
heel might have made her legs look good with a short skirt."
He gave a smirk in Jake's direction, man to man.

"Could you identify these as belonging to your wife?"

"You've got to be kidding me. Have you seen the number

of pairs of shoes she has? Besides, this is all scuffed and dirty. She would wear nothing like that."

EXCHANGING A LOOK, the detectives started a new line of questioning. "What about friends? Can you tell us the names and phone numbers of a few of her closest friends? People she might chat with on the phone or visit during the week while you're away."

"I already told you she didn't really have friends. I guess you'd describe her as more of an ice queen, kind of cold to people, and it took a lot to get to know her. Comes by it honestly, if you'd met her parents."

"There's nobody you can think of?"

Jackson shook his head. "We know a few people on our street, but not well. She never mentioned having coffee with any of them."

"And you think she'd mention it to you?"

"Certainly. I'm her husband. We shared everything."

Everything but childcare and seeing to their son's medical needs, Jake thought.

LEANING FORWARD, Brendan laced his fingers together and stared at Jackson. "I apologize if these next questions might make you uncomfortable, but you understand that we have to ask."

He was hesitant, but Jackson nodded. What was coming next?

"Was your wife having an affair?"

Jackson snorted, then one side of his mouth turned up. "No. I can tell you assuredly, no. She was not that type." Not imaginative enough, he thought, but didn't say that. "She wrapped her life around me and my son."

"How do you know what she did during the week when you were away?"

"You obviously do not know Elizabeth. Or just how ill our son is." He thought a minute about how to explain how sure he was. "She's a straight-shooter. That's one of the things that first attracted her to me." He almost surprised himself at remembering that.

"Okay. If you're sure, we'll leave that alone for now." Shifting in his chair, he leaned back on one elbow and glanced at Jackson sideways. "And you, Mr. Whitmore? Are you having an affair?"

Jackson's face turned red, then a deeper red. He leaned back against his chair, blustered and puffed out his chest and complained how this investigation was turning out to be about him when these incompetent police officers were supposed to be finding his wife.

They let him rant until he quieted somewhat.

"Mr. Whitmore, tell us what your week has been like. Start with when you left the house Monday morning and describe where you went, who you talked to and what you did."

Jackson's eyebrows raised. "Me? It's my wife and son you're supposed to be finding. My life's an open book; they are the ones who are missing. Plus, I have a confidentiality agreement in my job; I can't discuss clients, either who they are or what we talk about."

"For now, we don't need the details of your discussions with them, just your itinerary. We will get some of this from your credit and debit card statements, but would like to hear it from you."

"My credit card! Why are you looking at that? I gave my consent for you to look at my wife's statements but not mine."

"Mr. Whitmore, we don't need your permission. This is

now an official investigation since they have been missing over forty-eight hours. I would think that you would cooperate in every way, doing anything you could to help."

"I am," Jackson protested. "I am. Geez, I run down here every time you guys ask. I've given you access to our house and answered all your personal questions. And still you haven't found my son."

"Your son?"

"And my wife. You know what I mean."

Brendan feared that he was starting to get an idea of exactly what Jackson meant.

CHAPTER 31

*T*he police techs wrought their magic on the videotape from the gas station. They complained that they had little to work with since the tapes themselves were old and worn from so many re-recordings. But they managed some enhancements.

Some close-up work on the hand that opened the driver's side door of Elizabeth's car revealed that it belonged to a male, based on the amount of hair and its size. What looked like the bottom of a t-shirt was visible on the upper arm. Then, as the man got into the car, they had a not bad side shot of his body. They estimated him to be about five foot eleven, maybe two hundred pounds. His hair was longish below his ears, partially covering his stubbled chin. This was not a stylish long, but the look of someone who had not seen the inside of a barbershop in maybe years.

"There!" The tech stopped the frame. "There's the best shot we have of his profile." He handed Brendan and Jake photocopies of the shot. It was not great, what with the hair and the shadow created by the door frame, but better than nothing.

Jake asked his partner, "Does that look like the type of guy someone like Elizabeth would pick up with?"

THE TECH TOOK them through another part of the tape he thought they might find interesting. He started it from the point where Elizabeth stood at the counter, rummaging around in her bag. He froze the frame where she pulled out her wallet, then passed out enlarged pictures of her hand holding the wallet. She then pulled something thin from the wallet, holding it in her right hand. "Watch what happens next."

The film captured the look on the woman's face when she realized something was happening outside. Dropping her wallet, she ran out of the building. The next papers the tech handed them were blown-up images of her hand clutching a black card as that hand pushed open the door to the gas station. "Looks like she kept hold of something - her credit card, I'm guessing. We can't blow it up any better than that."

Brendan expected the film to switch to that captured by the outside camera. "No, just wait. There is something more you need to see," the tech said.

One camera behind the counter focused on what the employee would see and do. The back of Reggie's head followed Elizabeth's flight out the door. As he leaned forward to watch her, his hand rested on her bag. Looking around to see if anyone was watching, Reggie's left hand picked up the dropped wallet while his right hand swept her purse under the counter. He bent down and placed it on a shelf. He seemed so intent on squirreling away the purse he didn't realize that he held the opened wallet upside down. Something fluttered out of it, but the camera didn't catch it. They watched Reggie reach down, pick something up off the floor and stash it in the sole of his shoe.

"Got him!" Jake did a fist pump. "I knew that slime ball knew more than he said."

Brendan was already tapping on his keyboard. "Let's get his home address and pay him a visit."

CHAPTER 32

"*I* say it doesn't matter if we suspect that the husband's a sleaze. It's time."

The captain agreed. "We'll schedule a press release for two o'clock. Have the husband primed and ready."

But first there was time to talk to Reggie. Their searches turned up no current address for him. A call to his boss pointed to an apartment where the manager had never heard of him. Judging by the place, that meant little though. So, they caught Reggie at work instead of at home. His boss was there as well and nodded to the detectives to go ahead, take Reggie with them if it would help the case.

Protesting that he didn't know nothing about nothing, Reggie didn't pull against the hand wrapped around his bicep. After seeing the video clip, he realized that he would not get out of this one. "Yeah, I guess I took it. I just wanted to see what was in the bag; that woman acted so weird, running off like that." He warmed to his subject. "She took off without paying for her gas. Mr. Wilton doesn't deserve that; he's an okay boss. I thought that maybe we could take what she owed from her wallet, then the station wouldn't get ripped off." Mr. Wilton looked aghast at that idea.

"Show us what you did with it, Reggie," instructed Detective James.

With one detective on either side of him, they walked with Reggie down the road and through the park. Reggie showed them the trash can where he tossed the purse. "Can you get it for us?"

No way was Reggie sticking his hands in that mess. So, while Brendan held him, Jake gloved up and began searching. Didn't take long with only small things flung on top of it, part of a hot dog with ketchup, mustard and relish, a paper cup that might have held some darkish soda, an empty brown paper bag from a liquor outlet and an ice cream wrapper. Finally, no one had pulled the purse out by now, but the bag mostly obscured it. Besides, when you threw stuff in a trash can, did you really look inside the can first?

"Yeah, that looks like it," confirmed Reggie. But he denied taking anything out of it.

"What about the wallet?"

"I didn't steal any wallet out of that purse."

"Semantics, Reggie." He looked confused at that, so Brendan tried again. "We have you on film holding the wallet in one hand and the purse in the other before you stashed it behind the counter.

There was not much fight in Reggie. "I got mugged," he complained. "The neighborhood's all gone to shit. Some guy roughed me up and stole it." He led them to the area by the dumpster.

"Why didn't you report it?"

Reggie shrugged. They didn't really expect an answer.

.   .   .

"Show us where you've stayed this week."

"Oh, man, I'm on hard times right now, just staying with whichever friends I can."

"Take us there."

It didn't take that long, both places within easy walking distance from the park and from the dumpster. The first was a third-floor walk-up with the requisite old urine smells in the stairwell, stale cooking odors of fried foods and takeout. The door to the apartment opened as Jake rapped on it with the back of his hand. Responding to the gentle shove from behind, Reggie entered. "Hey, man," he said. His voice wavered as if he was unsure of his reception. The inhabitants barely looked up at Reggie's voice, but there was more movement when the two men and a woman saw that he was not alone.

Brendan showed his badge as murderous looks shot Reggie's way. One hand pushed deep into the crack in the stained sofa. The half-dressed young woman kept her hands behind her and backed into the kitchen.

"Has this guy been staying with you?" Eyes switched to Jake.

One guy nodded. The other said, "Yeah, he crashed here last night."

Jake took down their names; not one of them had phone numbers, then they left them to whatever pursuits they were doing today.

"Oh, man," said Reggie. "You've screwed me over so bad. Now I can never stay there again. They won't let anyone in who brings the cops around."

His Monday night resting place was worse - a basement one-room bachelor suite. There was a questionable mattress on the floor, bare, with a sleeping bag thrown over one corner, protecting a yellowish stain. Along one wall of the room stretched a counter that housed a hot plate and more dirty dishes than Brendan thought he owned. A couple of open cupboard doors showed storage space for dishes. The stains on the plates and bowls were off-putting, but tolerable. The mold and whatever grew on the ancient food bits was more than most stomachs could stand. The only inhabitant was a guy passed out in the corner. He was not dead; they could tell by his snoring, but Reggie's probing foot could not rouse him. Reggie knew the guy as Al, no last name. He didn't think that Al rented the place, he might have been just crashing there as well. He'd been there Monday with Reggie.

Although they had nothing to corroborate Reggie's story of being here Monday night, who would make stuff like this up?

THEY TOOK Reggie to the station with them. "Are you guys going to arrest me?"

"Should we?"

Reggie shut up.

Jake drew a sketch of the area, plotting Reggie's path from the gas station, through the park, to the dumpster, then to the basement where he stayed Monday night. "Does that look about right," he asked?

Reggie nodded.

"Now here's where we need your help." He began drawing a line between where Reggie spent the night and the gas station. "Is this how you walked to work Tuesday morning?"

"I guess so."

Jake pulled up Google Maps on his computer and turned the screen so Reggie could watch. "See here? Did you pass this Safeway on your way?"

He looked uncomfortable, but nodded again.

Brendan's finger followed a list of items in a folder. "It says here that a debit card belonging to Mrs. Whitmore, the woman we're trying to find, was used at this Safeway around eight Tuesday morning." He described the purchases "Did you buy these?"

Reggie looked around. Was there a way out of this one? They'd caught him on camera at the gas station. What if Safeway had the same kind of surveillance? They'd already got him on some stuff, but they were looking for a missing lady. Surely the penalty for that would be higher than boosting a bit of food. "Yeah, I stopped there for breakfast."

Silence.

"Okay, I know it was wrong, but geez, man, a guy gets hungry. Do you know how hard it is to make ends meet? Sure, I got a job and all, but it doesn't pay shit. She looked rich. If she could afford to just leave her purse lying around, she wouldn't miss the bit I put on her debit card. She was good for it, the tap went through."

"Hmm." Brendan was noncommittal. "Then that afternoon, someone used that same card to pick up beer. Some snacks as well." He lowered his head and looked over the top of his glasses at Reggie. "Was that you as well?"

They had him. Reggie was getting jittery. What were the penalties for using someone's card? He didn't buy much, wouldn't have been fifty bucks worth all together. He'd better get rid of that card, though.

"Then, Tuesday afternoon, Mrs. Whitmore's credit card was used to purchase drinks at this bar." Jake showed a picture of the establishment on his screen. "Was that you?"

Reggie's body backed up in his chair as he shook his head no. "No! No way, man."

Somehow, Brendan believed him. It didn't look like the place a low life like Reggie would frequent. One last question. "Did you buy smokes with her card at this place?" He pointed to Jake's screen.

"No way, man. I ain't never been there. Don't even know where it is."

Jake and Brendan looked at each other. Somehow, they thought Reggie was telling the truth. The last two locations were not in the area that Reggie frequented.

CHAPTER 33

*B*esides grumbling about having to make yet another trip to the police station, Jackson appeared rather pumped about appearing on camera. Brendan's concern was Jackson wouldn't follow the script they'd set for him, but take off in a direction all his own. He was a loose cannon, but they needed him; the public wanted to see a distraught father and husband appealing to them for help in finding his family. Hopefully tips would roll in then.

But first, they needed to prompt Jackson.

Jackson arrived dressed well - almost too well. Would a man whose family was missing for over forty-eight hours take the time to be as natty as this? Whatever. There wasn't time to tell him to return home to change.

He came across calm and collected. Brendan had seen a stillness come over the family of victims, an eerie stillness almost as if they were bracing themselves for the storm that might strike at any minute. Jackson's demeanor didn't quite fit that. If he had the kid stashed somewhere safe and sound, it would make sense. But so far, the detectives could not find any evidence of that, or complicity in the abduction.

Was this staged and Mrs. Whitmore left of her own accord? Or was this an abduction? And, where was the child?

THEY WERE in a private interview room where it was possible to find some quiet in the bustling station. They needed a distraction-free place to practice with Jackson, but also to ask some questions that were not of the comforting sort.

"Mr. Whitmore, please understand that we need to investigate all possibilities."

Jackson was fiddling with his cuff links, but he nodded.

"One thing we haven't talked about is the possibility that your wife took off - left of her own choosing."

"Why would she do that?"

"You tell us, Mr. Whitmore."

"She wouldn't. Why would she? She has everything she needs already. She lives in a nice house, has a kid she loves and a husband who works hard to provide for her."

Jake asked, "Ever think of the possibility that she might be lonely?"

Jackson scoffed. "She's not lonely - she's never alone. Timothy is with her twenty-four-seven."

"Sometimes a woman needs some adult companionship."

"That's what I'm for. I'm home every weekend."

Brendan tried another track. "You're away often four nights a week. Ever see anything lying around the house that doesn't seem familiar? Something that might belong to someone you don't know?"

Jackson denied it.

This guy doesn't get what I'm hinting at, thought Brendan. "Ever come home unexpectedly, like a day early or something?"

"A couple of times."

"Have there been any odd phone calls? Hang-ups when

you pick up? Your wife's cell ringing and she leaves the room to take the call?"

Jackson shook his head. "Nah, don't think so."

He needed to be more direct. "Mr. Whitmore, do you think that your wife might have an affair?"

This time Jackson snorted. "You have got to be kidding. She has everything she needs already. And before you ask, things are quite all right in the bedroom. I pride myself on that."

Did the guy have any idea how slimy he sounded?

Jake took over. "Is your wife a spontaneous person?"

"You have got to be kidding. She's just like her old man, planning and thinking out each step before she makes a move. You should see the way she researched things when Timothy first got his diagnosis of Wills or Wells or West or something like that. We have binders full of printouts, all organized with tabs separating aspects she looked into. Before giving him any of the medications they prescribe, she'd research each one, trying to tell me about the possible side-effects, drug interactions and stuff like that. Me? I say let the experts do their job. That's why they went to school for so long and get paid the big bucks."

"Could Elizabeth have done something impulsive, like suddenly decide to take a trip?"

"Not without telling me. Even then, I couldn't see her doing it. We haven't had a vacation in over a year. She says that Timothy is too sick to put in a new environment out of his routine." More bitterly, he continued, "She also says he's too sick to leave with a sitter for a weekend so we could get away together. That kid has way more of her time than I do. Even when I'm home, her son is still the center of her attention."

Brendan's turn. "You don't seem happy, Mr. Whitmore."

"Well, who would be if they pretty much lost their wife

when their kid got sick?" Perhaps he picked up something from their faces because he lowered his voice. "If you had kids, you'd know what it's like. You're the center of your wife's universe. You plan to have a child together, but the reality of that is that the kid needs attention, lots of it, and suddenly that same loving wife doesn't have time for you. Not much time, anyway. I work hard all week and when I come home, I expect to relax and to have things nice around me. That doesn't happen when your kid has unpredictable seizures." He shook his head. "It's an awful thing to watch."

"What do you do when Timothy has a seizure, Mr. Whitmore?"

"There's nothing you can do. Elizabeth tries to hold his head, so he doesn't hit it on anything, then we just wait it out. When it's over she turns him onto his side, calls it the recovery position. You can't just leave him like that, though. He usually pisses himself or worse when he has a seizure. He stinks and you have to clean him up. That takes Elizabeth's time, too. The kid is usually tired afterwards and will sometimes sleep for hours. You'd think that that would leave some togetherness time for Elizabeth and me, but no. She's jumping up all the time to go check on him. Kids really change your life."

Brendan cut Jake off. He could tell from the look on Jake's face that anything Jake said right now would not move the investigation forward, even if Jackson deserved whatever Jake had been about to say.

"Let's sum this up, Mr. Whitmore. You don't think that your wife is having an affair." He waited between each point for Jackson to shake his head no. "You don't think Elizabeth just took off." Negative. "What about if she got so overwhelmed with the responsibility that she couldn't face it anymore and took off?"

"No, she wouldn't do that. She's Little Miss

Responsibility, another thing she got from her father. Duty was something he talked about all the time, and it rubbed off on his only daughter."

"Sounds like you know your wife well."

"Of course I do. We've been married six years."

Jake wondered how well Mrs. Whitmore knew her husband.

"Just a couple more areas to cover, Mr. Whitmore. Could your wife have learned something that shocked her, something so startling that would cause her to take her child and bolt?

"No, like what?"

"What if she learned that her husband of six years was having an affair?"

Was there a slight hitch before Jackson's reply? "Ridiculous! Of course not." His foot tapped under the table.

"Anything else she might have found out that might have caused her to flee?"

"Like what? She leads a pretty ordinary life."

"And you, Mr. Whitmore? Do you lead an ordinary life?"

"Well, of course my life is more exciting than Elizabeth's. I'm a different type of person. She's a homebody. My job takes me out into the world. I travel. I talk to many people all the time, going places, meeting new contacts, dining out, you know."

"We don't yet, but we will. Hopefully by tomorrow we'll have more information on your contacts and phone calls and your, ah, dining out and we'll be talking to you about that then."

The foot tapping stopped then started up again, the pace perhaps just a tad more rapid.

The knock on the door interrupted any further questions. "The press talk starts in five minutes, sir. The Captain asks that you take your places now."

"Thanks. We'll be right there." Then, turning to Jackson, he said, "Remember, no deviating from the script. Keep exactly to what we told you to say. If you don't, it could jeopardize the safety of your family."

Facing the door, Jackson nodded his agreement.

BRENDAN LED THE PRESS CONFERENCE. "Thank you, ladies and gentlemen of the press for taking the time to be here. We need your help." He turned and pointed to the timeline that Jake had put up on the screen. With the laser beam, he pointed at the key areas as he spoke.

"This is a picture of Mrs. Elizabeth Whitmore. And this is her four-year-old son, Timothy. Sitting beside me is her husband, Mr. Jackson Whitmore." Jackson smiled, waved his hand and half rose to his feet. "Mr. Whitmore last saw his wife when he left for work Monday morning, two days ago. She was last seen by others Monday afternoon. She attended an appointment with her son's doctor, dropped off a prescription at her pharmacy, and said she'd be back to pick it up in half an hour. We believe that she then briefly did some grocery shopping before stopping for gas."

The screen switched to a picture of the outside of the gas station. "According to the station's video surveillance, Mrs. Whitmore put fuel into her car then entered the building to pay for that gas. Before she could pay, she saw a man get into her car and start to drive. She had presumedly left her son in that same car. She raced out of the station and jumped into the back seat of the car as it sped away. That is the last anyone has seen of either her or her son."

Jake projected a hazy, blown-up image of a man getting into the car. "This is all we have on the man. If anyone has information on his identity, we ask that you contact your nearest police station immediately or call the Crime Tips line."

"While we are all worried about Mrs. Whitmore, of even greater concern is the whereabouts of little Timothy Whitmore. We have a positive identification of Timothy with his mother at the drug store between approximately two thirty and three o'clock Monday afternoon. After that, nothing. Not only is this a missing four-year-old, but he is an ill four-year-old. He is a child with serious medical condition that requires continuous medication. We believe that his mother did not have the needed medications with her. She was to pick them up from the pharmacist."

He held up his hand to still the murmuring in the crowd. "If I may have your patience for a bit longer, Mr.Whitmore has something he would like to say to you." He handed the microphone to Jackson.

This is the part that intimidated many family members, getting up in front of an audience and the cameras. Jackson seemed unfazed by the attention. He stood smiling and confident until the flashes of light from the cameras died down. "Thank you. Thank you for coming here and thank you for your help to bring my wife and little boy safely back home. They mean the world to me. As you can imagine, these last two days have been trying, some of the most trying in my life. Not knowing where they are and if they are all right. Having the police look into every nook and cranny of our lives. Having our phone and credit records scrutinized by strangers. Well, it's been really awful, as I'm sure you understand." He received a nudge from Jake and looked down at the index card the detective thrust at him. He nodded that he understood.

"Timothy is a special little guy. We held him very dear to our hearts from the start, but when he was about six months old, he started having seizures. This was every parent's nightmare. But many tykes have febrile seizures, I think they're called, then grow out of them. Timothy didn't. In fact, they have continued to this day and gotten worse. He requires medication several times a day to keep them limited to the number that he presently goes through. We all go through having to watch our little boy…." His voice broke. Clearing his throat, he continued. "I know, I know. In this day and age, you'd think that doctors would have something to make this all go away, but that is not the case, or so I've been told. Anyway, it is crucial that my son have his meds. My wife was going to get his prescription refilled, but something interrupted her. So, Timothy is without these life-saving drugs. There is no telling the amount of brain damage he might suffer even now as we speak."

He let his voice crack, just a bit. "As of right now, we don't know what came over my wife. Did she leave with Timothy, taking off without thought for his medical needs? Or did she leave him somewhere and take off on her own? Either way, we cannot let a precious, innocent little boy suffer for the decisions of a flighty mother." He brought a pristine handkerchief from his pocket and delicately wiped under one eye.

Brendan's scowl deepened, and he rose to reach for the microphone. Before he could grab it, Jackson continued. "Please, if you have seen them, either of them, if you overheard something or if you know of anything suspicious, please contact these good detectives here by my side. Thank you." He sat down, wiping his eyes.

EACH TAKING AN ARM, Jake and Brendan frog-stepped Jackson out of the room. As soon as they were relatively alone, they rounded on the "distraught" father. "What the hell was that about?" Brendan's voice was too loud for where they were, but he was beyond caring. Before he could say more, Jackson shook off their hold.

Straightening his suit and adjusting his cuffs, Jackson explained. "I gave them what they want. They now have the image of a reckless, crazy woman alone with a defenseless child who needs saving. Don't you think they'll try all the harder now? The public will love this."

He swung back to face them. "Now do your job and bring me back my son." He walked off.

CHAPTER 34

*B*reakfast was toast. Just toast. No eggs, no jam, no butter. Elizabeth was trying to figure out the best way to convince Russell Rose that they needed to get groceries if they were going to stay here any longer. When she broached it last night, he said they could go for days without food, he'd often done it as a child. Wouldn't do them any harm. Might be fine for him, but she and Timothy had grown addicted to three meals a day - at least. And, with Timothy off his medications, she could not afford to add any more stressors to his system.

So far, he had remained calm. No preschooler tantrums and no more tantrums from the big guy either. She put that down to the fact that her son had charmed him. Who'd have thought? Well, she should have known since Timothy had that effect on most people. Hard to believe that he did it all without talking, but he did.

He had returned to his position from yesterday, kneeling behind the coffee table by Russell Rose's legs. The two of them were again watching Sesame Street. Timothy sang along to some jingles while she washed up the few breakfast plates, and she thought that she could hear a faint baritone joining in with Timothy. She shook her head at the complexities of that man. Still, she needed to work on figuring him out; it could mean their safety. Although she monitored her son while she cleaned the kitchen, she was less apprehensive about having him near Russell Rose. The man seemed bemused by her son. Hopefully, he'd grow to like him and maybe even want to take care of him.

~

THE ENDING CREDITS ROLLED, a signal to Timothy that it was time to move. Elizabeth had ready for him some paper boats and airplanes she had made from the pages of an old phone book. Simple toys, but what did a four-year-old know? His eyes lit up when he saw them, and immediately he plunked himself down on the dingy carpet and played. Elizabeth tried to keep her cringe to herself. This was not the time to worry about whatever might lurk in the fibers of that rug, since there was nothing she could do about it. It was better to keep him quiet and content for many reasons.

The television droned on and Russell Rose slumped back on the couch, eyes at half-mast as he watched. Then the tone on the television changed, and the image changed to a man sitting behind a desk talking about interrupting the programming for a public service announcement. Coming to the doorway, Elizabeth watched.

There on the screen were four men sitting at a table with a large screen behind them. And what? Was one of those men Jackson? "Turn it up, turn it up," she instructed Russell Rose. She moved closer.

On the screen flashed a picture of her - not the best picture, but it was clearly her, taken a few years ago. Her hair had been shorter then, but she was definitely recognizable.

As she listened to what the man in a suit was saying, the picture changed to one of Timothy. It was a formal portrait from last Christmas. Then there was one of her, Jackson and their son, taken as part of that Christmas package. Glancing over at a noise, she could almost feel Russell Rose vibrating. He was on his feet in front of the couch, all languorousness gone.

The next image was a grainy one of a man opening the driver's side door to her car and getting in. The gas pump was in the frame. Oh, thank god. That gas station must have had surveillance cameras.

The next picture that flashed on the screen was of Elizabeth as she reached for the back door and flung herself inside, legs ungracefully hanging out. Oh, they knew it was her. They had details on her car and now they knew that she was with it. The police would be on it and they'd be here for them soon.

But how would they know where they were? *She* didn't even know where they were.

"My face! They have my face and they've shown it to the world now." Russell Rose clenched and unclenched his fists as he paced, wheezing through his teeth. Elizabeth pulled her son out of his path and sent him into the kitchen to play.

The man turned on her and screamed, "How could you do that? How could you do that to me?"

Backing up, Elizabeth put up her arms, as if that could protect her. "What? What did I do?"

"You! You gave them those pictures."

It was like facing down an enraged grizzly. One who had lost his mind.

"What do you mean? How could I have done that? I've been with you the whole time."

"You left the house. Twice! You and your brat were in the back yard that night. Then you went out the front door yesterday. You snuck into the car." His pacing became more frenetic. "You've ruined everything. Now they'll come to take me back."

"Who? Who will come?" There was no answer, just the smacking sound of a fist hitting the palm of his hand.

Moving around the man, she turned her attention back to the television. He'd already made her miss some of it. Now Jackson was standing before the microphone. Her eyes teared up. Her husband. Never had he looked so dear to her. And so handsome, she thought. Was that a new suit?

Using the remote, she turned up the volume in time to catch these words:

"As of right now, we don't know what came over my wife. Did she leave with Timothy, taking off without thought for his medical needs? Or did she leave him somewhere and take off on her own? Either way, we cannot let a precious, innocent little boy suffer for the decisions of a flighty mother."

It took a few seconds for those words to register. "What! Flighty!" What the hell? Was Jackson actually talking about her? She, the person who kept their family together, ticking along? The person who attended to all of their son's medical needs? Who managed their finances? Flighty?

"Well, you took a dive into a moving car." Russell Rose pointed at the screen. "It showed it right there."

She turned on him, all her ire over the current insult, the slur on her character and their present predicament pouring out. "It was MY car! And you had MY son in it!" Gone was the composed Elizabeth. "This is all your fault. Look what you've done. You've ruined all of our lives. You…" She remembered who she was talking to. Daddy always said, "Don't let your emotions get the best of you." She needed to remain calm so she could think. She was all that Timothy had now. It was her turn to pace.

Grabbing the remote, she flicked through the channels, hoping to find a replay or even a station that put a more accurate spin on her predicament. Across the bottom of the screen, words scrolled. "Did this local young mother run off with her lover, abducting her own son? Or were both mother and son abducted? Anyone who has seen this car, or this woman is asked to contact the police immediately."

"Abduct my son!? I took him to a freaking doctor's appointment. They can ask Dr. Muller; he saw me. So did Mr. Rexton. I left my purse at the gas station! Who would take off and leave their purse behind? Geez!" She ran both hands through her hair.

Russell Rose picked up the remote. Funny. When she lost it, he seemed to get quieter. Think, Elizabeth, think. She was on her own. Daddy was gone, and it now looked like the other man in her life, her husband, was not looking out for her either. Daddy had tried to warn her about him. The only time she had gone against her father, and now he turned out to be right.

"Hey," said Russell Rose, pointing the remote at the television. "There you are again."

Yep, her fifteen-minute claim to fame for the world to see, and her character defamed by no less than her husband. This time she listened intently. No, the police didn't say those things about her. They were asking for the public's help in locating her, her son, and her car. Surely people had seen them, and the calls would pour in even now as she watched the announcement.

There was Jackson standing up again, looking poised and put together, not at all like a frantic husband whose family had been missing for two days. Now he was speaking; at first his words were about what you would expect, and she felt her body soften. She had misheard the first time, that was all.

Then he continued. "As of right now, we don't know what

came over my wife. Did she leave with Timothy, taking off without a thought for his medical needs? Or did she leave him somewhere and take off on her own? Either way, we cannot let a precious, innocent little boy suffer for the decisions of a flighty mother."

Was it possible to bust your own teeth through clenching them so tightly together? The cords in her neck stood out, and her nails bit into her hands. How could he say those things about her? She had never given him even one moment, one iota of hint that she took anything but spectacular care of their son. Hell, she did it all!

Now a still of Russell Rose's profile filled the screen. This time the image was clearer than in the previous broadcast. "Anyone who has seen this man is asked to contact the police."

Russell Rose shot to his feet. "We gotta run. Come on, get out of here."

"Where? Why?"

"They'll know it's me and this is the first place they'll look." He glanced around him. "Where's that kid?" He took a step toward the door. "No, we can leave him here."

"We are not leaving my child alone."

"He'll be fine. We'll put him in the basement. I spent lots of time there, and I was okay."

Elizabeth screeched at him. "We are not putting my child in any basement. And what in God's name would give you the idea that you are okay?" Those were not words she could pull back, even though she wished with her whole heart that she could. The silence filled the air, weighing down her chest, making it hard to draw in air. The fight went out of her eyes, replaced by fear.

Those dark eyes bore into hers.

CHAPTER 35

*B*rendan and Jake seethed as they returned to their desks. "The bastard…" The Captain was waiting for them.

"You guys were supposed to rehearse with him before the press conference."

"We did, over and over. The guy went off-script."

"Okay. Maybe he harmed the case, maybe he didn't. It tells us something about him though. This was not a scene of domestic bliss, apparently. You have new avenues to follow - two things. Find out who was boinking whom and follow the money."

~

THEY STARTED with what they knew about Elizabeth first. No records of arrest, not even a single parking ticket ever. Are people really that squeaky clean wondered Jake. Apparently, this woman was. Easier to do when you're buffered by that much cash.

"Don't think you can get a better credit rating than this.

Never overdue on a payment, never paid a cent of interest on her credit cards, conservative investments with steady growth."

"I've traced her husband's credit score and it's not nearly as pristine. Looks like he doesn't make a bad income but lives beyond his means." He showed a page to Brendan. "Hard to understand when it looks like they pretty much lived off the wife's money."

Brendan followed her spending patterns. Nothing flashy, good quality clothes from shops his wife would only visit in her dreams, but she didn't upgrade her wardrobe often. Monthly payments to a company who did her yard work and another for the weekly cleaning inside the house. She'd had the same service providers for several years. No charges at expensive dining establishments or overnights at hotels - none of the usual signs of someone having an affair. No one they had talked to spoke ill of her. She might just be what she appeared to be.

~

THERE WAS a knock on the door frame. "Hey detective, I've got a couple things here that might interest you." A uniformed officer held out a print-out. "We've tracked the numbers on that phone you gave us. Only two numbers on it, either incoming or calls made from it. Here they are. The one is a burner, but the other has a name attached to it. Haven't had time to track it yet, though.

"This came through and thought you'd want to see it right away. It's a missing person report that came in Monday night. It's for an adult, so we sat on it for forty-eight hours. The report's from St. Bartholemew's Center - you know that mental institution."

"I don't think we call them that anymore."

"Yeah, well, you know what I mean. Seems this guy has been in that nut house on and off on both voluntary and then involuntary status for years. Looks like he took a walk on Monday and never returned. It says here that he requested a release to attend his grandmother's funeral but was denied. So, he walked."

"Probably happens a lot at places like that that aren't locked down."

"They say that this guy left upset. His grandmother died, and he wanted to go to her place. Not just her funeral, but her house. Staff there didn't think he was stable enough right now to be out on his own. Apparently, it comes and goes with him, good spells and bad. This was not one of the good times."

"Lots of crazies out walking the streets."

"Yeah, but then the facility calls this afternoon. Some of their staff saw your bulletin on TV and they think they recognized this guy."

That got Jake's and Brendan's attention. "Who is he?"

"If we've got the right guy, he's Russell Rose Allen. Single, white male, aged thirty-five."

"Does he have a sheet?"

"Yeah, crimes against property. His juvie records are sealed."

"Where's he live?"

"Here's the address of his grandmother's house. It's a little place outside the town of Bathinghurst."

Jake and Brendan had one last question.

"Is he dangerous?"

~

THE WEIGHT of dread that had been hovering around Elizabeth's shoulders for the past day-and-a-half seeped into her bones, intertwining with her sinews. What was going to happen to them? Who could she count on? Daddy was gone. Now, Jackson had turned on her. He wasn't coming to rescue them. Timothy had only his mother to protect him. And she was busy antagonizing the unstable man who held their future in his hands.

A loud thunk interrupted the stare-off. Immediately Elizabeth moved toward her little boy where he lay prone on the kitchen floor.

Behind her, Russell Rose followed. "What's wrong with him?" His voice was growly and unlike that of the fellow who recently watched Sesame Street with a child.

"He's had a seizure."

"*Again?* Geez, does it never end? He's not jerking around this time; maybe you're wrong."

"No, this is a drop seizure, a different kind. And no, it does not ever end, especially when he doesn't have his medication. They'll get worse and do him brain damage." As she cradled her son, she gave Russell Rose a bitter look over her shoulder. "Thanks to *you*."

"Did he piss himself?"

Elizabeth whirled to face this man, this creature who brought such peril into their lives. "You…" He wasn't listening.

Russell Rose stood transfixed, his gaze following small and random movements around the room, near the doorway. Elizabeth's eyes turned toward what had this deranged man mesmerized. All she saw was a buzzing fly.

A fly. The guy got distracted by a fly. "Are you listening to me?" She demanded. She needed to get through to him just how ill Timothy was.

With lightning speed, Russell Rose's right hand shot out. Elizabeth flinched, but he paid her no mind. His fist wrapped around the fly. Moving to the outside door, he opened it and let the fly go free. "Everything deserves to live," he said. "Until it doesn't."

～

"Got it," Brendan said as he grabbed his jacket. "We're on our way to Bathinghurst and the home of the late Mrs. Rose."

Jake punched the address into the car's GPS. "What did they say this perp's name is again?"

"Russell Rose Allen."

"He *goes* by that name? Who'd name a guy Rose?"

"Someone with a sick sense of humor."

CHAPTER 36

*J*ake's pocket vibrated. Pulling out a phone, he showed Brendan the one that Jackson had left behind in the interview room. He looked at the number and recited it aloud to his partner. Then, he pressed the button to accept the call, saying nothing.

"Hello, hello," a female voice said. "Jackson? Are you there?"

Turning on the radio so it wasn't quite bringing in a station properly, Jake raised his voice slightly above the static. "Kind of hard to hear you. Can you hear me?"

"Not well. I thought these phones were better than this. Why'd you buy us such cheapo ones?"

Jake waited.

"Oh, well. What's happening? You didn't call me today." Silence.

"Jackson? You still there?" She waited. "Jackson, this isn't funny. Wait! Is this Jackson?" The line went silent.

"We're getting a ping," said Jake. "Yeah, the guys are on it."

"Without a name or account, though, that won't do us much good."

~

"I lost it."

"You what?"

"I lost it. I left it somewhere, or it slipped out of my pocket. I'm not used to carrying around two of the things, you know. And they make them bigger these days. Need to make pockets bigger to match."

"I called, and some guy answered. At first I thought it was you."

"Probably some bum picked it up. I'll buy another one."

~

The next time the phone rang, Jake accepted the call, put it on speaker, but said nothing.

"Hey Whitmore, what's with the silent treatment. We had a deal. I haven't heard from you in two days."

Needing to keep him on the line longer, Jake took a stab at conversation. "I had nothing to report."

"You're still saying you don't know where she is."

"Yeah."

"We need to meet. Tonight, at the usual."

"Can't. Car trouble. What about the Denny's in the Heritage Mall? I can walk there."

"You have got to be shitting me."

"No, I mean it. Things are really stressful."

"Well, grow a pair or it's going to get more stressful. Don't keep us waiting." The call ended.

"Damn," said Brendan. "Got a location but not a time."

"We've got a few hours to set up surveillance. I'll call this in."

∼

NARROWING it down to the two most likely suspects from the restaurant, those men were now trailed twenty-four/seven. Well, at least for a few days, depending on budget constraints. Brendan would not like to be Jackson; these men were not happy about being stood up. They weren't the type of guys you'd want to tick off.

Their next phone call to the phone Jake held confirmed it. There was little need for Jake to hold up his end of the conversation as the guy ranted and swore at him for being a no-show. Jake doubted that there were many people who blew this guy off, at least not more than once.

His rant winding down somewhat, the guy continued. "So, you think you're a movie star now and don't have to mix with the likes of us. Well, not true. We saw your stunt on TV, then the news about the guy who nabbed your wife and kid. We're on to him now. If we find out you arranged it to double-cross us, your life will be worth shit. If you didn't do it, then we'll grab them from him. He looks like low-class help. You should have done better." The call ended.

"Looks like this Russell Rose Allen is suddenly a popular guy."

"Yeah. We'd better find him first."

∼

FOLLOWING THE DIRT ROAD, Jake and Brendan obeyed the GPS's directions, slowing as they neared their destination. Pulling off the road and parking behind a bluff, they left the car, unsnapping their holsters for their weapons. There was no sign of the local back-up they'd requested.

Approaching with caution, they saw no sign of movement. At the end of the road a small house in poor repair was planted among grass and weeds that had not seen a mower in years. Tire tracks were evident and indentations where a car had rested not long ago.

Careful to remain out of sight of any windows, each man took a side, planning to meet at the back of the house. What they found was a fence six-feet tall, with no discernible gate. They met at the back of the fence, believing that the other would have found the way in. No such luck. Grabbing the top of the fence, Jake boosted himself up enough to peer inside. "Nothing but more long grass," he reported.

Trading sides, they circled along the fence, meeting back by the front door. Weapons drawn; Brendan tried the door. It swung open at his touch, not latched. After sharing a look and head nod, both men entered the door fast, Brendan going to the right and low, Jake to the left and high. Weapons following their gazes, they saw no one. On a gouged coffee table sat a plate and fork with what looked like remnants of egg glued to it. Next to that was a paper airplane and a television remote control.

Jake advanced into what looked like a kitchen; Brendan entered the hallway. Nothing. No one. While Brendan eyed the closed door leading off the kitchen, Jake opened the back door. He was gone only seconds, with nothing to report from the backyard.

"Cover me." Brendan put his back to the wall, reaching with one hand to quickly open the closed door. The men listened and waited. Nothing. "Mrs. Whitmore," Brendan called. "Mr. Allen. Can you hear me? This is the police." Nothing. "Come out with your hands up."

Not even a spider scurrying, thought Jake. He nodded to

Brendan as he threw on the light switch, then backed away. Still nothing. He stood with just one eye and his gun around the corner to the basement stairs as Brendan carefully descended. This was the part of police work they dreaded. The reward of finding the person they sought could be so quickly replaced with the danger of getting attacked.

While Jake guarded the upstairs, Brendan searched the basement. Disgusting place. A pile of ratty blankets balled near the foot of the stairs. Mouse droppings and the remnants of a rodent nest in its midst. Nearby were rusted mini toy cars. Had some child actually played here?

"I hear something coming," called Jake.

"Nothing down here."

The men moved toward the front window, seeing two sheriff cars pull up directly in front of the house. Well, there go tire tracks, thought Brendan. Pulling out their badges, he and Jake moved to the front step to meet the other lawmen.

"Thanks for coming." He filled them in on the search they'd just made. With six of them, they could be more thorough.

The kitchen showed evidence of recent cooking, although the fridge held scant provisions. They hit the jackpot in the bathroom. Draped over the shower rail were items of clothing that would fit a small boy. And they were damp. Someone had washed, then hung them here not long ago. Bagging the items, they hoped that Jackson would be able to identify the jeans and underwear as belonging to his son.

The house smelled of old lady. There was no other way Jake could think to describe it. Sweat, old food, talcum powder, muscle rub, moth balls, and body odor. Doilies backed the couch and chairs, yellow with grime and hair grease. Dust littered every surface, except in the kitchen and the dresser in one bedroom. Had someone tried to clean up? That room drew their attention. Unlike one of the other bedrooms where the bed covers were a mess, this one had pillows fluffed and a bedspread neatly made up. Jake bagged the pillows; maybe they hid hairs that could be matched to those belonging to Elizabeth or Timothy. As he lifted the second pillow, Brendan leapt for the bed. His gloved hands retrieved something small and shiny. The earring matched nothing else in this house. Just from its feel, he knew that it was real. There was no other evidence of fine jewelry in this home. It probably cost more than this whole house. He checked the clasp. No, the backing was attached. Someone had deliberately removed the earring, replaced the backing, and left it under the pillow. Bless Elizabeth if she was trying to leave them clues. Surely Jackson would be able to tell if this belonged to his wife?

~

"No, we ain't going in. The place is crawling with cops. There's no way the broad and kid are there." He listened. "Okay. Meet you back in the city."

CHAPTER 37

$\mathcal{O}$n the road again. There should have been some comfort in the familiarity of her car, but there wasn't. No comfort to be had at all.

Russell Rose made them leave the house immediately, no time to bring a change of clothes for Timothy or to grab the bit of food they had left.

He drove as ferociously as he looked. Elizabeth silently thanked Daddy for buying her such a sturdy car. A cheaper model would have broken over these potholes. The only shining moment was Timothy. He shrieked with glee at the bumps and the seconds when they'd be airborne until crashing back onto the so-called road.

"Where are we going?"

No response. Elizabeth wondered if there was even a person inside that shell.

EVENTUALLY THE DIRT road gave way to gravel, then narrow, chipped pavement. Then they were back on the highway, heading back to the city, back to where they had fled from two days before. This was the place Russell Rose was so anxious to leave. Elizabeth opened her mouth to ask why they were returning but stopped herself. It was to her advantage to be back on familiar turf; she'd never understand the reasoning of a mad man, anyway.

For now, there were more pressing matters.

"Can we stop for something to eat?"

"No."

"Timothy has had nothing since breakfast. His seizures get worse when his body's under additional stress."

No comment. Several minutes later, Russell Rose spoke. "Does he like having seizures?"

"What? No!"

"Are they painful?"

Elizabeth's shoulders slumped. She really didn't know. She hoped not, but Timothy couldn't tell her. From what she read of adults describing seizures, there seemed a wide variation in how they're experienced; none of it positive. "No," she said in a small voice. "I don't think so."

"Is there anything good about them?"

"No!"

"He keeps on having them."

"Yes, and it's worse because he doesn't have his medicine!"

"Have you ever considered euthanasia?"

~

Her nodding head hit her chest with a jerk. The bump woke her up as Russell Rose turned her car into the overgrown lot of a seedy motel. A light blinked on the overhead sign, advertising "Vac n y". The two-story building sprawled left from a dimly lit office. The grimy windows obscured the view inside.

"We're not stopping here," asserted Elizabeth.

Russell Rose simply turned his head to look at her.

Guess we are, thought Elizabeth. Never had she even noticed places like this, except in movies. They really existed, but were a far-cry from the Ritz-type hotels which she had experienced. She could see her mother's shudders at the thought of stepping foot in such a dive.

"Get us a room."

"What?"

"What didn't you understand about that? Get. Us. A. Room."

"No. Why don't you?" Maybe she could grab Timothy and run while he was inside. He'd never see them through the filth on those windows.

"I can't show my face, thanks to you."

Me? This guy was nuts and getting nuttier by the day.

His knife glinted in the on-and-off neon light.

"Okay, okay." She reached across to unbuckle Timothy from his car seat.

"Leave him here."

"What? No. No way. He comes with me."

"He's my insurance, lady, that you don't do anything stupid in there, like give them my name."

No, but she could give *her* name, she thought. Maybe ask to use the phone. Have them call the police. There were ways this could play out in her favor.

THERE WAS NO PHONE BOOTH, no public phone. The pimply kid behind the desk wouldn't let her use his cell phone. "There's a phone in your room," he told her. He accepted her credit card and entered her name into the book. No computer system. The way he scrawled her name, no one would ever know it was her. When he turned the book for her to sign, she inked her full name in exquisite care, doing her primary school penmanship teacher proud.

"Please," she begged. "Please call the police and tell them I'm here. They're looking for me. We need help."

The buds plugged into the kid's ears likely blocked out most of what she said; she could hear the hip hop blasting from across the desk. She tried again. In block letters in the ledger, she wrote HELP! We're kidnapped by Russell Rose Allen. This is Elizabeth and Timothy Whitmore. Call police.

There was a time when she would have instructed this motel worker, or anyone she encountered to call her husband, but not anymore. Slipping off her wedding ring, she stuck it between the pages. Maybe someone would see it. Jackson would have a fit to learn that she'd taken it off. She gave a little smile.

The kid handed back her credit card, shut the ledger and slid it under the counter, without even looking at what she had written. Tears stung her eyes. Surely someone would read it before too long. Maybe this kid's shift was nearly over. With a swift look over her shoulder to the waiting car, she tried once more. The windows obscured her, she hoped. Reaching across the counter, she made a grab for the kid's arm. He yanked it back. "Please," she asked. "Please call the police." From the dilated pupils and aroma of non-medicinal weed that wafted from him, she feared he was not a fan of interacting with the police. Worried about leaving Timothy alone with that mad man any longer, she took the room key and left.

.

CHAPTER 38

"*A*bout time we heard from you."

"*Yeah, well, I've been busy.*"

"*Hey, what's with this number?*"

"*I lost my burner. This is my personal phone.*"

"*You're calling me from your own phone?*" *His voice rose an octave by the last word.*

"*Well, you wanted to hear from me.*"

"*You dumb shit. Destroy that phone as soon as we hang up.*"

"*Sure.*" *Right, like he would. His life was stored in that phone.*

"*Make this fast. You're not wasting my time like you did earlier this evening.*"

"*What?*"

"*We don't have time for this, you dumb ass.*"

"*Just wanted to make sure that you got the name of the guy who took them. You saw that on TV, right?*"

"*We did. I have my, ah, associates on the way to his house in godforsaken Bathinghurst. If they're there, we'll get 'em.*" *His partner interrupted. "Hold on," he ordered.*

He was back in a minute. "You're in luck, Jackson, old buddy.

We just got a ping on your wife's credit card. They used it at a motel on the edge of the city. I'm getting the address now."

They made a plan, or rather, Jackson listened to the plan. They'd meet at that motel.

"You go in and get your kid." He wanted no part in offing kids. "Do what you need to do to your wife. And yes, you're getting your hands dirty this time. Then, take your kid and get out. We'll go in and clean up after your wife."

"What about this Allen character?"

"He'll no longer be a bother to anyone."

Finalizing the details, the guy had one last admonition. "Oh, and our fee? It's just doubled."

JACKSON RETURNED to where Barbara waited in the car with the rear-view mirror angled toward her passenger seat, as she applied a fresh coat of lipstick.

"They found them."

"Oh, thank god." At least she thought it was good. She was getting used to it being just her and Jackson. But the addition of Elizabeth's money would certainly elevate their status. "Now what?"

"They're holed up in some motel. We'll meet there. You and I'll go in and get Timothy while they take care of Elizabeth and that Allen creep."

Barbara didn't ask what taking care of meant. She didn't really care, as long as she got to live in style.

Jackson leaned over and squeezed her hand. "Just a while longer. In an hour or so, we'll have Timothy with us, and all this will be over."

Timothy. Oh, goodie, thought Barb.

THEIRS WAS a room on the second floor. Why he hadn't given them one closer to the office, closer to help, was a mystery. There was only one other vehicle parked in front of the motel, and given the amount of rust and the two flat tires that made it list to the left, it didn't belong to a current tenant. Maybe that was good. If any cops drove by, her car would stand out.

Their steps echoed on the metal stair rungs as Russell Rose led the way. Elizabeth was slower, lugging a slumbering Timothy. He was sleeping more than usual now; maybe a sequela from all the seizures he'd had. His damp crotch straddled her hip as she mounted the stairs with him, far past worrying about the urine being transferred to her slacks. Luckily there'd still been some nighttime Pull-Ups in the car. She'd snagged them as she lifted Timothy from his car seat. They'd need the diapers.

Ahead of them, Russell Rose mumbled to himself. He'd snatched the key from her hand as soon as she returned to the car. She'd watched carefully, but he pocketed the car keys. He wasn't that crazy.

He stopped in front of a door and worked the key in the lock. When it didn't open, he wrenched harder on the knob, turning the key hard enough Elizabeth feared it would break in the lock. What was she thinking? That would be good. The clerk would have to come up here, or call a locksmith; one more chance to plead for help.

Russell Rose gave up with a kick to the door and moved on to the next one. What was he doing? She watched as he tried three doors in a row. Didn't he even look at the tag attached to the key fob? In large numbers it stated which room the key fit. Elizabeth wouldn't enlighten him. The longer they stood out on the open balcony that ran the length of the second floor, the more opportunity there was for someone to spot them and call for help.

The fourth door was the charm. The key wiggled loosely in the old lock and gave way abruptly. Russell Rose, used now to trying to bully his way into a room, stumbled off-balance into the doorway.

Elizabeth took a quick look over her shoulder. Was this an opportunity to run? While she debated, a hairy hand reached out and grabbed her arm, yanking her into the room. The door slammed behind her as she struggled to keep her hold on her son.

CHAPTER 39

Getting her balance, Elizabeth gently laid her son on the far side of the bed. She cringed to think of what may be on that coverlet, but she couldn't hold on to him any longer. While Russell Rose muttered to the door, she took the three short steps it took to reach the minuscule bathroom, wet a facecloth and brought it back to rinse her son's face.

"Hey! Get away from him."

What?

Russell Rose charged at her, a look she'd not yet seen on his face. Towering over her, he backed her away from the bed, from her child.

"What's the matter with you?" Elizabeth asked.

"Get back. You've done enough. I'll look after him now. He's my responsibility."

"Your responsibility?" She didn't get this.

"Gran said so."

Oh, lord. He'd gone right off his rocker.

"There." He pointed at the room's only chair, a wooden thing perched near a counter that doubled as desk and table.

When she didn't move, he jerked her arm roughly, propelling her into the chair.

Keeping herself and the chair from tipping over, Elizabeth's hair partially obscured her vision. Gone were the days of a tidy chignon.

Russell Rose charged around the room. First, he tore off the cord running from the wall to the phone, the cord between the phone's base and the receiver. Then he went to the blinds and ripped off their cords. Turning, he approached Elizabeth.

Oh, no. No, no, he wouldn't. He'd never….

Yanking both her and the chair around, Russell Rose clenched both of her wrists in one hand, pulling them tightly behind her back.

WITH EACH OF her legs tied to a chair rung and her arms secured behind her back, Russell Rose lost interest in her. And in Timothy, thank god.

The man paced in a u-shape around the cramped hotel room, talking to himself. Some words came through, but mostly they were a blur to Elizabeth's mind. Timothy slept. Elizabeth's head lolled forward.

"HE STINKS."

Those words she understood. And he was right. "I could bathe him and change him if you untied me. Then he'd smell better."

"No!" His agitation increased, the ramblings more intense.

"Maybe just let me wash him off with a cloth." Had he heard her? She had to keep trying. He wouldn't hurt the child, would he, just because the odor offended him? How to get through to him? "Look, if you tied my hands in front, I think I could take his clothes off. Put on a diaper. If you handed me a wet towel, I could clean him, then he wouldn't smell." Hopefully, speaking softly would work.

Abruptly Russell Rose left. Seconds later there was the sound of taps running in the bathroom. Then he returned with a wet towel draped over one shoulder.

Roughly, he jerked on her arms, untying them. He repositioned her arms in front, allowing some slack. Then he picked her up, chair and all, depositing her with a thud onto the floor by the bed. "Be fast."

Crooning softly to her semi-conscious child, with difficulty, she pulled off his damp and moldering pants. She winced when she realized that Russell Rose had wet the towel with cold water. In Timothy's current state, he didn't flinch as she tried gently giving him a sponge bath. Drying him with the small bit of the towel that hadn't been under the faucet, she pulled on the diaper, thankful that she had at least one spare. She didn't do an outstanding job attaching it, with the limited use of her hands, and the dead weight of the child. At least the diaper was semi in place. Checking that Russell Rose's back was to them, awkwardly she used one hand to remove the backing from one earring, then tugged out the metal stem. She slid the earring under the pillow. Sorry, Daddy.

Clunking and rattling, the old air-conditioning unit started up. While it had been cool in the room before, now the temperature would drop. With bare legs, Timothy would chill quickly. She tugged on the bedspread, firmly corralling her mind from considering all the activities and deposits that might live on the material. She pulled it up and over his legs, covering him to the waist. She wanted to do a better job of wrapping him up, but she was suddenly airborne, then deposited back in the chair's original position.

"Get away from that boy," came the order. "He is my responsibility now. You've done enough."

SINCE RUSSELL ROSE didn't resume his rants, she hoped he'd entered a more rational state. "What happens now?" she asked.

"Now? We wait."

"Wait? What are we waiting for?"

"We'll know when the time is right."

"Right for?"

He looked at her like she was dense. "You know that this has to end, right?"

Elizabeth wasn't sure that her definition of *end* matched that of the man standing in front of her.

"There is a time to live and a time to die. To everything there is a season."

Oh god, oh god, oh god, she screamed in her mind, each syllable rising in a crescendo. She shook her head from side to side.

"WHO GOES FIRST, you or the kid?"

CHAPTER 40

*T*hink, Elizabeth, think. Now's the time for a plan. Put that first-year psychology class to use.

SHE OPENED HER MOUTH, but nothing intelligent rushed to her tongue. Stall. That was all she could come up with. Engage him in talk. Maybe get philosophical. An errant part of her gave a hysterical giggle. Right. Now she was losing it, too.

"WHAT DO YOU MEAN 'GO FIRST'?" She feared she knew, but anything to stall for time.

"I want to be fair about this. I thought and can't figure out which is best. I asked Granny, but she's not answering me."

"Why won't she answer you?"

"She does that sometimes. Especially when I was in the cellar; she'd never answer me then, no matter how much I cried. 'Some things don't deign a response', she'd say."

A part, mind you, a tiny part, of Elizabeth's heart

mourned for the tiny child this man had once been. An innocent boy raised by a woman who sounded like the bats in her belfry had run amok.

Russell Rose interrupted her reverie. "Here's how I see it. Parents love their child. When you're responsible for something, you care about it. It was really hard for me to kill my dog. Man, I loved that thing. It was my best friend. Well, next to Gran, that is. But, he was in pain and had to go It was the kindest thing." Then Russell Rose was gone, lost in his thoughts.

With a slight shake of his head, his mind seemed to come back to her, to the reality of the three of them in this moldy, ancient motel room. "If you love Timothy, it will be hard for you to watch him die. I don't want to cause you undue pain. So, it would be better for you if you died first."

Elizabeth's mind tried to wrap itself around the logic. This man was talking about sparing her pain, yet he intended to kill her, kill both her and her son.

"On the other hand, Timothy is mental. He doesn't talk. He probably won't understand when I tell him why these things must be done. He might not realize why I am killing his mother first. It might frighten him, and he'll be upset. I don't wish to be cruel."

He let those words sink in.

"So, maybe it would be better if I kill the boy first. Put him out of his misery."

∽

THE WAIST-HIGH WEED growth and the detritus strewn about provided concealment for the law enforcement team that followed Jackson to the motel. A second group of unmarked cars trailed a safe distance behind the men from the Denny's restaurant. The good guys were behind, but hopefully, not by much.

The tap on Jackson's mobile phone paid off. Who'd have thought he'd be dumb enough to use that phone to call the hired kidnappers. They had enough recorded to lay charges, if not assure convictions.

The safety of the woman and child - no, Elizabeth and Timothy - this had become personal, was paramount, even more important than nabbing these schemers.

"AM I CRAZY?"

As a hoot owl was the immediate response in Elizabeth's head. She clamped down on that. Cajole him. Keep him talking. Get him on their side. Don't insult him or do anything to make him act impulsively. As if an impulse would be worse than his thoughtful plans.

"No."

He looked directly at her. "No?"

She shook her head. "If you were, would you even know to ask that question?"

"Maybe not."

"Would a crazy person be able to hold a rational conversation like this?"

"No, you're right." His gaze penetrated hers, then he smiled. "Thank you. That helps. I'm about to kill a child. If you told me I was crazy, I would know that this is something I shouldn't do, and I'd stop. If I'm not crazy, then this is a logical move, the right thing to do." He smiled. "I had some doubts, you know. You've helped."

CHAPTER 41

imothy lay unmoving. Somewhere along the way, he'd lost one shoe. His feet dangled over the side of the bed; one too-big sock half-off his little foot. His eyes were at half-mast, fatigue over-taking him after that last seizure. Usually, he'd sleep for hours in the aftermath.

Sleep, she implored her son. Rest so you don't have this scene implanted on your brain the way every excruciating detail is on mine, she thought.

Russell Rose pulled out the butcher knife and whet stone he'd brought from his grandmother's kitchen, the one he'd been waving around, the one he'd been sharpening in every idle moment. "Respect your tools," Granny said. "If you sharpen it before every use, it'll serve you well." The sharpening action was repetitive, soothing, and practical. "You must look after your tools."

ELIZABETH CONTINUED to work at the ties binding her to the chair. She had movement now in her lashed-together wrists -

not much, but some. Thankfully, Russell Rose listened to her when she complained that it hurt too much to have her hands tied behind her. Then, when Timothy needed his diaper changed, Russell Rose altered the way the ropes bound her arms, tying each wrist separately, then together, leaving some hand movement so she could manipulate her son's clothing and the diaper. If she could either widen the space between her hands or slip one hand free....

Her legs made less progress, each bound to a chair leg. But she was inching the chair closer to the bed where her son lay. The progress felt infinitesimal, but she didn't want Russell Rose to notice, and push her back again.

RUSSELL ROSE MOVED to the bed, staring down at Timothy. Did he even see him as a child? Timothy was no threat to him. He'd done no one any harm. His only fault was to have her for a mother, a mother who left her small son alone and unprotected while she went to pay for gas.

Russell Rose passed the knife from hand to hand, contemplating the child. Timothy's eyes opened, and he gazed at Russell Rose. He gave him a wide smile. Elizabeth's heart broke.

"It won't be long now, little man," Russell Rose assured him. "Your suffering is almost over. I will do my duty to you."

Oh God, oh God. Elizabeth sped up her efforts to hump the chair over toward the pair at the bed. She planted her feet on the filthy shag carpet, leaned forward, pushed up and tried to edge the chair in the bed's direction. Sometimes she progressed, sometimes the chair seemed to settle back to where it was. Her legs were raw from the chair legs grating at her skin with each effort to move.

Would she make it in time? And, when she got there, what

could she do? Russell Rose had at least a hundred pounds and eight inches on her. Plus, he had a weapon, while she had neither hands nor feet free. She had to save her son. She flexed and relaxed her wrists, over and over. It was easier now that the rope was slick with her blood. The stinging of her scraped skin didn't register; her only thought to get her hands free and snatch Timothy away from this monster.

How had he tied this rope? Coils remained firmly around each wrist, the length of rope in between each wrist seemed to lengthen. Yes, she could now spread her hands about four inches apart. If she could only ease the loose part to one wrist and slip a hand out. She was sure that then she'd be able to untie herself and get free.

RUSSELL ROSE RAISED THE KNIFE. He was speaking, but his mutterings didn't reach Elizabeth's ears. She prayed that whatever he was saying, Timothy didn't understand. Russell Rose shifted the grip on his knife. Now it poised in the air above his head, and above Timothy's thin chest. Russell Rose made swiping motions in the air, once, twice, three times, bringing the knife back to its initial position.

Out of time, out of time, rang in Elizabeth's head. What could she do? Pushing her weight onto her feet again, this time she leaned forward, far forward. The rickety chair groaned, but came with her. Not too far, not too far, she warned herself as the chair threatened to throw her forward onto her face. She balanced in time to prevent that disaster. Now she was semi erect, with the chair glued to her back like a tortoise's shell.

Hopping, shuffling, she crept forward, closer to her child and the crazy man with the knife. If she pushed into him, that might buy them a few seconds, but then what? She'd still be tied to this chair. Russell Rose would still have the knife. And what if pushing him caused the knife to fall from his hands onto Timothy? The steel of that knife would penetrate flesh and bone as easily as it would water.

Russell Rose seemed lost in his mutterings. Thank God whatever was going on in his mind kept his attention; he didn't seem to know that Elizabeth was getting closer. Now, now with just a foot or so to go. Now would be a good time to employ her plan. What plan? She had none. She had nothing.

Frantically she pulled her hands apart, then relaxed them. That initial slack she thought she'd achieved wasn't changing. Maybe the ropes were the way they'd always been, and she just imagined she was making progress.

Her mind raced through the possibilities. Nothing that might work as a weapon was within reach. The sparse hotel room offered little.

On the nightstand to her right was the phone, with the cord that Russell Rose had torn from the wall. Is there a way she could use that cord to strangle the man? She could pick it up, yeah, but how would she reach up to wrap it around his neck? From her crouched position, her arms might reach his shoulder blades.

The only other object around was the bedside lamp. It looked like something from forty years ago, a fat ceramic base in browns and oranges, with a burned orange shade. Maybe, just maybe. Could she stretch her wrists far enough to wrap her hands around its base? Was it hefty enough to deliver a fatal blow?

Just a few more mincing steps and she'd be close enough. She prayed that she got there before Russell Rose finished whatever incantations he was doing and let that knife drop into Timothy.

Timothy's body stiffened. His eyes lost focus and looked up and to the right. Then the tremors began. Another seizure. That got Russell Rose's attention. He watched, sort of like gawkers at a train wreck.

There. No, almost, almost. Her knees almost touching the back of Russell Rose's, she leaned to the right, stretching her hands for the lamp's base. Not quite - only her fingers touched it. Another hop and, yes! Clawing at it, her fingers hit the edge, then the middle, the finally were over the apex and she could pick it up.

God, it was heavy, heavier than she'd thought. Good. The better to bash his head in with.

Russell Rose stopped talking, stiffened, and glanced at the hotel room door. Thumps came from the other side, heavy thuds.

It distracted him. Now. Elizabeth grabbed the lamp. It slipped from her hands, leaving bloodstains on its surface. She rubbed her hands on the tabletop, hoping to wipe off some sweat and blood. She tried again. Yes, she had it this time. She shifted her hands just a bit higher, spreading her wrists as far apart as the ropes would allow.

Channeling her inner kiai from those karate lessons she took in college, Elizabeth rose onto her toes, swinging the lamp in an arc toward Russell Rose's head, letting loose her kiai with more force than a yell had ever come from her body.

Russell Rose's attention shifted from the noise at the door to what was behind him.

Elizabeth's aim was sound; she had no choice. Yes, it would connect with the side of his head. She could see him falling to the floor unconscious. Then she'd scoop Timothy up in her arms and race them out of here. Oh, yeah. There was the minor matter of the ropes, but she'd figure that out.

As the lamp was about to smash into the nutcase's head, it jerked back. The cord! It remained connected to the wall. Instead of colliding with Russell Rose's head, it caught his shoulder, just grazing his temple. He slumped to the left.

CHAPTER 42

*M*ore noise at the door, almost like kicking noises, and then it flew open.

Jackson stood there, his legs spread wide, knees bent, both hands gripping a pistol.

Elizabeth had never been so relieved to see her husband.

His eyes met hers. Then there was a pfft sound and Elizabeth felt like someone had punched her in the shoulder. Her balance precarious at best, she went down, that same shoulder enduring her impact with the stained carpet. She wiggled to take her weight off the shoulder. She slid, her head passing the foot of the bed. If she could get to Jackson, he'd help her.

Russell Rose staggered to his feet. There was that airy sound again, and Russell Rose slumped to the floor. He lay where he crumpled, a pool of red spreading under his back.

Pushing on her elbow, ignoring the pain, Elizabeth's head rose enough to see her son's feet come onto the bed, then move across the soiled bedspread. Jackson had their son under the arms, dragging him across the bed, taking him to safety. Hoisting him over his shoulder, Jackson turned to the door.

"Here," he said to someone. "Take him. I gotta go back and finish her. I didn't get a clear shot, and she's still moving."

"Eww." That was a woman's voice. "He's wet. The kid has pissed himself!"

"Take him! He's just a child. He likely had another seizure."

"Oh, gross!"

"Drop your weapon and put your hands in the air." That was another unfamiliar voice.

"Now, now, now. Lay the child on the ground." Still another voice.

Footsteps pounding up the stairs. It sounded like the whole cavalry was there.

"Lady, if you drop that child over the railing, you'll be in a world of hurt you'll never recover from."

Child? What child could be out there but Timothy? Elizabeth frantically tried to wiggle her way toward the door. She made no progress with the chair attached to her. The pain in her shoulder screamed white hot as she put all her weight on it, trying, trying to edge closer to the door and her son. Why was she so weak?

The man's voice continued. "Ease him back onto this side of the railing, then lay him on the ground. Gently. Yes, that's it." A muffled voice, a few second's pause and then his voice again. "I need an ambulance here." Then, clearer now, "Back away from the child three steps. That's it. Now down on the ground, face down, with your hands behind your head. Now!"

More footsteps. A man appeared in the doorway, gun and eyes scanning the room. He took a step in and repeated his scan. He spied Elizabeth. "Are you all right, ma'am? You're safe now." He took two more steps into the room, not lowering his gun. "Make that two ambulances," he yelled over his shoulder. He checked the bathroom, then trained his gun on Russell Rose. "No, we need three ambulances."

He left and yelled out the door, "Medics!"

Voices beyond the door recited, "You're under arrest for attempted murder. You have the right to remain silent…" Another voice started the same speech. What were they doing out there? Shouldn't they be in here saying this to Russell Rose?

The man pulled a bag from his pocket and wrapped Russell Rose's knife in it. He felt Russell Rose's neck, then turned to Elizabeth. "Mrs. Whitmore?" he said.

She nodded.

"I'll have you untied in a sec, then we'll get that shoulder looked at."

He said more, but his voice seemed to get farther and farther away. Then she knew no more.

EPILOGUE

*H*olding herself stiffly, taking care not to jar her injured arm, Elizabeth tried to get comfortable in the creaky leather chair. By her feet, Timothy played with his Etch-a-Sketch.

"You have our deepest sympathies for all that you have been through, you and your son."

Elizabeth nodded. "Thank you." She rubbed the bare spot on her left finger where her rings once sat.

The lawyer wasn't ready to let this go. "Your father would roll over in his grave if he knew what Mr. Whitmore did to you." He shook his head. "Unbelievable. But rest assured, we've got your back. Our firm served your daddy, and we'll look after you."

He opened a file folder, spread the contents and turned the papers to face his client. "I've started your divorce proceedings. Under the circumstances, things will move expeditiously, without contest. We've already secured all your financial accounts; your soon-to-be-ex-husband has no access to any of your private or shared accounts."

Elizabeth signed on the indicated spots, but it took time

as she insisted on reading every single word. No longer would she blindly trust a man. That Elizabeth was gone.

~

ENJOYED THIS STORY? The author would be grateful if you would leave a review at GONE. Reviews are how new readers find the work.

~

WOULD YOU LIKE A FREE STORY? Get *Anything for Her Son.* You'll learn more about the police officer, Jake and how he meets Keira and her son, Daniel. Jake and Keira become close friends with Elizabeth and Timothy in *TRUST*, book two of this series. Download it free at https://dl.bookfunnel.com/a27d9uzou0.

~

The psychological thriller series
When Bad Things Happen:

GONE - Book One
TRUST - Book Two
SELFISH - Book Three
INSTINCT - Book Four
REASONS WHY - Book Five
MINE - Book Six
SANCTUM - Book Seven
When Bad Things Happen Box Set (books 1-3)
YOUNG ANNA - short story (free)

Elizabeth's story continues in TRUST.

After surviving a kidnapping and betrayal at her husband's hands, Elizabeth wants only to cocoon with her son now that they're safely home.

But the judge decrees that she must get outside help for her son or the State will take over his custody and care.

Trusting no one, she has three choices:
- Comply with the ruling, as scary as that may be
- Ignore the judge's order and hope that all will be well (how likely is that), considering how her life has gone?
- take her medically fragile son and flee.

Elizabeth thought that after all they'd been through, the bad parts were over. Guess not.

Read the first three chapters of TRUST below.

∿

Would you like a free story?
Anything For Her Son is a tale about a mother's love for her autistic child. Grab your free copy at https://dl. bookfunnel.com/a27d9uzou0

∿

A PSYCHOLOGICAL THRILLER

TRUST

WHEN BAD THINGS HAPPEN BOOK 2

SHARON MITCHELL

PROLOGUE TO TRUST

TRUST

After surviving a kidnapping and betrayal at her husband's hands, Elizabeth wants only to cocoon with her son now that they're safely home.

But the judge decrees that she must get outside help for her son or the State will take over his custody and care.

Trusting no one, she has three choices:
- Comply with the ruling, as scary as that may be
- Ignore the judge's order and hope that all will be well (how likely is that), considering how her life has gone?
- take her medically fragile son and flee.

Elizabeth thought that after all they'd been through, the bad parts were over. She was wrong, so very wrong.

"*L*ook at me, Timothy. Look at mommy." Elizabeth watched her son closely, watching for any sign that he heard her or even noticed her presence. She lowered herself further, trying to put her face directly in front of his.

Timothy turned his head to avoid her, intent on the object he'd sent spinning. His gaze intent, his concentration never swerving.

Elizabeth sat back on her heels and sighed. She closed her eyes and tilted her face upwards, willing the tears not to fall. How could she feel this way about her son, her only child? She loved him with fierce determination and would lay down her life for him in an instant. She had proved that just a month ago. But such frustration overshadowed this overwhelming love.

After surviving their ordeal, she had thought that she and Timothy would be closer than ever. After all, it was just the two of them now, two against the world, making their way together. She would keep him safe at all costs this time.

Steeling her determination to connect with this little man, Elizabeth tried again. With babies, she'd read how you should have tummy time, when you would both lay on the floor together playing and examining objects. As the child became a toddler, that changed to floor time, where you'd sit on the floor and play together.

Timothy had no problems playing on the floor; in fact, that was how he preferred to spend his time these days. The problem was that that play time did not include her. Her little boy did not seem to need her, to want her.

Reaching into the bottom drawer for another pot lid, Elizabeth tried to mimic her son's actions. She set the lid carefully on its side and, with the thumb and first two fingers of her right hand, gave it a spin. The lid twirled nicely in a circle once, twice, then wobbled as its arcs became erratic and toppled.

Timothy's hand shot out and caught it before it touched the floor. Moving it out of his mother's reach, he set it in perfect, practiced spin. He angled his body away from his mom and set a third pot lid spinning.

TRYING NOT to feel the sting of rejection, Elizabeth rose to make herself a cup of tea. She needed to do something with her hands, something to push back the hurt.

Life had not gone the way she'd expected this last while. Who could have guessed what her life would become? But throughout it all, despite it all, the one thing she had never imagined was that this distance between her and her only child would grow.

CHAPTER 1 OF TRUST

"Come on, Timothy. Hurry up. We don't want to be late for Dr. Muller." Elizabeth threw back her head and let out a breath. Now she'd blown it. She'd said the two words guaranteed to make her son balk - hurry and late. It never failed.

Elizabeth hated being late. Absolutely hated it. Growing up, tardiness had been a strict no-no. It showed a lack of respect for other people's time. It presented you as a disorganized person, someone not in control of themselves. That would never do for a properly brought up young lady. Ah, she missed her parents.

Forcing herself to relax her shoulders, take two deep breaths, and paste a smile on her face, she got down to her son's level. "Timothy, Dr. Muller is waiting for us. You know how much you like going to his office. He has that wooden train you can play with."

That got her son's attention. He adored that train on the colorful wooden tracks. No matter how long they might have to sit in the waiting room, as long as he could push that train in its endless loop, he was content.

259

. . .

MID-MORNING TRAFFIC WAS LIGHT. She planned her
appointments that way, especially now since she no longer
took the direct, predictable route to the doctor's office, or to
anywhere else. No more distracted driving for her.
Elizabeth's eyes scanned the road in front, through the rear-
view mirror and both sides constantly, watching for
anything out of the ordinary, any sign of danger. You could
never be too careful. She knew that only too well.

Pulling into the parking lot behind the office, she kept her
hands on the steering wheel, the engine running, and the
doors locked as she surveyed the lot. A mom and two small
children left the building, heading for an SUV. A man
carrying a briefcase hurried from a BMW to the back door,
his head down, one hand working his phone. He did not
glance in her direction.

Assured that no one had her in their sights, Elizabeth
chided herself for her paranoia. But is it really paranoia
when someone is actually out to get you? No, she reminded
herself. We're safe now. They've been caught and it could
never happen again.

Sure, tell that to my pounding heart, she told herself.

Pasting on that fake smile she feared she was perfecting,
Elizabeth looped the strap of her purse over her head and
across one shoulder. This kept both of her hands free. She
got out of the car, taking another careful look around the
vicinity. Somewhat reassured that there was no one around
who meant them harm, she opened the back door. Leaning
in, she undid Timothy's seatbelt. Before helping him from
the car, she again checked that no one was paying them
undue attention.

Thankful for the parking space so close to the entrance,

she pressed the button to lock her car doors and set the alarm.

SEEING Dr. Muller felt like meeting up with an old friend. Pitiful, Elizabeth thought, that your son's doctor was almost your only friend. Still, she trusted him and extended that trust to very few people.

Pulling the journal from her purse, she offered it to the doctor. As a pediatric neurologist, Dr. Peter Muller saw all sorts of parents. Elizabeth was one of his favorites. Her dedication to her son was obvious. Plus, she followed his instructions, intelligently weighing options, reporting side-effects, and partnering in Timothy's care. It wasn't always like that.

The journal recorded everything that Timothy had eaten over the last two weeks, the time and dose of each medication, any possible reactions, and data about how he spent his time, his responsiveness, developmental milestones, and any verbalizations. Of most pressing concern were the records of seizure activity.

Timothy's seizures were not under control. They were working on that or had been before the kidnapping. Being off his meds for almost a week had taken a toll on his small body, and his seizure activity increased. They were getting them back under control. Perusing Elizabeth's notes, Dr. Muller smiled.

"Good, good," he said. "We're getting back on track, aren't we?"

"Yes, or getting there. There's been no tonic-clonic seizures since, well, since we got home and back on these meds. The absence seizures are lessening, too, or at least that I've noticed those small moments where he seems to freeze, then comes back."

"I see that. Good. Don't beat yourself up about noticing them. Some happen briefly and no one, not even the best mom in the world has her eyes on her child one hundred percent of the time." He smiled. "And I'm including you among the best moms."

"Right. A mom that allows her child to get kidnapped and go without life-sustaining medications."

"We've been through this before. You cannot continue to beat yourself up for things that were beyond your control. You held up admirably and you and your little man are safe, mainly thanks to your efforts."

Elizabeth gave a half-smile. "Thanks. It's just hard, you know. So many what-ifs run through my mind."

"Understandable."

Elizabeth's one shoulder raised, then lowered.

"How are *you* sleeping?" Dr. Muller's gaze searched hers.

"Me? I'm fine," she assured him quickly. "I think that Timothy is sleeping better now. I'm not sure, but I think that since we started this ketogenic diet, he sleeps through the night."

"Yes, other parents remark on that, as well. While this diet isn't the first thing that we try with one so young, for some kids with intractable seizures, it can be worth a try, at least until we get things settled down."

"But, back to you. How are *you* doing?"

"I'm focusing on Timothy these days and on trying to get our lives back to normal. I'm working on getting us into a routine, one that's calm and predictable."

"You deserve some time to veg out and regroup. Everything you've been through would throw someone not as strong as you."

"Strong? No. We wouldn't have been in that position if I were strong."

"Nonsense. But that kind of talk isn't helpful. Have you

thought more about my suggestions of counselling you and for some form of play therapy for Timothy?"

Elizabeth shifted in her seat. "Not really. Things are still all so new, and I feel like we're in recovery mode."

Dr. Muller nodded. "Understandable. You *are* in recovery mode and will be for some time. That's why a good counselor would be helpful. You'll need help in figuring out how to move on from this. Even though you're safe now, the trauma remains imprinted in your mind. You need help in dealing with it."

She shrugged. "Maybe." She smiled up at him. "I don't mean to seem ungrateful, and I appreciate your concern. But I only seem to have so much energy right now, and it is all directed at Timothy and helping him to get better.

"I wanted to ask you about something else." She checked to see that the train held Timothy engrossed. "I'm worried. Yes, the seizures are better, but there are other changes in him since, well, since we got back home." She checked again, but her son ran the train along the floor along a track that only he could see. "I've lost him." Tears smarted her eyes. "He's here with me, but it feels like he isn't. There was a time when we were close, almost like any mother and son. I know that he has never been the most affectionate child, and he's always happily done his own thing. I used to be proud of the way he could amuse himself for hours. But lately, it's almost as if he doesn't need me, doesn't see me. He's content by himself and doesn't seem to want me to enter into his world." Now the tears came. She hastily turned her face; Timothy should not see her like this.

Dr. Muller handed over a box of tissue gave her a minute to get herself under control. "And you think that this has increased since your ordeal?"

She nodded.

"Have you considered that this might be a reaction to

what the two of you went through? His way of processing events that would be hard for an adult to understand, let alone a preschooler, and one with limited language skills?"

"I've thought of all kinds of things, including that this is his way of punishing me for letting so many bad things happen to us."

"He's four, Elizabeth. That's a pretty elaborate punishment plan for a small child to concoct and maintain, don't you think?"

"Yeah." She gave a half-smile. "I only think that when I'm feeling, well, you know."

Elizabeth's lips formed a firm line. She shook her head. "I can't bear the thought of strangers around Timothy." She held up her hand. "Not even professionals recommended by *you.*"

Dr. Muller waited.

"Maybe one day, I'll be ready," Elizabeth continued. Then I'll think about counseling. But for now, I want to get used to life with just the two of us. That's our reality, so we'd better get comfortable with it. We're all each other needs."

CHAPTER 2 OF TRUST

A knock. Elizabeth's eyes darted to the front door, reassured when she saw that the deadbolt was in place. Although how could it not be when she must check it dozens of times a day?

The knock came again. Maybe if she ignored it, whoever would go away. For weeks the press hounded them, but she thought that she, Timothy, and her husband, Jackson had become yesterday's news. Still, you never knew when a lone reporter would try to make a name for himself.

She turned on the outside security camera. The grainy picture showed a woman, turned away from the door and laughing at someone out of the lens' range. She looked vaguely familiar, maybe a newscaster she'd seen on television.

The woman turned toward the door and rang the bell. Now she recognized her - a neighbor.

They had the sort of neighbors to whom you would nod politely in passing or wave a hand to when driving by. Pleasant, but they didn't really know any of them. Jackson, well Jackson worked a lot and was rarely home. At least, that's what Elizabeth used to *believe* he was doing.

The woman wasn't giving up. She leaned into the doorbell and raised and lowered the door knocker repeatedly. What was up with her? Could she not take a hint?

"Elizabeth, I know that you're in there. I saw when your car drove up. It's me, Cynthia, your neighbor. I'll just take a minute of your time." She waited. When there was nothing, she added, "I know that you must be gun-shy with the press. Believe me, I'm alone and have nothing to do with those vultures. Just give me a couple minutes, please. I'm on your side and want to help."

Elizabeth had had it with trusting that people were supposedly on her side. Look where that had got her - almost dead. But this woman wasn't going away. Nothing she'd yelled through the door was worthy of calling the police. Besides, she was just a little woman; Elizabeth could probably take her in a fight. *Now where had that come from? She, Elizabeth Whitmore in a fight? Her mother would roll over in her grave.* She grinned to herself.

Anyone who could bring a smile to her face these days deserved a few seconds of her time. Raising her voice, she hollered, "Coming", as if she'd been at the back of the house. *Imagine me yelling. Oh, my poor mother would faint dead away at such unbecoming behavior.*

She smoothed her hair back, then opened both deadbolts, then the latch. She left the screen door closed and locked. Pasting on her best prep-school girl smile, she greeted her neighbor.

"Hi! I'm Cynthia from next door." She pointed over her left shoulder. "I'm not sure you remember me. I introduced myself when we first moved in. Cynthia Blythe." She held out her right and used her left to open the screen door. It didn't budge.

Looking over her shoulder to make sure that Timothy had not come downstairs, Elizabeth unlatched the door and stepped out onto the step. "Hello. I'm Elizabeth Whitmore. It's nice to meet you again." She gave the woman's hand a delicate, quick squeeze.

"You have my deepest sympathies for everything that you and your son have been through. You have my admiration, and I'm so glad that you're all right. We were so worried when we heard on the news that you were missing."

"Thank you. We're fine now."

That last bit gave Cynthia pause. "Yes. Well, I'm sure you are, but it will take some getting over."

Elizabeth gave her formal smile. Her mother's words rang in her head - "Keep yourself to yourself." Apt advice. Look what letting others in had led to.

Cynthia's smile faltered just slightly, but she plowed on. "Look. I understand." At Elizabeth's look, she stopped. "Well, no, I don't, really. No one could unless they've been through the exact same thing. But I'd like to understand, and I'd like to help."

"Thank you, but we're fine."

For a small woman, Cynthia had some bulldog tendencies. "I've been watching. No, I'm not a noisy neighbor, just concerned. Once I called the police when those reporters tried looking in your windows when you weren't home. A few times I drove them off with threats of reporting them." At Elizabeth's look, she hurried on. "No, I didn't talk to them. Ever. Sure, they tried asking me questions about you and your husband, but I never answered them, not once. I wouldn't do that.

"I get what it's like when strangers are intrusive. Believe me, I know. I also get that feeling, that preservation instinct that tells you to just cocoon at home with your child. I also know that that can't continue forever. Sometimes you need to let someone else in, to let them help." She took a big breath and continued nervously. "I'm a private person, too. Really. And, before this I would not have dreamed of pushing myself on you. But you need help, and from the look of the amount of company you've had lately, I think you could use a friend."

"Thank you, but we are quite all right on our own. Thank you for coming over." Elizabeth opened the door and was halfway inside when she heard something.

She and Cynthia turned at the squeal and giggle that came from Elizabeth's front yard.

"Amy, I told you to stay on our grass."

The little girl raced around the lawn, followed by, and following a grinning ball of fluff with a tail that looked like it was about to wag right off. The child and dog rolled on the ground together, making it hard to tell which of the two was the most energetic.

Cynthia turned back to Elizabeth. "Sorry about that." She waved a hand toward the duo. "My daughter, Amy and Blitz, her dog. Blitz is over a year old now, but you'd think she was still a pup."

There was noise behind her, and Elizabeth turned to see that her son had entered the foyer. She let out an unladylike squeal as something furry brushed by her shins and attacked Timothy. He tumbled to the ground with the squirming bundle of white fluff in his arms. His face bathed with who knows what sort of doggie breath. Thank god those sounds coming from the canine weren't snarls, but yips of what seemed to be welcome.

And what was that other noise? Giggles! Actual giggles coming from her son's throat. When was the last time she heard such a thing?

The door pushed open behind her and the little girl from next door jumped into the fray, rolling, and laughing with Timothy and Blitz.

"I'm so sorry. Here, let me separate these monsters and get them out of your house." Cynthia's flush started at her cheeks and filled all the skin down to her collarbones.

Elizabeth's shock receded and her mama bear instinct rose. While she knew that Timothy was not being harmed by either the dog or the little girl. He had allergies. Likely. They didn't know for sure yet, but he might have all sorts of allergies. She knew that many kids reacted to cat and dog dander, but since her son had never been close to animals, she didn't know if he would have a reaction. Any sort of reaction could bring on a seizure.

Cynthia took a leap and her right foot landed on a dangling dog leash. "Got ya." She dragged the dog off the children. "If you don't mind, I'll just tie him out here to your railing." Without waiting for permission, she left, secured the dog to the front step, then let herself back inside. As Cynthia brushed by, and toed off her sneakers, Elizabeth glanced down, noticing the perfect dog print on one of her own cream, suede shoes.

In that brief time, Amy had spied Timothy's wooden blocks scattered about the living room floor. "Cool," she said, as she darted into the room. "Wanna play?"

Timothy sat down several feet away from this strange girl and watched as she began building, chattering non-stop the whole time.

"She'll rarely let him get a word in. She's my little chatterbox."

"Timothy doesn't say much." Elizabeth watched as Timothy followed Amy's lead and attached wheels to a larger block.

"Looks like they'll be entertained for a while."

A while? Did they think that they'd been invited in?

CHAPTER 3 OF TRUST

Cynthia awkwardly balanced the china teacup between her thumb and index finger. It clattered when she placed it onto its saucer. "Sorry. I'm more used to mugs, I guess."

Elizabeth nodded. While courtesy required that she offer tea or coffee, she was not prepared to be besties with anyone, and that included her neighbor. They would have a civilized cup of tea, then go back to the nodding acquaintance they'd enjoyed for the past few years.

Cynthia had other ideas. "I've been following your case on the news."

Elizabeth stiffened. Although she tried to keep her facial expression passive, her eyes gave her away.

Cynthia raised both hands. "Sorry. I'm not trying to be nosy. Honestly! Yeah, I know more about you than you know about me; your life is news.

"That's why I came over today. *Your* life may be news, and people all over are paying attention, but you might not want Timothy to hear it all. I know that the two of you have been going to the trial most days. It's mentioned in the news reports on the court case's progress.

"Soon, the parts about his father will come up." She pointed in the living room's direction, where they could hear Amy's almost non-stop voice. "Things will be discussed there, and accusations made about your husband that you might not want Timothy to hear."

There was a fine line between aloof and haughty and Elizabeth had perfected it. "I can watch out for my son on my own, thank you. He will be fine; I will take care of him."

"Of course, you will. But there will be times when you must testify. You'll be up front in the courtroom and Timothy cannot be with you. You wouldn't want him to hear some of that, anyway."

The judge, the social worker and now this noisy neighbor - all people trying to insert themselves into her life - hers and Timothy's.

But Cynthia echoed worries that plagued Elizabeth's mind, worries that she'd shoved deep and labelled as things to think about down the road. That day was not here yet, but was coming up. Soon.

"The reason I came over was to offer to watch Timothy sometimes while you're in court. Amy and I are almost often home, and as you see; the kids get along great."

"Thank you for your offer, but Timothy and I are a team. Where I go, he goes. I need him with me, and we stick together.

"And now, it's time for his nap." She rose. "I'll see you out."

~

ANOTHER KNOCK. Since they'd lived here, they could go weeks without someone rapping on their door. So now, just when she wanted to be left alone, it becomes a daily occurrence?

Elizabeth turned on the outdoor cameras. All but one showed no one. She watched for a few moments to be sure the man at the door didn't have an accomplice lurking somewhere around her property. Assured that the rest of the yard was clear, she turned her attention to the screen that showed the front door. As the man's profile turned towards the lens, her breath caught. What was *he* doing here? She'd not seen Detective Jake Dean since they'd been rescued in that hotel room. The door knocker sounded again.

Surely, he wasn't here to warn her of some new threat. Lord love a duck. How many people could there be who were out to get her? Wasn't five of them enough, all behind bars now?

She pressed the speaker. "Mr. Dean. How may I help you?"

"Good day, Ms. Whitmore. I wasn't sure if you'd remember me."

"I'd hardly forget many moments of that day." She altered her tone. "Thank you again for coming to our aid."

"You're welcome. Just doing my job." He shifted his feet. "May I come in and speak to you for a few moments?"

Elizabeth debated. She really did not want to have to deal with anyone right now. She couldn't seem to throw off the exhaustion that had settled on her shoulders and focusing on herself and Timothy was the max effort she could put in on these non-trial days. But he might have important news. Talking through the door suited her, but she owed this man more courtesy than that.

"Just a minute, please." She undid first the top deadbolt, then the lower one, before releasing the lock in the doorknob and opening the main door.

Jake went for the screen door's handle, but it was locked.

As Elizabeth released the final lock and stepped back, he pulled open the screen and entered the foyer, brushing his shoes on the mat.

He held out his hand. "I wanted to check up on you, to see how you and Timothy are doing."

"Is that part of your normal duties?"

"Sometimes." His grin was sheepish. "Well, not often, although we'd like to have the time to do more follow-up." He trailed Elizabeth into the living room.

Elizabeth's head came up, wary. Anything out of the ordinary worried her these days.

Jake held up his hands. "No, no, there's nothing wrong or nothing new with the case." He rubbed the back of his head. "It's just that you and your son have stuck in my mind. You went through more in a week than most people suffer in a lifetime. My partner, Brendan, wanted to come, too, but he got tied up at work, and couldn't get away. But he'll be by sometime."

They sat in the living room and he continued. "I have a soft spot for kids." He amended that. "I never used to think much about them until I was posted to schools as a liaison officer. Then I became involved with a single mom and her son - my girlfriend and her little boy. Daniel is the same age as your Timothy. I keep thinking that if it had been Keira going through your ordeal, I'd really like for her to have a friend. Some friends."

When there was no reply, he added, "Keira's like you - she's tough."

He sees me as tough, Elizabeth thought. He's probably the first person in my life to ever put that word together in the same sentence as me.

"Tough on the outside, at least," Jake continued. "She's had to be. I admire that kind of grit."

"People do what they have to do at the time." No biggie. When the life of your child is at stake, there's no choice.

"Not true. In my line of work, I see all sorts of reactions to adversity." He glanced around, seeing signs that a child lived there, but no Timothy. "How is the little guy?"

"He's fine, thank you." Her primly folded hands didn't fidget. That's not what a lady did. She forced herself to sit back.

Jake regarded Elizabeth. Something about her reminded him of his Keira. His. Funny how he was starting to think of her that way. And Daniel. He brought himself back to the woman in front of him. She didn't look open to a heart-to-heart. That's a relief. Touchy-feely wasn't his thing, either; he was a man of action, of doing and letting the feelings work themselves out. "I thought that Timothy might enjoy a playmate. Maybe I could bring Keira and Daniel by sometime and let the boys get together."

Elizabeth's default reaction was obvious. No. Hell, no, Jake thought, if he was reading her correctly. Well. He'd gotten through Keira's defences and if he could do that, this woman's guard should be easy.

"I thought that Timothy could use a friend."

"He has me," assured Elizabeth. "That's all he needs for now." She'd worry about more later.

"Sometimes just playing with another kid can get his mind off things rather that dwelling on the bad that happened."

"My son does not dwell. He plays fine here, by himself and with me." That latter bit was perhaps a stretch, but in time, it would be true. True enough for this man, anyway.

Jake rubbed his hands up and down his thighs and stood up. "Well, thanks for your time and I'm glad that you're doing all right." He walked to the door, turning with one hand on the knob. "I'll be back again and maybe bringing Keira and

Daniel with me next time." Before she could protest, he added, "Just for a little play." He shut the door behind him before she could say more.

Yeah, right, thought Elizabeth as she engaged the door locks. Like that is ever going to happen.

❧

Read *TRUST: A Psychological Thriller* - Book Two in the series
When Bad Things Happen
http://www.Books2Read.com/Trust

❧

Did you find Timothy intriguing? Check out these other novels featuring autistic kids:
Autism Goes to School
Autism Runs Away
Autism Belongs
Autism Talks and Talks
Autism Grows Up
Autism Goes to College - Jeff's Coming of Age Story
Autism Box Set (the first 5 books in the series)

ABOUT THE AUTHOR

Dr. Sharon A. Mitchell lives on a farm, with her nearest neighbor several miles away. Doesn't that seem like the ideal setting to spark the imagination? She takes long walks with her hundred-pound German Shepherd dogs, Pickles and Dill. (She didn't name them - don't blame her).

She's working on her sixth psychological thriller novel for the *When Bad Things Happen* series.

Besides two, (almost three), short stories tied to that series, she's written six novels in another series, each featuring an autistic child or young adult. Two nonfiction books accompany that autism series.

Sharon's been a teacher, counselor, psychologist and consultant for decades and continues to teach university classes to soon-to-be teachers and administrators.

Dr. Sharon A. Mitchell is author of the psychological thriller series When Bad Things Happen:

·*GONE*

·*TRUST*

·*SELFISH*

- *INSTINCT*

-*REASONS WHY*

-*MINE*

-*SANCTUM*

- *When Bad Things Happen Box Set (Books 1-3)*

·*YOUNG ANNA* (a short story)

·*Anything for Her Son* (prequel short story)

Would you like a free story?

Anything For Her Son is a tale about a mother's love for her autistic child. And the mom in the story plays a key role in helping Elizabeth in TRUST. Grab your free copy at https://dl.bookfunnel.com/a27d9uzou0

She's also written a series of six novels, each featuring a child or young adult on the autism spectrum:

·*Autism Goes to School*
·*Autism Runs Away*
·*Autism Belongs*
·*Autism Talks and Talks*
·*Autism Grows Up*
·*Autism Goes to College*
·*Autism Box Set* (contains the first five stories in this series)

In addition, there are two nonfiction books:

·*Autism Questions Parents Ask & the Answers They Seek*
·*Autism Questions Teachers Ask & the Answers They Seek*

Dr. Sharon A. Mitchell has two passions - writing and kids who learn differently. Well, four passions actually - her family and also their family farm.

When it comes to autism and those whose brains are uniquely wired, she gets it. She's been a teacher, counselor, school psychologist, district consultant and autism consultant for decades. She has presented to thousands at conferences and workshops. She teaches university classes to wanna-be-teachers and to school administrators on inclusion strategies and students who learn differently.

Romance creeps into many of the novels because, well, isn't that what life's about?

 bookbub.com/authors/sharon-a-mitchell
amazon.com/Dr-Sharon-A-Mitchell/e/B008MPJCYA
twitter.com/autismsite

ALSO BY SHARON A. MITCHELL

Gone

Trust

Selfish

Instinct

Reasons Why

Mine

Sanctum

Young Anna (short story)

Anything for Her Son (short story)

When Bad Things Happen Box Set (Books 1-3)

Autism Goes to School

Autism Runs Away

Autism Belongs

Autism Talks and Talks

Autism Grows Up

Autism Goes to College

Autism Box Set

Autism Questions Parents Ask & the Answers They Seek

Autism Questions Teachers Ask & the Answers They Seek

Would you like a free story?

Anything For Her Son is a tale about a mother's love for her autistic child. And the mom in the story plays a key role in helping Elizabeth in TRUST. Grab your free copy at https://dl. bookfunnel.com/a27d9uzou0

Manufactured by Amazon.ca
Bolton, ON